AN EYE
F·O·R
JUSTICE

AN EYE F·O·R JUSTICE

THE THIRD PRIVATE EYE WRITERS OF AMERICA ANTHOLOGY

EDITED BY

ROBERT J. RANDISI

THE MYSTERIOUS PRESS

New York • London • Tokyo • Sweden

The Mysterious Press, 129 West 56th Street, New York, N.Y. 10019

Printed in the United States of America

First Trade Paperback Printing: September 1989
10 9 8 7 6 5 4 3 2 1

Library of Congress Cataloging-in-Publication Data

An Eye for justice : the third Private-Eye Writers of America anthology / [edited
by] Robert J. Randisi.
   p.   cm.
   Contents: Introduction and reminiscence / by Richard S. Prather—Candala /
George C. Chesbro—Marble Mildred / Max Allan Collins—Black in the snow /
Michael Collins—The Judas target / Wayne D. Dundee—State of grace / Loren
D. Estleman—Non sung smoke / Sue Grafton—Left for dead / Bob Kantner—
DDS 10752 Libra / John Lutz and Josh Pachter—Dead copy / Arthur Lyons—
Incident in a neighborhood tavern / Bill Pronzini—The vanishing virgin /
Robert J. Randisi—The safest place in the world / James M. Reasoner—
Hollywood guns / L.J. Washburn.
   ISBN: 0-89296-979-2 (pbk.) (U.S.A.)
       0-89296-980-6 (pbk.) (Can.)
   1. Detective and mystery stories, American. I. Randisi, Robert J. II.
Private Eye Writers of America.
PS648.D4E9 1988   88-4197
813'.0872'08—dc19   CIP

CONTENTS

AN EYE F·O·R JUSTICE

RICHARD S. PRATHER

INTRODUCTION

When Bob Randisi asked me if I would write an introduction to this, the third in the continuing series of Private Eye Writers of America anthologies, I said, without thinking much about it, "Sure. I'd love to."

But, since then, I've thought about it and now realize what a rare privilege this pleasant labor has been—particularly for me; particularly at this peculiarly significant time in my personal P.I. frolic. (I may get around to explaining that comment more fully a bit later.)

So I welcome this opportunity to introduce you to—some as new and intriguing acquaintances and some as old friends of yours (and mine)—some of the best writers in the business, who here happen to be writing about the good-guy-up-against-the-bad-guys investigator, or "private eye."

I love all of these P.I.s, hard-boiled or soft-boiled, youthful and horny or arthritic and bitter, male or female, naive or cynical, invulnerable or flawed; but that's partly because I love *writers*, admire them, respect them, enjoy them. And I mean almost any kind of writer, with the possible exception—no, the absolutely certain exception—of blank-verse poets. But I admire none of them more than the men and women who create private-eye novels, and stories like those you are about to enjoy.

Enjoy. That's the key word here. Because you have a treat, several treats, in store. And in the end that's what it's all about:

Were you *entertained*, did you *enjoy*? Maybe as a bonus you'll learn something new along the way. (Is it really true that with DNA fingerprinting blood or semen can identify a suspect as positively as do fingerprints? Is human flesh really tasteless, as de Maupassant declared after tasting a bite? Can latent fingerprints be made visible by the vapors from plain old supermarket Super Glue even months after the burglar deposited them on a doorknob?)

These tidbits, by the way, are not from the following stories, but they're all true tidbits—I wanted you to learn *something* exciting from this introduction. What you will learn from the stories themselves is as yet a mystery, which should always include some suspense, so you will have to discover that for yourself by buying—do not borrow it, and do not steal it or a P.I. will get you—and reading the book.

I do, perhaps excessively, admire (to repeat myself) these clever and surprising and sometimes astonishing creators of private-eye novels and stories; but there are a number of good reasons that justify my enthusiasm and bias. For one:

I've a hunch that almost anybody can write a stream-of-consciousness story that many readers will assume must be wonderfully profound and meaningful because they personally can't understand a word of it; or a shapeless and sprawling tale of unmotivated characters who, as in real true life, stumble from scene to scene without logic or apparent reason; or 300 pages without a recognizable beginning or middle or end. But it requires either a "natural" writer or a pro who's learned his trade—both of which categories you'll find in the pages that follow, sometimes happily in the same individual—to create memorable characters in conflict, both the good guys and bad guys acting from recognizable, believable motives, plus an interesting or even unique puzzle with threads dangling every which way but captured and at last hey prestoed together (or if not a puzzle, then at least friction and mounting suspense) in a story that grabs, interests, pleases, and in the end satisfies.

Which, I predict, fairly describes most, if not all of the stories you are about to read. Some are by established pros like George C. Chesbro, the Collinses, Max Allan and Michael, Loren D. Estleman, and Arthur Lyons; some by talented young tigers (or tigresses) represented here by Rob Kanter, L.J. Washburn, and Sue Grafton.

Some of them devise plots, or merely fragments of them, in their heads—or simply start writing and let creation occur "between the pen and the paper," in Gertrude Stein's interesting phrase. Others plot laboriously, in detail, on pages or pounds of paper before writing that socko first line, "Naked, she stood in the window and watched the approach of her lover across the lawn" (from Jack Woodford, somewhere). I'm of the pounds-of-paper school: I "plot," sometimes endlessly, and know in advance where every scene will go and why, and what leads into it and issues from it, before I begin the first draft. Others—like Loren D. Estleman (here included), or Elmore Leonard—start with a title or line or whole scene or maybe book in their heads and just get going and let it flow. One way is not better than the other; what counts is the result and whether or not it works. No matter how the authors represented in *An Eye for Justice* get their lines onto the blank pages, what they do works. As you will see.

Another reason for my pro-P.I. and pro-P.I. writer bias: These stories have *heroes*. Occasionally you may have to stand back and squint askance in order to recognize the virtue, but the fictional private eye, in whatever guise or disguise he may appear, *is* heroic, a heroic *individual*, not a member of the Mob or even the mob but apart from (and often opposed to) it, a self-employed entrepreneur with a gun (sometimes) tilting courageously against crimedoers, or suspicious windmills, or organized crookdom, or Evil. Even if he's over fifty or the hill and crippled by rheumatiz or the trauma of yesterday's gunplay, he limps *toward*, not away from; and it might successfully be argued that he's fiction's purest example of Emersonian self-reliance, the individual who, in a society where more than half the entire population either works for governmental bureaucracy or cashes checks handed out by it, says, "Please, just stay the hell out of my way," or "You mother, I'd rather do it myself." In my book (or books) that's not too shabby. I like it. A lot.

Speaking of my books, a final and undoubtedly self-soothing reason for my bias in favor of P.I. writers, including those who appear here, is because what they do I do also, and have done for a good many years. Between 1950 and 1975, forty-one of my books were published and thirty-eight of them were in the continuing series about my own private eye, Shell Scott. By 1975, those books had sold many millions of copies . . . and then my P.I. and I allakazam disappeared—until Shell's reappearance in *The Amber Effect* eleven years later.

Allow me to digress here briefly, please, if I may (and how can you stop me?), for a word about Bob. This thing has been on my mind, eating at my brain like a big worm, and I have to get rid of it before it lays eggs and hatches them. Bob, or Robert J. Randisi, who dreamed up PWA, and put together those first two anthologies and most of this one, among too many other things, is a phenomenon who fills me with vast unease.

Until I met Bob—in May 1986 I believe it was, in a dimly illumined New York bistro—I thought I'd banged out a fair number of books in the twenty-five years before my involuntary retirement. But, at some point during the scintillating conversation, Randisi stopped scintillating and casually mentioned that he'd written "more than a hundred" books since 1980, all of which were either published or on their way to that condition. A likely story, I thought; a *likely* story. Look, I have, myself, written forty-one, or forty-two . . . *How* many? Since *when*?

Well, that was several months ago, and I believe the total is now a hundred and fifteen—if you want to believe a person who stops scintillating entirely when he's still sober. The man is obviously doing something unfair, if not actually illegal and very likely felonious. I suspect that his goal now is, during each of fifty weeks in the next year, to: write a novel, edit a collection, put together an anthology, host a convention, correspond with everybody, explore Africa, and in his spare time write short stories. Why during only fifty weeks when there are fifty-two weeks in a year? Well, hell, a man has to relax, and study, and improve himself, or he'll stay stuck in the same old rut, won't he?

I've deliberately mentioned this to prove that there are harmful persons about who look like regular people, and in fairness and generosity to publishing Croesuses so they won't get mad at me. Or, that is, as evidence that some of the cruelest things are done to writers not by publishers but by other *writers*. Which can be a more painful experience for a sensitive artist than having sex with a rock.

Writing this possibly unusual introduction has been a privilege and pleasure for me. Because it's fair to say that I know, at least as well as most, what the fourteen writers represented herein by their creative issues were up against when they started, the odds they had to beat, what they had to overcome along the way to here. And because I'm sure that curiosities similar to those I've hinted at have happened to most if not all of the authors here included. Similar fun things and also worse, perhaps much worse.

Yet it is also certain that, for every author who cries out, bewildered in the wilderness, "What the hell happened to my *title*? What happened to my *book*?" or even on occasion "What happened to my *money*, my *fortune*, which I have been expecting would soon arrive *hugely*?" there will be a publisher, or publisher's representative, or soft-eyed and steel-balled attorney prepared to argue soothingly that, while all of these trifles may not impress us instantly as wonderful, they are in the end good, for how could we appreciate sunstroke if we knew not moonbeams? How could we really-truly appreciate the evanescent splendor of life if nobody ever tried to kill us?

This is, of course, a little bit like Dracula responding to the lady who shrieked, "Out! From my bedroom, stay out, *out*!" by crooning soothingly, "Don't vorry, my dahling, I'll only put my head in." Still, these can be cogent and convincing arguments, especially should one be bleeding profusely from the involuntary transfusions.

You, dear reader, may not comprehend all of this fully. But you can bet your bucks that Bill Pronzini and Wayne Dundee and James Reasoner and Josh Pachter and John Lutz do. And who, you may ask, are all those people? They are, at last, the writers who wrote this book. And unless there is among them a brand-new, sparkling-eyed, clean-cut, handsomely profiled, gift-wrapped, and just-beginning one, whom I've mistaken for somebody else, each of them is already a seasoned, scarred, piranha-bitten, persistent, courageous, self-starting, determined, battered-but-unbowed survivor. Performing for your pleasure right here in this here circus, some recklessly on the high wire without a net, some feeding the elephants, some as clowns or acrobats or sideshow barkers, depending upon the spirit that moves them. But each and every one speaks in a strong and unique voice worth listening to.

There are, I'm sure you know, literally *millions* of "writers" and gonna-bes and one-days and next-years—but each of these winners has done it and has made it, at least made it to here. And each of them therefore deserves your respect, possibly your gratitude, and certainly your undivided attention.

Give it to them.

Here they are: fourteen of the best.

Enjoy.

GEORGE C. CHESBRO

CANDALA

Perhaps the most unusual P.I. to appear in this collection is George C. Chesbro's dwarf detective Robert "Mongo the Magnificent" Frederickson. Mongo is an ex-circus performer turned criminology professor, who works on the side as a P.I. Many of Mongo's recent cases have entered into the realm of the fantastic, but in "Candala" Mongo deals with an uncommon case involving a common problem: the unforeseen consequences of bigotry gone mad.

1

Indiri Tamidian wafted into my downtown office like a gossamer breath of incense from some Hindu temple in her native India. Her young, lithe body rippled beneath the rustling silk folds of her sari; her coal black eyes, sheened by that enormous zest for life which was Indiri's very quintessence, smoldered in their sockets. Blue-black hair tumbled to her shoulders, perfectly complementing the translucent, light chocolate colored flesh of her face. Indiri was stunningly beautiful. And troubled; the light from her eyes could not disguise the fact that she had been crying.

Self-pity, unexpected and unbidden, welled up within me like a poisonous cloud, a hated stench from a dark, secret place deep inside my soul. Some thoughts have teeth; just as it is dangerous for an artist to search too hard for the murky headwaters of his power, it is folly for a dwarf to entertain romantic thoughts of beautiful women. I fall into the second category.

I pushed the cloud back to its wet place and clamped the lid on. I stood and smiled as Indiri glanced around her.

"So this is where the famous criminologist spends his time when he's not teaching," Indiri said with a forced gaiety that fell just short of its mark.

I grunted. "You could have seen the criminology professor anytime on campus, even if you are majoring in agriculture," I said easily. "You didn't have to come all the way down here."

"I didn't come to see the professor," Indiri said, leaning forward on my desk. "I came to see the detective. I would like to hire you."

"Now what would a lovely, intelligent young woman like you want with a seedy private detective?" Immediately my smile faded. The girl's flesh had paled, isolating the painted ceremonial dot in the center of her forehead, lending it the appearance of an accusing third eye. It had been a stupid thing to say. Worse, it had sounded patronizing, and Indiri Tamidian was not a woman to be patronized. "How can I help you, Indiri?"

"I want you to find out what's bothering Pram."

"What makes you think anything is bothering him?"

"He hasn't called or come to see me for a week. Yesterday I went over to his room and he refused to see me."

I turned away before my first reaction could wander across my face. Pram Sakhuntala was one of my graduate students, and a friend of sorts. A good athlete, Pram often worked out with me in the gym as I struggled to retain and polish the skills that were a legacy of the nightmare years I had spent headlining with the circus as Mongo the Magnificent. Like Indiri, Pram was part of a U.N.-funded exchange program designed to train promising young Indians for eventual return to their own land, where their newly acquired skills could be put to optimum use. Pram was taking a degree in sociology, which explained his presence in one of my criminology sections. He was also Indiri's fiancé and lover. Or had been. Losing interest in a woman like Indiri might be an indication that Pram was losing his mind, but that was his business. It certainly did not seem the proper concern of a private detective, and that's what I told Indiri.

"No, Dr. Frederickson, you don't understand," Indiri said, shaking her head. "There would be no problem if it were simply a matter of Pram not loving me anymore. That I could understand and accept. But he *does* love me, as I love him. I know that because I see it in his eyes; I feel it. Perhaps that sounds silly, but it is true."

It did not sound silly; Indiri came from a people who had produced the *Kama Sutra*, a land where life is always a question of basics. "Still, you don't have any idea what could have caused him to stop seeing you?"

"I'm not sure," Indiri said hesitantly.

"But you do have a suspicion."

"Yes. Do you know Dr. Dev Reja?"

"Dev Reja. He's chairman of Far Eastern Studies." I knew him, and didn't like him. He strode about the campus with all the imperiousness of a reincarnated Gautama Buddha with none of the Buddha's compensating humility.

"Yes," Indiri said softly. "He is also the advisor to the Indo-American Student Union, and coordinator of our exchange program. Last week Pram told me that Dr. Dev Reja had asked to speak with him. I don't know if there's any connection, but it was after that meeting that Pram changed toward me."

It suddenly occurred to me that I had not seen Pram for more than a week. He had missed my last class. This, in itself, was not significant. At least it hadn't seemed so at the time.

"What could Dev Reja have said to Pram that would cause him to change his attitude toward you?"

"That is what I would like you to find out for me, Dr. Frederickson."

I absently scratched my head. Indiri reached for her purse and I asked her what she was doing.

"I don't know how much you charge for your services," the girl said, looking straight into my eyes. "I don't have too much—"

"I only charge for cases," I said abruptly. "So far, this doesn't look like anything I could help you with." Tears welled in Indiri's eyes. "Not yet, it doesn't," I added quickly. "First I'll have to talk to Dr. Dev Reja before I can decide whether or not there's going to be any money in this for me. If I think there's anything I can do, we'll talk about fees later."

I was beginning to feel like the editor of an advice to the lovelorn column, but the look Indiri gave me shook me right down to my rather modest dwarf toes and made it all worthwhile.

2

Famous. That was the word Indiri had used—half in jest, half seriously—to describe me. It was true that I'd generated some heat and some headlines with my last two cases, both of which I'd literally stumbled across. But *famous*? Perhaps. I never gave it much thought. I'd had enough of fame; Mongo the Magnificent had been famous, and that kind of freak fame had almost destroyed me. What Indiri—or anyone else, for that matter, with the possible exceptions of my parents and Garth, my six-foot police detective brother—could not be expected to understand were the special needs and perspective of a four-foot-seven-inch dwarf with an I.Q. of 156 who had been forced to finance his way to a Ph.D. by working in a circus, *entertaining* people who saw nothing more than a freak who just happened to be a highly gifted tumbler and acrobat. Long ago I had developed the habit of not looking back, even to yesterday. There were just too many seemingly impossible obstacles I had already crossed, not to mention the ones coming up; the look of disbelief in the eyes of an unsuspecting client seeing me for the first time, choking back laughter at the idea of a *dwarf* trying to make it as a private detective.

I squeezed the genie of my past back into its psychic bottle as I neared the building housing the Center for Far Eastern Studies. Mahajar Dev Reja was in his office. I knocked and went in.

Dev Reja continued working at his desk a full minute before finally glancing up and acknowledging my presence. In the meantime I had glanced around his office; elephant tusks and other Indian trinkets cluttered the walls. I found the display rather gauche compared to the Indian presence Indiri carried *within* her. Finally Dev Reja stood up and nodded to me.

"I'm Frederickson," I said, extending my hand. "I don't think we've ever been formally introduced. I teach criminology."

Dev Reja considered my hand in such a way that he gave the impression he believed dwarfism might be catching. But I left it there and finally he took it.

"Frederickson," Dev Reja said. "You're the circus performer I've heard so much about."

"Ex-performer," I said quickly. "Actually, I'd like to speak to you about a mutual acquaintance. Pram Sakhuntala."

That raised Dev Reja's eyebrows a notch and I thought I detected a slight flush high on his cheekbones.

"My time is limited, Mr.—Dr.—Frederickson. How does your business with Pram Sakhuntala concern me?"

I decided there was just no way to sneak up on it. "Pram has been having some difficulty in my class," I lied. "There's an indication his troubles may stem from a talk he had with you." It wasn't diplomatic, but Dev Reja didn't exactly bring out the rosy side of my personality. "I thought I would see if there was any way I could help."

"He *told* you of our conversation?" This time his reaction was much more obvious and recognizable; it was called anger. I said nothing. "*Candala!*" Dev Reja hissed. It sounded like a curse.

"How's that?"

"Pram asked you to come and see me?"

"*Is* Pram in some kind of trouble?"

Dev Reja's sudden calm was costing him. "It must have occurred to you before you came here that any discussion Pram and I may have had would be none of your business. You were right."

I didn't have to be told that the interview was at an end. I turned and walked to the door past a blown-up photograph of a tiger in an Indian jungle. It was night and the eyes of the startled beast glittered like fractured diamonds in the light of the enterprising photographer's flash. In the background the under-brush was impenetrably dark and tangled. I wondered what had happened to the man who took the shot.

Pram showed up at the gym that evening for our scheduled workout. His usually expressive mouth was set in a grim line and he looked shaky. I made small talk as we rolled out the mats and began our warm-up exercises. Soon Pram's finely sculpted body began to glisten, and he seemed to relax as his tension melted and merged with the sweat flowing from his pores.

"Pram, what's a 'candala'?"

His reaction was immediate and shocking. Pram blanched bone white, then jumped up and away as though I had grazed his stomach with a white-hot poker.

"Where did you hear that?" His words came at me like bullets from the smoking barrel of a machine gun.

"Oh, Dr. Dev Reja dropped it in conversation the other day and I didn't have time to ask him what it meant."

"He was talking about me, wasn't he?!"

Pram's face and voice were a torrent of emotions, a river of tortured human feeling I was not yet prepared to cross. I'd stuck my foot in the water and found it icy cold and dark. I backed out.

"As far as I know, it had nothing to do with you," I said lamely. Pram wasn't fooled.

"You don't usually lie, Professor. Why are you lying now?"

"What's a 'candala,' Pram? Why don't you tell me what's bothering you?"

"What right do you have to ask me these questions?"

"None."

"Where did you get the idea of going to see Dr. Dev Reja?"

Like it or not, it seemed I'd just been pushed right into the middle of the water. This time I struck out for the other side. "Indiri's been hurt and confused by the way you've been acting," I said evenly. "Not hurt for herself, but for you. She thinks you may be in some kind of trouble, and she asked me to try to help if I can. She loves you very much, Pram. You must know that. If you are in trouble, I can't help you unless you tell me what it's all about."

Pram blinked rapidly. His skin had taken on a greenish pallor and for a moment I thought he would be sick. The fire in his eyes was now banked back to a dull glow as he seemed to stare through and beyond me. Suddenly he turned and, still in his gym clothes, walked out of the gym and into the night. I let him go. I had already said too much for a man who was working blind.

I showered and dressed, then made my way over to the women's residence where Indiri was staying. I called her room and she immediately came down to meet me in the lobby. I wasted no time.

"Indiri, what's a 'candala'?"

The question obviously caught her by surprise. "It's a term used to refer to a person of very low caste," she said quietly, after a long hesitation. "A candala is what you in the West could call an 'untouchable.' But it is even worse—I'm sorry to have to tell you these things, Dr. Frederickson. I love my country, but I am so ashamed of the evil that is our caste system. Mahatma Gandhi taught us that it was evil, and every one of our leaders have followed his example. Still, it persists. I am afraid it is just too deeply ingrained in the souls of our people."

"Don't apologize, Indiri. India has no monopoly on prejudice."

"It's not the same, Dr. Frederickson. You cannot fully understand the meaning and implications of *caste* unless you are Indian."

I wondered. I had a few black friends who might give her an argument, but I didn't say anything.

"Actually," Indiri continued, "the most common name for an untouchable is 'sutra.' A candala is—or was—even lower."

"Was?"

"You rarely hear the word anymore, except as a curse. Once, a candala was considered absolutely apart from other men. Such a man could be killed on the spot if he so much as allowed his shadow to touch that of a man in a higher caste. However, over the centuries it was realized that this practice ran counter to the basic Indian philosophy that every man, no matter how 'low,' had *some* place in the social system. In Indian minds—and in day-to-day life—the concept of candala fell under the weight of its own illogic."

"Go on."

"Candalas were forced to wear wooden clappers around their necks to warn other people of their presence. They were allowed to work only as executioners and burial attendants. They were used to cremate corpses, then forced to wear the dead man's clothing."

I shuddered involuntarily. "Who decides who's who in this system?"

"It is usually a question of birth. A person normally belongs to the caste his parents belonged to, except in the case of illegitimate children who are automatically considered sutras."

"What about Pram?" I said, watching Indiri carefully. "Could he be a sutra, or even a candala?"

I had expected some kind of reaction, but not laughter. It just didn't go with our conversation. "I'm sorry, Dr. Frederickson," Indiri said, reading my face. "That just struck me as being funny. Pram's family is Ksatriyana, the same as mine."

"Where does a Ksatriyana fit into the social scheme of things?"

"A Ksatriyana is very high," she said. I decided it was to her credit that she didn't blush. "Ksatriyana is almost interchangeable with Brahman, which is usually considered the highest caste. Buddha himself was a Ksatriyana. A member of such a family could never be considered a sutra, much less a candala."

"What about Dr. Dev Reja? What's his pedigree?"

"He is a Brahman."

I nodded. I had no time to answer Indiri's unspoken questions; I still had too many of my own. I thanked her and left. The subject of our conversation had left a dusty residue on the lining of my mind and I gulped thirstily at the cool night air.

I needed an excuse to speak to Pram so I picked up his clothes from the common locker we shared in the gym and cut across the campus to his residence.

It was a small building, a cottage really, converted into apartments for those who preferred a certain kind of rickety individuality to the steel-and-glass anonymity of the high-rise student dorms. There was a light on in Pram's second-floor room. I went inside and up the creaking stairs. The rap of my knuckles on the door coincided with another sound that could have been a chair tipping over onto the floor. I raised my hand to knock again, and froze. There was a new sound, barely perceptible but real nonetheless; it was the strangling rasp of a man choking to death.

I grabbed the knob and twisted. The door was locked. I had about three feet of space on the landing and I used every inch of it as I stepped back and leaped forward, kipping off the floor, kicking out with my heel at the door just above the lock. It gave. The door flew open and I hit the floor, slapping the wood with my hands to absorb the shock and immediately springing to my feet. The scene in the room branded its image on my mind even as I leaped to right the fallen chair.

Two factors were responsible for the fact that Pram was still alive: He had changed his mind at the last moment, and he was a lousy hangman to begin with. The knot in the plastic clothesline had not been tied properly and there had not been enough slack to break his neck; he had sagged rather than fallen through the air. His fingers clawed at the thin line, then slipped off. His legs thrashed in the air a good two feet above the floor; his eyes bulged and his tongue, thick and black, protruded from his dry lips like an obscene worm. His face was blue. He had already lost control of his sphincter and the air was filled with a sour, fetid smell.

I quickly righted the chair and placed it beneath the flailing feet, one of which caught me in the side of the head, stunning me. I fought off the dizziness and grabbed his ankles, forcing his feet onto the chair. That wasn't going to be enough. A half-dead, panic-stricken man with a rope around his neck choking the life out of him doesn't just calmly stand up on a chair. I jumped up beside him, bracing and lifting him by his belt while, with the other hand, I stretched up and went to work on the knot in the clothesline. Finally it came loose and Pram suddenly went limp. I ducked and let Pram's body fall over my shoulder. I got down off the chair and carried him to the bed. I put my ear to his chest; he was still breathing, but just barely. I grabbed the phone and called for an ambulance. After that I called my brother.

3

Pram's larynx wasn't damaged and, with a little difficulty, he could manage to talk; but he wasn't doing any of it to Garth.

"What can I tell you, Mongo?" Garth said. He pointed to the closed door of Pram's hospital room where we had just spent a fruitless half hour trying to get Pram to open up about what had prompted him to try to take his own life. "He says nobody's done anything to him. Actually, by attempting suicide, he's the one who's broken the law."

I muttered a carefully selected obscenity.

"I didn't say I was going to press charges against him," Garth grunted. "I'm just trying to tell you that I'm not going to press charges against anyone else either. I can't. Whatever bad blood there is between your friend and this Dev Reja, it obviously isn't a police matter. Not until and unless some complaint is made."

I was convinced that Pram's act was linked to Dev Reja, and I'd hoped that a talk with Pram would provide the basis for charges of harassment—or worse—against the other man. Pram had refused to even discuss the matter, just as he had refused to let Indiri even see him. I thanked my brother for his time and walked him to the elevator. Then I went back to Pram's room.

I paused at the side of the bed, staring down at the young man in it who would not meet my gaze. The fiery rope burns on his neck were concealed beneath bandages, but the medication assailed my nostrils. I lifted my hands in a helpless gesture and sat down in a chair beside the bed, just beyond Pram's field of vision.

"It does have something to do with Dev Reja, doesn't it, Pram?" I said after a long pause.

"What I did was a terrible act of cowardice," Pram croaked into the silence. "I must learn to accept. I *will* learn to accept and live my life as it is meant to be lived."

"Accept what?" I said very carefully, leaning forward.

Tears welled up in Pram's eyes, brimmed at the lids, then rolled down his cheeks. He made no move to wipe them away. "My birth," he said in a tortured whisper. "I must learn to accept the fact of my birth."

"What are you talking about? You are a Ksatriyana. Indiri told me."

Pram shook his head. "I am a . . . sutra." I tried to think of a way to frame my next question, but it wasn't necessary. Now Pram's words flowed out of him like pus from a ruptured boil. "You see, I am adopted," Pram continued. "That I knew. What I did not know is that I am illegitimate, and that my real mother was a sutra. Therefore, on *two* counts, I am a sutra. Dr. Dev Reja discovered this because he has access to the birth records of all the Indian exchange students. He had no reason to tell me until he found out that Indiri and I intended to marry. It was only then that he felt the need to warn me."

"*Warn* you?" The words stuck in my throat.

"A sutra cannot marry a Ksatriyana. It would not be right." I started to speak but Pram cut me off, closing his eyes and shaking his head as though he was in great pain. "I cannot explain," he said, squeezing the words out through lips that had suddenly become dry and cracked. "You must simply accept what I tell you and know that it is true. I know why Dr. Dev Reja called me a candala; he thought I had gone to you to discuss something which has nothing to do with someone who is not Indian. It does not matter that it was said in anger, or that he was mistaken in thinking it was me who had come to you; he was right about me being a candala. I have proved it by my actions. I have behaved like a coward. It is in my blood."

"If you want to call yourself a fool, I might agree with you," I said evenly. "Do you think Indiri gives a damn what caste you come from?" There was a rage building inside me and I had to struggle to keep it from tainting my words.

Pram suddenly looked up at me. Now, for the first time, life had returned to his eyes, but it was a perverted life, burning with all the intensity of a fuse on a time bomb. "Having Indiri know of my low station would only increase my humiliation. I have told you what you wanted to know, Dr. Frederickson. Now you must promise to leave me alone and to interfere no further."

"You haven't told me anything that makes any sense," I said, standing up and leaning on the side of the bed. "A few days ago you were a fairly good-looking young man, a better than average student deeply loved by the most beautiful girl on campus. Now you've refused to even see that girl and, a few hours ago, you tried to take your own life. You're falling apart, and all because some silly bastard called you a *name!* Explain *that* to me!"

I paused and took a deep breath. I realized that my bedside manner might leave something to be desired, but at the moment I felt Pram needed something stronger than sympathy; something like a kick in the ass. "*I'm* not going to tell Indiri," I said heatedly. "*You* are. And you're going to apologize to her for acting like such a . . . jerk. Then maybe the three of us can go out for a drink and discuss the curious vagaries of the human mind." I smiled to soften the blow of my words, but Pram continued to stare blankly, shaking his head.

"I am a candala," he said, his words strung together like a chant. "What I did was an act of pride. Candalas are not allowed pride. I must learn to accept what my life has—"

I couldn't stand the monotonous tones, the corroding, poisonous mist that was creeping into his brain and shining out through his eyes; I struck at that sick light with my hand. Pram took the blow across his face without flinching, as if it was someone else I had hit. The nurse who had come into the room had no doubts as to whom I had hit and she didn't like it one bit. I shook off her hand and screamed into Pram's face.

"A name means nothing!" I shouted, my voice trembling with rage. "What the hell's the *matter* with you?! You can't allow yourself to be defined by someone else! You must define *yourself*! Only *you* can determine what you are. Now stop talking crazy and pull yourself together!"

But I was the one being pulled—out of the room by two very husky young interns. I continued to scream at the dull-faced youth in the bed even as they pulled me out through the door. I could not explain my own behavior, except in terms of blind rage and hatred in the presence of some great evil that I was unable to even see, much less fight.

Outside in the corridor I braced my heels against the tiles of the floor. "Get your goddam hands off me," I said quietly. The two men released me and I hurried out of the hospital, anxious to get home and into a hot bath. Still, I suspected even then that the smell I carried with me out of that room was in my mind, and would not be so easily expunged.

"He's changed, Dr. Frederickson," Indiri sobbed. I pushed back from my desk and the Indian girl rushed into my arms. I held her until the violent shuddering of her shoulders began to subside.

"He's told you what the problem is?" Pram had been released

from the hospital that morning, and it had been my suggestion that Indiri go to meet him.

Indiri nodded. "He's becoming what Dr. Dev Reja says he is."

I didn't need Indiri to tell me that. I knew the psychiatrist assigned to Pram and a little gentle prodding had elicited the opinion that Pram had, indeed, accepted Dev Reja's definition of himself and was adjusting his personality, character, and behavior accordingly. It had all been couched in psychiatric mumbo jumbo, but I had read Jean Paul Sartre's existential masterpiece, *Saint Genet*, and that was all the explanation I needed.

"How do you feel about what he told you?" I said gently. Indiri's eyes were suddenly dry and flashing angrily. "Sorry," I added quickly. "I just had to be sure where we stood."

"What can we do, Dr. Frederickson?"

If she was surprised when I didn't answer she didn't show it. Perhaps she hadn't really expected a reply, or perhaps she already knew the answer. And I knew that I was afraid, afraid as I had not been since, as a child, I had first learned I was different from other children and had lain awake at night listening to strange sounds inside my mind.

4

I burst into the room and slammed the door behind me. My timing was perfect; Dev Reja was about halfway through his lecture.

"Ladies and gentlemen," I intoned, "class is dismissed. Professor Dev Reja and I have business to discuss."

Dev Reja and the students stared at me, uncomprehending. Dev Reja recovered first, drawing himself up to his full height and stalking across the room. I stepped around him and positioned myself behind his lectern. "Dismiss them now," I said, drumming my fingers on the wood, "or I deliver my own impromptu lecture on bigotry, Indian style."

That stopped him. Dev Reja glared at me, then waved his hand in the direction of the students. The students rose and filed quickly out of the room, embarrassed, eager to escape the suppressed anger that crackled in the air like heat lightning before a summer storm.

"What do you think you're doing, Frederickson?" Dev Reja's voice shook with outrage. "This behavior is an utter breach of professional ethics, not to mention common courtesy. I will have this brought up—"

"Shut up," I said easily. It caught him by surprise and stopped the flow of words. He stared at me, his mouth open. My own voice was calm, completely belying the anger and frustration behind the words. "If there's anyone who should be brought before the Ethics Committee, it's you. You're absolutely unfit to teach."

Dev Reja walked past me to the window, but not before I caught a flash of what looked like pain in his eyes. I found that incongruous in Dev Reja, and it slowed me. But not for long.

"Let me tell you exactly what you're going to do," I said to the broad back. "I don't pretend to understand all that's involved in this caste business, but I certainly can recognize rank prejudice when I see it. For some reason that's completely beyond me, Pram has accepted what you told him about himself, and it's destroying him. Do you know that he tried to kill himself?"

"Of course I know, you fool," Dev Reja said, wheeling on me. I was startled to see that the other man's eyes were glistening with tears. I was prepared for anything but that. I continued with what I had come to say, but the rage was largely dissipated; now I was close to pleading.

"You're the one who put this 'untouchable' crap into his head, Dev Reja, and you're the one who's going to have to take it out. I don't care how you do it; just do it. Tell him you were mistaken; tell him he's really the reincarnation of Buddha, or Gandhi. Anything. Just make it so that Pram can get back to the business of living. If you don't, you can be certain that I'm going to make your stay at this university—and in this country—very uncomfortable. I'll start with our Ethics Committee, then work my way up to your embassy. I don't think they'd like it if they knew you were airing India's dirty laundry on an American campus."

"There's nothing that can be done now," Dev Reja said in a tortured voice that grated on my senses precisely because it did not fit the script I had written for this confrontation. Dev Reja was not reacting the way I had expected him to.

"What kind of man are you, Dev Reja?"

"I am an Indian."

"Uh-huh. Like Hitler was a German."

The remark had no seeming effect on the other man and I found that disappointing.

"Dr. Frederickson, may I speak to you for a few minutes without any interruption?"

"Be my guest."

"I detest the caste system, as any right-thinking man detests a system that traps and dehumanizes men. However, I can assure you that Pram's mentality and way of looking at things is much more representative of Indian thinking than is mine. The caste system is a stain upon our national character, just as your enslavement and discrimination against blacks is a stain upon yours. But it *does* exist, and must be dealt with. The ways of India are deeply ingrained in the human being that is Pram Sakhuntala. I can assure you this is true. I know Pram much better than you do, and his reaction to the information I gave him proves that I am correct."

"Then why did you give him that information? Why did you give him something you knew he probably couldn't handle?"

"Because it was inevitable," Dev Reja said quietly. "You see, Dr. Frederickson, you or I could have overcome this thing. Pram cannot, simply because he is not strong enough. Because he is weak, and because he would have found out anyway, for reasons which I think will become clear to you, he would have destroyed himself, and Indiri as well. This way, there is a great deal of pain for Pram, but the catastrophe that would otherwise be is prevented."

"I don't understand."

"Pram was going to marry a Ksatriyana. Don't you suppose Indiri's family would have checked the circumstances of Pram's birth before they allowed such a marriage to take place? I tell you they would, and then things would have been much worse for everyone involved."

"But he could have married her and lived here."

"Ah, Dr. Frederickson, he could *still* do that, couldn't he? But I think you will agree that that does not seem likely. You see, what you fail to understand is that Pram is an *Indian*, and his roots are in India. Pram's adoptive parents are extremely liberal and far-seeing people. Not at all like most people in India, in the United States or, for that matter, in the world. Pram himself failed to learn the great truth that was implicit in his adoption. I know that if Pram was to attempt to return to India and marry Indiri—as he would most certainly have done if I had not told him what I did—he would have been ridiculed and derided by Indiri's family; perhaps even stoned for even presuming to do such a thing. In other words, Dr. Frederickson, Pram has the same options he had before: to marry Indiri or not; to live here or in India. I'm sure Indiri is as indifferent to Pram's origins as his own family is. He is not able to do this because, as you say, the knowledge that *he* could come from sutra origins is destroying him. You see, in effect, Pram is prejudiced against himself. I had hoped that telling him the truth as I did would give him time to adjust, to prepare himself."

I suddenly felt sick at the image of a young man doing battle with shadows; Pram had had a glittering treasure within his grasp and had ended with an empty pot at the end of a fake rainbow. And all because of a label he had swallowed and internalized but which, for him, was no more digestible than a stone.

"I didn't know you'd said those things to him," I said lamely. "But now he's obsessed with this candala thing."

"I'm afraid you'll have to take the responsibility for that, Dr. Frederickson."

"You said it."

"In anger, without thinking. You felt the need to repeat it."

I could feel a cloak of guilt settling over my shoulders. I made no attempt to shrug it off for the simple reason that Dev Reja was right.

"It doesn't really matter, Dr. Frederickson. Even without you the problem would still remain. However, now I am curious. What would you have done in my place?"

I wished I had an answer. I didn't. I was in over my head and knew it.

"All right," I said resignedly, "what do we do now?"

"What we have been doing," Dev Reja said. "Help Pram the best we can, each in our own way."

"He has a psychiatrist looking after him now. The university insisted."

"That's good as far as it goes," Dev Reja said, looking down at his hands. "Still, you and I and Indiri must continue to talk to him, to try to make him see what you wanted him to see: that a man is not a label. If he is to marry Indiri and return to India, he must strengthen himself; he must prepare an inner defense against the people who will consider his love a crime."

"Yes," I said, "I think I see." It was all I said, and I could only hope Dev Reja could sense all of the other things I might have said. I turned and walked out of the classroom, closing the door quietly behind me.

* * *

Pram's soul was rotting before my eyes. He came to class, but it was merely a habitual response and did not reflect a desire to actually learn anything. Once I asked him how he could expect to be a successful sociologist if he failed his courses; he had stared at me blankly, as though my words had no meaning.

He no longer bathed, and his body smelled. The wound on his throat had become infected and suppurating; Pram had wrapped it in a dirty rag which he did not bother to change. His very presence had become anathema to the rest of his class, and it was only with the greatest difficulty that I managed to get through each lecture that Pram attended. Soon I wished he would no longer come, and this realization only added to my own growing sense of horror. He came to see me each day, but only because I asked him to. Each day I talked, and Pram sat and gave the semblance of attention. But that was all he gave, and it was not difficult to see that my words had no effect; I could not even be sure he heard them. After a while he would ask permission to leave and I would walk him to the door, fighting back the urge to scream at him, to beat him with my fists.

The infected wound landed him back in the hospital. Three days later I was awakened in the middle of the night by the insistent ring of the telephone. I picked it up and Indiri's voice cut through me like a knife.

"Dr. Frederickson! It's Pram! I think something terrible is going to happen!"

Her words were shrill, strung together like knots in a wire about to snap. "Easy, Indiri. Slow down and tell me exactly what's happened."

"Something woke me up a few minutes ago," she said, her heavy breathing punctuating each word. "I got up and went to the window. Pram was standing on the lawn, staring up at my window."

"Did he say anything, make any signal that he wanted to talk to you?"

"No. He ran when he saw me." Her voice broke off in a shudder, then resumed in the frightened croak of an old woman. "He was wearing two wooden blocks on a string around his neck."

"Wooden blocks?"

"Clappers," Indiri sobbed. "Like a candala might wear. Do you remember what I told you?"

I remembered. "In what direction was he running?"

"I'm not sure, but I think Dr. Dev Reja's house is in that direction."

I slammed down the phone and yanked on enough clothes to keep from being arrested. Then, still without knowing exactly why, I found myself running through the night.

My own apartment was a block and a half off campus, about a half mile from Dev Reja's on-campus residence. I hurdled a low brick wall on the east side of the campus and pumped my arms as I raced across the rolling green lawns.

I ran in a panic, pursued by thoughts of clappers and corpses. My lungs burned and my legs felt like slabs of dough; then a new surge of adrenalin flowed and I ran. And ran.

The door to Dev Reja's house was ajar, the light on in the living room. I took the porch steps three at a time, tripped over the door jamb and sprawled headlong on the living room floor. I rolled to my feet; and froze.

Pram might have been waiting for me, or simply lost in thought, groping for some last thread of sanity down in the black, ether depths where his mind had gone. My mouth opened, but no sound came out. Pram's eyes were like two dull marbles, too large for his face and totally unseeing.

Dev Reja's naked corpse lay on the floor. The handle of a kitchen knife protruded from between the shoulder blades. The clothes Dev Reja should have been wearing were loosely draped over Pram. The room reeked with the smell of gasoline.

Candala. Pram had made the final identification, embracing it completely.

I saw Pram's hand move and heard something that sounded like the scratching of a match; my yell was lost in the sudden explosion of fire. Pram and the corpse beside him blossomed into an obscene flower of flame: its petals seared my flesh as I stepped forward.

I backed up slowly, shielding my face with my hands. Deep inside the deadly pocket of fire Pram's charred body rocked back and forth, then fell across Dev Reja's corpse. I gagged on the smell of cooking flesh.

Somewhere, thousands of miles and years from what was happening in the room, I heard the scream of fire engines, their wailing moans blending with my own.

MAX ALLAN COLLINS

MARBLE MILDRED

"Marble Mildred" is another of Max Collins's miniature historical gems featuring P.I. Nathan Heller, an ex-cop in the corrupt Chicago of the 1930s. The first Heller novel, True Detective, *won the Shamus Award for Best P.I. Novel of 1983. The subsequent Heller novels,* True Crime *and* The Million-Dollar Wound, *were nominated for the same award in 1984 and 1986. Max Collins has had a Nate Heller story in each of the three PWA anthologies; this is the lengthiest, and the best.*

In June 1936, Chicago was in the midst of the Great Depression and a sweltering summer, and I was in the midst of Chicago. Specifically, on this Tuesday afternoon, the ninth to be exact, I was sitting on a sofa in the minuscule lobby of the Van Buren Hotel. The sofa had seen better days, and so had the hotel. The Van Buren was no flophouse, merely a moderately rundown residential hotel just west of the El tracks, near the LaSalle Street Station.

Divorce work wasn't the bread and butter of the A-1 Detective Agency, but we didn't turn it away. I use the editorial "we," but actually there was only one of us, me, Nathan Heller, "president" of the firm. And despite my high-flown title, I was just a down-at-the-heels dick reading a racing form in a seedy hotel's seedy lobby, waiting to see if a certain husband showed up in the company of another woman.

Another woman, that is, than the one he was married to; the dumpy, dusky dame who'd come to my office yesterday.

"I'm not as good-looking as I was fourteen years ago," she'd said, coyly, her voice honeyed by a Southern drawl, "but I'm a darn sight younger looking than *some* women I know."

"You're a very handsome woman, Mrs. Bolton," I said, smiling, figuring she was fifty if she was a day, "and I'm sure there's nothing to your suspicions."

She had been a looker once, but she'd run to fat, and her badly hennaed hair and overdone makeup were no help; nor was the raccoon stole she wore over a faded floral print housedress. The stole looked a bit ratty and in any case was hardly called for in this weather.

"Mr. Heller, they are more than suspicions. My husband is a successful businessman, with an office in the financial district. He is easy prey to gold diggers."

The strained formality of her tone made the raccoon stole make sense, somehow.

"This isn't the first time you've suspected him of infidelity."

"Unfortunately, no."

"Are you hoping for reconciliation, or has a lawyer advised you to establish grounds for divorce?"

"At this point," she said, calmly, the Southern drawl making her words seem more casual than they were, "I wish only to know. Can you understand that, Mr. Heller?"

"Certainly. I'm afraid I'll need some details . . ."

She had them. Though they lived in Hyde Park, a quiet, quietly well-off residential area, Bolton was keeping a room at the Van Buren Hotel, a few blocks down the street from the very office in which we sat. Mrs. Bolton believed that he went to the hotel on assignations while pretending to leave town on business trips.

"How did you happen to find that out?" I asked her.

"His secretary told me," she said, with a crinkly little smile, proud of herself.

"Are you sure you need a detective? You seem to be doing pretty well on your own . . ."

The smile disappeared and she seemed quite serious now, digging into her big black purse and coming back with a folded wad of cash. She thrust it across the desk toward me, as if daring me to take it.

I don't take dares, but I do take money. And there was plenty of it: a hundred in tens and fives.

"My rate's ten dollars a day and expenses," I said, reluctantly, the notion of refusing money going against the grain. "A thirty-dollar retainer would be plenty . . ."

She nodded curtly. "I'd prefer you accept that. But it's all I can afford, remember; when it's gone, it's gone."

I wrote her out a receipt and told her I hoped to refund some of the money, though of course I hoped the opposite, and that I hoped to be able to dispel her fears about her husband's fidelity, though there was little hope of that, either. Hope was in short supply in Chicago, these days.

Right now, she said, Joe was supposedly on a business trip; but the secretary had called to confide in Mrs. Bolton that her husband had been in the office all day.

I had to ask the usual questions. She gave me a complete description (and a photo she'd had foresight to bring), his business address, working hours, a list of places he was known to frequent.

And, so, I had staked out the hotel yesterday, starting late afternoon. I didn't start in the lobby. The hotel was a walk-up, the lobby on the second floor; the first floor leased out to a saloon, in the window of which I sat nursing beers and watching people stroll by. One of them, finally, was Joseph Bolton, a tall, nattily attired businessman about ten years his wife's junior; he was pleasant looking, but with his wire-rimmed glasses and receding brown hair was no Robert Taylor.

Nor was he enjoying feminine company, unless said company was already up in the hotel room before I'd arrived on the scene. I followed him up the stairs to the glorified landing of a lobby, where I paused at the desk while he went on up the next flight of stairs (there were no elevators in the Van Buren) and, after buying a newspaper from the desk clerk, went up to his floor, the third of the four-story hotel, and watched from around a corner as he entered his room.

Back down in the lobby, I approached the desk clerk, an older guy with rheumy eyes and a blue bow tie. I offered him a buck for the name of the guest in Room 3C.

"Bolton," he said.

"You're kidding," I said. "Let me see the register." I hadn't bothered coming in earlier to bribe a look because I figured Bolton would be here under an assumed name.

"What it's worth to you?" he asked.

"I already paid," I said, and turned his register around and looked in it. Joseph Bolton it was. Using his own goddamn name. That was a first.

"Any women?" I asked.

"Not that I know of," he said.

"Regular customer?"

"He's been living here a couple months."

"Living here? He's here every night?"

"I dunno. He pays his six bits a day, is all I know. I don't tuck him in."

I gave the guy half a buck to let me rent his threadbare sofa. Sat for another couple of hours and followed two women upstairs. Both seemed to be hookers; neither stopped at Bolton's room.

At a little after eight, Bolton left the hotel and I followed him over to Adams Street, to the Berghoff, the best German restaurant for the money in the Loop. What the hell—I hadn't eaten yet either. We both dined alone.

That night I phoned Mrs. Bolton with my report, such as it was.

"He has a woman in his room," she insisted.

"It's possible," I allowed.

"Stay on the job," she said, and hung up.

I stayed on the job. That is, the next afternoon I returned to the Van Buren Hotel, or anyway to the saloon underneath it, and drank beers and watched the world go by. Now and then the world would go up the hotel stairs. Men I ignored; women that looked like hookers I ignored. One woman, who showed up around four-thirty, I did not ignore.

She was as slender and attractive a woman as Mildred Bolton was not, though she was only a few years younger. And her wardrobe was considerably more stylish than my client's—high-collared white dress with a bright colorful figured print, white gloves, white shoes, a felt hat with a wide turned-down brim.

She did not look like the sort of woman who would be stopping in at the Van Buren Hotel, but stop in she did.

So did I. I trailed her up to the third floor, where she was met at the door of Bolton's room by a male figure. I just got a glimpse of the guy, but he didn't seem to be Bolton. She went inside.

I used a pay phone in the saloon downstairs and called Mrs. Bolton in Hyde Park.

"I can be there in forty minutes," she said.

"What are you talking about?"

"I want to catch them together. I'm going to claw that hussy's eyes out."

"Mrs. Bolton, you don't want to do that . . ."

"I most certainly do. You can go home, Mr. Heller. You've done your job, and nicely."

And she had hung up.

I'd mentioned to her that the man in her husband's room did

not seem to be her husband, but that apparently didn't matter. Now I had a choice: I could walk back up to my office and write Mrs. Bolton out a check refunding seventy of her hundred dollars, goddamnit (ten bucks a day, ten bucks expenses—she'd pay for my bribes and beers).

Or I could do the Christian thing and wait around and try to defuse this thing before it got even uglier.

I decided to do the latter. Not because it was the Christian thing—I wasn't a Christian, after all—but because I might be able to convince Mrs. Bolton she needed a few more days' work out of me, to figure out what was really going on here. It seemed to me she could use a little more substantial information, if a divorce was to come out of this. It also seemed to me I could use the money.

I don't know how she arrived—whether by El or streetcar or bus or auto—but as fast as she was walking, it could've been on foot. She was red in the face, eyes hard and round as marbles, fists churning as she strode, her head floating above the incongruous raccoon stole.

I hopped off my bar stool and caught her at the sidewalk.

"Don't go in there, Mrs. Bolton," I said, taking her arm gently.

She swung it away from me, held her head back and, short as she was, looked down at me, nostrils flared. I felt like a matador who dropped his cape.

"You've been discharged for the day, Mr. Heller," she said.

"You still need my help. You're not going about this the right way."

With indignation she began, "My husband . . ."

"Your husband isn't in there. He doesn't even get off work till six."

She swallowed. The redness of her face seemed to fade some; I was quieting her down.

Then fucking fate stepped in, in the form of that swanky dame in the felt hat, who picked that very moment to come strolling out of the Van Buren Hotel like it was the goddamn Palmer House. On her arm was a young man, perhaps eighteen, perhaps twenty, in a cream-color seersucker suit and a gold tie, with a pale complexion and sky-blue eyes and corn-silk blond hair. He and the woman on his arm shared the same sensitive mouth.

"Whore!" somebody shouted.

Who else? My client.

I put my hand over my face and shook my head and wished I was dead, or at least in my office.

"Degenerate!" Mrs. Bolton sang out. She rushed toward the slender woman, who reared back, properly horrified. The young man gripped the woman's arm tightly; whether to protect her or himself, it wasn't quite clear.

Well, the sidewalks were filled with people who'd gotten off work, heading for the El or the LaSalle Street Station, so we had an audience. Yes we did.

And Mrs. Bolton was standing nose to nose with the startled woman, saying defiantly, "I am *Mrs.* Bolton—you've been up to see my husband!"

"Why, Mrs. Bolton," the woman said, backing away as best she could. "Your husband is not in his room."

"Liar!"

"If he were in the room, I wouldn't have been in there myself, I assure you."

"Lying whore . . ."

"Okay," I said, wading in, taking Mrs. Bolton by the arm, less gently this time, "that's enough."

"Don't talk to my mother that way," the young man said to Mrs. Bolton.

"I'll talk to her any way I like, you little degenerate."

And the young man slapped my client. It was a loud, ringing slap, and drew blood from one corner of her wide mouth.

I pointed a finger at the kid's nose. "That wasn't nice. Back away."

My client's eyes were glittering; she was smiling, a blood-flecked smile that wasn't the sanest thing I ever saw. Despite the gleeful expression, she began to scream things at the couple: "Whore! Degenerate!"

"Oh Christ," I said, wishing I'd listened to my old man and finished college.

We were encircled by a crowd who watched all this with bemused interest, some people smiling, others frowning, others frankly amazed. In the street the clop-clop of an approaching mounted police officer, interrupted in the pursuit of parking violators, cut through the din. A tall, lanky officer, he climbed off his mount and pushed through the crowd.

"What's going on here?" he asked.

"This little degenerate hit me," my client said, wearing her bloody mouth and her righteous indignation like medals, and she grabbed the kid by the tie and yanked the poor son of a bitch by it, jerking him silly.

It made me laugh. It was amusing only in a sick way, but I was sick enough to appreciate it.

"That'll be all of that," the officer said. "Now what happened here?"

I filled him in, in a general way, while my client interrupted with occasional non sequiturs; the mother and son just stood there looking chagrined about being the center of attention for perhaps a score of onlookers.

"I want that dirty little brute arrested," Mrs. Bolton said, through an off-white picket fence of clenched teeth. "I'm a victim of assault!"

The poor shaken kid was hardly a brute, and he was cleaner than most, but he admitted having struck her, when the officer asked him.

"I'm going to have to take you in, son," the officer said.

The boy looked like he might cry. Head bowed, he shrugged and his mother, eyes brimming with tears herself, hugged him.

The officer went to a call box and summoned a squad car and soon the boy was sent away, the mother waiting pitifully at the curb as the car pulled off, the boy's pale face looking back, a sad cameo in the window.

I was at my client's side.

"Let me help you get home, Mrs. Bolton," I said, taking her arm again.

She smiled tightly, patronizingly, withdrew her arm. "I'm fine, Mr. Heller. I can take care of myself. I thank you for your assistance."

And she rolled like a tank through what remained of the crowd, toward the El station.

I stood there a while, trying to gather my wits; it would have taken a better detective than yours truly to find them, however, so, finally, I approached the shattered woman who still stood at the curb. The crowd was gone. So was the mounted officer. All that remained were a few horse apples and me.

"I'm sorry about all that," I told her.

She looked at me, her face smooth, her eyes sad; they were a darker blue than her son's. "What's your role in this?"

"I'm an investigator. Mrs. Bolton suspects her husband of infidelity."

She laughed harshly—a very harsh laugh for such a refined woman. "My understanding is that Mrs. Bolton has suspected that for some fourteen years—and without foundation. But at this point, it would seem moot, one would think."

"Moot? What are you talking about?"

"The Boltons have been separated for months. Mr. Bolton is suing her for divorce."

"What? Since when?"

"Why, since January."

"Then Bolton *does* live at the Van Buren Hotel, here?"

"Yes. My brother and I have known Mr. Bolton for years. My son Charles came up to Chicago recently, to find work, and Joe— Mr. Bolton—is helping him find a job."

"You're, uh, not from Chicago?"

"I live in Woodstock. I'm a widow. Have you any other questions?"

"Excuse me, ma'am. I'm sorry about this. Really. My client misled me about a few things." I tipped my hat to her.

She warmed up a bit; gave me a smile. Tentative, but a smile. "Your apology is accepted, mister . . . ?"

"Heller," I said. "Nathan. And your name?"

"Marie Winston," she said, and extended her gloved hand.

I grasped it, smiled.

"Well," I said, shrugged, smiled, tipped my hat again, and headed back for my office.

It wasn't the first time a client had lied to me, and it sure wouldn't be the last. But I'd never been lied to in quite this way. For one thing, I wasn't sure Mildred Bolton knew she *was* lying. This lady clearly did not have all her marbles.

I put the hundred bucks in the bank and the matter out of my mind, until I received a phone call, on the afternoon of June 14.

"This is Marie Winston, Mr. Heller. Do you remember me?"

At first, frankly, I didn't; but I said, "Certainly. What can I do for you, Mrs. Winston?"

"That . . . incident out in front of the Van Buren Hotel last Wednesday, which you witnessed . . ."

"Oh yes. What about it?"

"Mrs. Bolton has insisted on pressing charges. I wonder if you could appear in police court tomorrow morning, and explain what happened?"

"Well . . ."

"Mr. Heller, I would greatly appreciate it."

I don't like turning down attractive women, even on the telephone; but there was more to it than that: the emotion in her voice got to me.

"Well, sure," I said.

So the next morning I headed over to the south Loop police court and spoke my piece. I kept to the facts, which I felt would pretty much exonerate all concerned. The circumstances were, as they say, extenuating.

Mildred Bolton, who glared at me as if I'd betrayed her, approached the bench and spoke of the young man's "unprovoked assault." She claimed to be suffering physically and mentally from the blow she'd received. The latter, at least, was believable. Her eyes were round and wild as she answered the judge's questions.

When the judge fined young Winston one hundred dollars, Mrs. Bolton stood in her place in the gallery and began to clap. Loudly. The judge looked at her, too startled to rap his gavel and demand order; then she flounced out of the courtroom very girlishly, tossing her raccoon stole over her shoulder, exulting in her victory.

An embarrassed silence fell across the room. And it's hard to embarrass hookers, a brace of which were awaiting their turn at the docket.

Then the judge pounded his gavel and said, "The court vacates this young man's fine."

Winston, who'd been hangdog throughout the proceedings, brightened like his switch had been turned on. He pumped his lawyer's hand and turned to his mother, seated behind him just beyond the railing, and they hugged.

On the way out Marie Winston, smiling gently, touched my arm and said, "Thank you very much, Mr. Heller."

"I don't think I made much difference."

"I think you did. The judge vacated the fine, after all."

"Hell, I had nothing to do with that. Mildred was your star witness."

"In a way I guess she was."

"I notice her husband wasn't here."

Son Charles spoke up. "No, he's at work. He . . . well, he thought it was better he not be here. We figured *that woman* would be here, after all."

" 'That woman' is sick."

"In the head," Charles said bitterly.

"That's right. You or I could be sick that way, too. Somebody ought to help her."

Marie Winston, straining to find some compassion for Mildred Bolton, said, "Who would you suggest?"

"Damnit," I said, "the husband. He's been with her fourteen years. She didn't get this way overnight. The way I see it, he's got a responsibility to get her some goddamn *help* before he dumps her by the side of the road."

Mrs. Winston smiled at that, some compassion coming through after all. "You have a very modern point of view, Mr. Heller."

"Not really. I'm not even used to talkies yet. Anyway, I'll see you, Mrs. Winston. Charles."

And I left the graystone building and climbed in my '32 Auburn and drove back to my office. I parked in the alley, in my space, and walked over to the Berghoff for lunch. I think I hoped to find Bolton there. But he wasn't.

I went back to the office and puttered a while; I had a pile of retail credit-risk checks to whittle away at.

Hell with it, I thought, and walked over to Bolton's office building, a narrow, fifteen-story, white granite structure just behind the Federal Reserve on West Jackson, next to the El. Bolton was doing all right—better than me, certainly—but as a broker he was in the financial district only by a hair. No doubt he was a relatively small-time insurance broker, making twenty or twenty-five grand a year. Big money by my standards, but a lot of guys over at the Board of Trade spilled more than that.

There was no lobby really, just a wide hall between facing rows of shops—newsstand, travel agency, cigar store. The uniformed elevator operator, a skinny, pockmarked guy about my age, was waiting for a passenger. I was it.

"Tenth floor," I told him, and he took me up.

He was pulling open the cage doors when we heard the air crack, three times.

"What the hell was that?" he said.

"It wasn't a car backfiring," I said. "You better stay here."

I moved cautiously out into the hall. The elevators came up a central shaft, with a squared-off "c" of offices all about. I glanced quickly at the names on the pebbled glass in the wood-partition walls, and finally lit upon BOLTON AND SCHMIDT, INSURANCE BROKERS. I swallowed and moved cautiously in that direction as the door flew open and a young woman flew out—a dark-haired dish of maybe twenty with wide eyes and a face drained of blood, her silk stockings flashing as she rushed my way.

She fell into my arms and I said, "Are you wounded?"

"No," she swallowed, "but somebody is."

The poor kid was gasping for air; I hauled her toward the bank of elevators. Even under the strain, I was enjoying the feel and smell of her.

"You wouldn't be Joseph Bolton's secretary, by any chance?" I asked, helping her onto the elevator.

She nodded, eyes still huge.

"Take her down," I told the operator.

And I headed back for that office. I was nearly there when I met Joseph Bolton, as he lurched down the hall. He had a gun in his hand. His light brown suitcoat was splotched with blood in several places; so was his right arm. He wasn't wearing his eyeglasses, which made his face seem naked somehow. His expression seemed at once frightened, pained, and sorrowful.

He staggered toward me like a child taking its first steps, and I held my arms out to him like daddy. But they were more likely his last steps: he fell to the marble floor and began to writhe, tracing abstract designs in his own blood on the smooth surface.

I moved toward him and he pointed the gun at me, a little .32 revolver. "Stay away! Stay away!"

"Okay, bud, okay," I said.

I heard someone laughing.

A woman.

I looked up and in the office doorway, feet planted like a giant surveying a puny world, was dumpy little Mildred, in her floral housedress and raccoon stole. Her mug was split in a big goofy smile.

"Don't pay any attention to him, Mr. Heller," she said, lightly. "He's just faking."

"He's shot to shit, lady!" I said.

Keeping their distance out of respect and fear were various tenth-floor tenants, standing near their various offices, as if witnessing some strange performance.

"Keep her away from me!" Bolton managed to shout. His mouth was bubbling with blood. His body moved slowly across the marble floor like a slug, leaving a slimy red trail.

I moved to Mrs. Bolton, stood between her and Bolton. "You just take it easy . . ."

Mrs. Bolton, giggling, peeked out from in back of me. "Look at him, fooling everybody."

"You behave," I told her. Then I called out to a businessman of about fifty near the elevators. I asked him if there were any doctors in the building, and he said yes, and I said then for Christsake go get one.

"Why don't you get up and stop faking?" she said teasingly to her fallen husband, the Southern drawl dripping off her words. She craned her neck around me to see him, like she couldn't bear to miss a moment of the show.

"Keep her away! Keep her away!"

Bolton continued to writhe like a wounded snake, but he kept clutching that gun, and wouldn't let anyone near him. He would cry out that he couldn't breathe, beating his legs against the floor, but he seemed always conscious of his wife's presence. He would move his head so as to keep my body between him and her round cold glittering eyes.

"Don't you mind Joe, Mr. Heller. He's just putting on an act."

If so, I had a hunch it was his final performance.

And now he began to scream in pain.

I approached him and he looked at me with tears in his eyes, eyes that bore the confusion of a child in pain, and he relented, allowed me to come close, handed me the gun, like he was offering a gift. I accepted it, by the nose of the thing, and dropped it in my pocket.

"Did you shoot yourself, Mr. Bolton?" I asked him.

"Keep that woman away from me," he managed, lips bloody.

"He's not really hurt," his wife said, mincingly, from the office doorway.

"Did your wife shoot you?"

"Just keep her away . . ."

Two people in white came rushing toward us—a doctor and a nurse—and I stepped aside, but the doctor, a middle-aged, rather heavyset man with glasses, asked if I'd give him a hand. I said sure and pitched in.

Bolton was a big man, nearly two hundred pounds I'd say, and pretty much dead weight; we staggered toward the elevator like drunks. Like Bolton himself had staggered toward me, actually. The nurse tagged along.

So did Mrs. Bolton.

The nurse, young, blond, slender, did her best to keep Mrs. Bolton out of the elevator, but Mrs. Bolton pushed her way through like a fullback. The doctor and I, bracing Bolton, couldn't help the young nurse.

Bolton, barely conscious, said, "Please . . . please, keep her away."

"Now, now," Mrs. Bolton said, the violence of her entry into the elevator forgotten (by her), standing almost primly, hands folded over the big black purse, "everything will be all right, dear. You'll see."

Bolton began to moan; the pain it suggested wasn't entirely physical.

On the thirteenth floor, a second doctor met us and took my place hauling Bolton, and I went ahead and opened the door onto a waiting room where patients, having witnessed the doctor and nurse race madly out of the office, were milling about expectantly. The nurse guided the doctors and their burden down a hall into an X-ray room. The nurse shut the door on them and faced Mrs. Bolton with a firm look.

"I'm sorry, Mrs. Bolton, you'll have to wait."

"Is that so?" she said.

"Mrs. Bolton," I said, touching her arm.

She glared at me. "Who invited you?"

I resisted the urge to say, *you did, you fucking cow,* and just stood back while she moved up and down the narrow corridor between the offices and examining rooms, searching for a door that would lead her to her beloved husband. She trundled up and down, grunting, talking to herself, and the nurse looked at me helplessly.

"She *is* the wife," I said, with a facial shrug.

The nurse sighed heavily and went to a door adjacent to the X-ray room and called out to Mrs. Bolton; Mrs. Bolton whirled and looked at her fiercely.

"You can view your husband's treatment from in here," the nurse said.

Mrs. Bolton smiled in tight triumph and drove her taxicab of a body into the room. I followed her. Don't ask me why.

A wide glass panel looked in on the X-ray room. Mrs. Bolton climbed onto an examination table, got up on her knees, and watched the flurry of activity beyond the glass, as her husband lay on a table being attended by the pair of frantic doctors.

"Did you shoot him, Mrs. Bolton?" I asked her.

She frowned but did not look at me. "Are *you* still here?"

"You lied to me, Mrs. Bolton."

"No, I didn't. And I didn't shoot him, either."

"What happened in there?"

"I never touched that gun." She was moving her head side to side, like somebody in the bleachers trying to see past the person sitting in front.

"Did your husband shoot himself?"

She made a childishly smug face. "Joe's just faking to get everybody's sympathy. He's not really hurt."

The door opened behind me and I turned to see a police officer step in.

The officer frowned at us, and shook his head as if to say "Oh, no." It was an understandable response: it was the same cop, the mounted officer, who'd come upon the disturbance outside the Van Buren Hotel. Not surprising, really—this part of the Loop was his beat, or anyway his horse's.

He crooked his finger for me to step out in the hall and I did.

"I heard a murder was being committed up on the tenth floor of 166," he explained, meaning 166 West Jackson. "Do you know what happened? Did you see it?"

I told him what I knew, which for somebody on the scene was damned little.

"Did she do it?" the officer asked.

"The gun was in the husband's hand," I shrugged. "Speaking of which . . ."

And I took the little revolver out of my pocket, holding the gun by its nose again.

"What make is this?" the officer said, taking it.

"I don't recognize it."

He read off the side: "Narizmande Eibar Spair. Thirty-two caliber."

"It got the job done."

He held the gun so that his hand avoided the grip; tried to break it open, but couldn't.

"What's wrong with this thing?" he said.

"The trigger's been snapped on empty shells, I'd say. After six slugs were gone, the shooter kept shooting. Just once around wouldn't drive the shells into the barrel like that."

"Judas," the officer said.

The X-ray room's door opened and the doctor I'd shared the elevator and Bolton's dead weight with stepped into the hall, bloody and bowed.

"He's dead," the doctor said, wearily. "Choked to death on his own blood, poor bastard."

I said nothing; just glanced at the cop, who shrugged.

"The wife's in there," I said, pointing.

But I was pointing to Mrs. Bolton, who had stepped out into the hall. She was smiling pleasantly.

She said, "You're not going to frighten me about Joe. He's a great big man and as strong as a horse. Of course, I begin to think he ought to go to the hospital this time—for a while."

"Mrs. Bolton," the doctor said, flatly, with no sympathy whatsoever, "your husband is dead."

Like a spiteful brat, she stuck out her tongue. "Liar," she said.

The doctor sighed, turned to the cop. "Shall I call the morgue, or would you like the honor?"

"You should make the call, Doctor," the officer said.

Mrs. Bolton moved slowly toward the door to the X-ray room, from which the other doctor, his smock blood-spattered, emerged. She seemed to lose her footing, then, and I took her arm yet again. This time she accepted the help. I walked her into the room and she approached the body, stroked its brow with stubby fingers.

"I can't believe he'd go," she said.

From behind me, the doctor said, "He's dead, Mrs. Bolton. Please leave the room."

Still stroking her late husband's brow, she said, "He feels cold. So cold."

She kissed his cheek.

Then she smiled down at the body and patted its head, as one might a sleeping child, and said, "He's got a beautiful head, hasn't he?"

The officer stepped into the room and said, "You'd better come along with me, Mrs. Bolton. Captain Stege wants to talk to you."

"You're making a terrible mistake. I didn't shoot him."

He took her arm; she assumed a regal posture. He asked her if she would like him to notify any relatives or friends.

"I have no relatives or friends," she said, proudly. "I never had anybody or wanted anybody except Joe."

A crowd was waiting on the street. Damn near a mob, and at the forefront were the newshounds, legmen and cameramen alike. Cameras were clicking away as Davis of the *News* and a couple of others blocked the car waiting at the curb to take Mrs. Bolton to the Homicide Bureau. The mounted cop, with her in tow, brushed them and their questions aside and soon the car, with her in it, was inching into the late afternoon traffic. The reporters and photogs began flagging cabs to take quick pursuit, but snide, boyish Davis lingered to ask me a question.

"What were you doing here, Heller?"

"Getting a hangnail looked at up at the doctor's office."

"Fuck, Heller, you got blood all over you!"

I shrugged, lifted my middle finger. "Hell of a hangnail."

He smirked and I smirked and pushed through the crowd and hoofed it back to my office.

I was sitting at my desk, about an hour later, when the phone rang.

"Get your ass over here!"

"Captain Stege?"

"No, Walter Winchell. You were an eyewitness to a homicide, Heller! Get your ass over here!"

The phone clicked in my ear and I shrugged to nobody and got my hat and went over to the First District Station, entering off Eleventh. It was a new, modern, nondescript high rise; if this was the future, who needed it.

In Stege's clean little office, from behind his desk, the clean little cop looked out his black-rimmed, round-lensed glasses at me and said, "Did you see her do it?"

"I told the officer at the scene all about it, Captain."

"You didn't make a statement."

"Get a stenographer in here and I will."

He did and I did.

That seemed to cool the stocky little cop down. He and I had been adversaries once, though were getting along better these days. But there was still a strain.

Thought gripped his doughy, owlish countenance. "How do you read it, Heller?"

"I don't know. He had the gun. Maybe it was suicide."

"Everybody in that building agrees with you. Bolton's been having a lot of trouble with his better half. They think she drove him to suicide, finally. But there's a hitch."

"Yeah?"

"Suicides don't usually shoot themselves five times, two of 'em in the back."

I had to give him that.

"You think she's nuts?" Stege asked.

"Nuttier than a fruitcake."

"Maybe. But that was murder—premeditated."

"Oh, I doubt that, Captain. Don't you know a crime of passion when you see it? Doesn't the unwritten law apply to women as well as men?"

"The answer to your question is yes to the first, and no to the second. You want to see something?"

"Sure."

From his desk he handed me a small slip of paper.

It was a receipt for a gun sold on June 11 by the Hammond Loan Company of Hammond, Indiana, to a Mrs. Sarah Weston.

"That was in her purse," Stege said, smugly. "Along with a powder puff, a hanky, and some prayer leaflets."

"And you think Sarah Weston is just a name Mrs. Bolton used to buy the .32 from the pawn shop?"

"Certainly. And that slip—found in a narrow side pocket in the lining of her purse—proves premeditation."

"Does it, Captain?" I said, smiling, standing, hat in hand. "It seems to me premeditation would have warned her to get *rid* of that receipt. But then, what do I know? I'm not cop." From the doorway I said, "Just a detective."

And I left him there to mull that over.

In the corridor, on my way out, Sam Backus buttonholed me.

"Got a minute for a pal, Nate?"

"Sam, if we were pals, I'd see you someplace besides court."

Sam was with the Public Defender's office, and I'd bumped into him from time to time, dating back to my cop days. He was a conscientious and skillful attorney who, in better times, might have had a lucrative private practice; in times like these, he was glad to have a job. Sam's sharp features and receding hairline gave the smallish man a ferretlike appearance; he was similarly intense, too.

"My client says she employed you to do some work for her," he said, in a rush. "She'd like you to continue—"

"Wait a minute, wait a minute—your client? Not Mrs. Mildred Bolton?"

"Yes."

"She's poison. You're on your own."

"She tells me you were given a hundred-dollar retainer."

"Well, that's true, but I figured I earned it."

"She figures you owe her some work, or some dough."

"Sam, she lied to me. She misrepresented herself and her intentions." I was walking out the building and he was staying right with me.

"She's a disturbed individual. And she's maintaining she didn't kill her husband."

"They got her cold." I told him about Stege's evidence.

"It could've been planted," he said, meaning the receipt. "Look, Bolton's secretary was up there, and Mrs. Bolton says he and the girl—an Angela something, sounds like 'who-you'—were having an affair."

"I thought the affair was supposed to be with Marie Winston."

"Her, too. Bolton must've been a real ladies' man. And the Winston woman was up there at that office this afternoon, too, before the shooting."

"Was she there during the shooting, though?"

"I don't know. I need to find out. The Public Defender's office doesn't have an investigative staff, you know that, Nate. And I can't afford to hire anybody, and I don't have the time to do the legwork myself. You owe her some days. Deliver."

He had a point.

I gathered some names from Sam, and the next morning I began to interview the participants.

"An affair with Joe?" Angela Houyoux said. "Why, that's nonsense."

We were in the outer office of BOLTON AND SCHMIDT. She'd given me the nickel tour of the place: one outer office, and two inner ones, the one to the south having been Bolton's. The crime scene told me nothing. Angela, the sweet-smelling dark-haired beauty who'd tumbled into my arms and the elevator yesterday, did.

"I was rather shaken by Mrs. Bolton's behavior at first—and his. But then it became rather routine to come to the office and find the glass in the door broken, or Mr. Bolton with his hands cut from taking a knife away from Mrs. Bolton. After a few weeks, I grew quite accustomed to having dictation interrupted while Mr. and Mrs. Bolton scuffled and fought and yelled. Lately they argued about Mrs. Winston a lot."

"How was your relationship with Mrs. Bolton?"

"Spotty, I guess you'd call it. Sometimes she'd seem to think I was interested in her husband. Other times she'd confide in me like a sister. I never said much to her. I'd just shrug my shoulders or just look at her kind of sympathetic. I had the feeling she didn't have anybody else to talk to about this. She'd cry and say her husband was unfaithful—I didn't dare point out they'd been separated for a year and that Mr. Bolton had filed for divorce and all. One time . . . well, maybe I shouldn't say it."

"Say it."

"One time she said she 'just might kill' her husband. She said they never convict a woman for murder in Cook County."

Others in the building at West Jackson told similar tales. Bolton's business partner, Schmidt, wondered why Bolton bothered to get an injunction to keep his wife out of the office, but then refused to mail her her temporary alimony, giving her a reason to come to the office all the time.

"He would dole out the money, two or three dollars at a time," Schmidt said. "He could have paid her what she had coming for a month, or at least a week—Joe made decent money. It would've got rid of her. Why parcel it out?"

The elevator operator I'd met yesterday had a particularly wild yarn.

"Yesterday, early afternoon, Mr. Bolton got on at the ninth floor. He seemed in an awful hurry and said, 'Shoot me up to eleven.' I had a signal to stop at ten, so I made the stop and Mrs. Bolton came charging aboard. Mr. Bolton was right next to me. He kind of hid behind me and said, 'For God's sake, she'll kill us both!' I sort of forced the door closed on her, and she stood there in the corridor and raised her fist and said, 'Goddamnit, I'll fix you!' I guess she meant Bolton, not me."

"Apparently."

"Anyway, I took him up to eleven and he kind of sighed and as he got off he said, 'It's just hell, isn't it?' I said it was a damn shame he couldn't do anything about it."

"This was yesterday."

"Yes, sir. Not long before he was killed."

"Did it occur to you, at the time, it might lead to that?"

"No, sir. It was pretty typical, actually. I helped him escape from her before. And I kept her from getting on the elevator downstairs, sometimes. After all, he had an injunction to keep her from 'molesting him at his place of business,' he said."

Even the heavyset doctor up on thirteen found time for me.

"I think they were *both* sick," he said, rather bitterly I thought.

"What do you mean, Doctor?"

"I mean that I've administered more first aid to that man than a battlefield physician. That woman has beaten her husband, cut him with a knife, with a razor, created commotions and scenes with such regularity that the patrol wagon coming for Mildred is a commonplace occurrence on West Jackson."

"How well did you know Bolton?"

"We were friendly. God knows I spent enough time with him, patching him up. He should've been a much more successful man than he was, you know. She drove him out of one job and another. I never understood him."

"Oh?"

"Well, they live, or lived, in Hyde Park. That's a university neighborhood. Fairly refined, very intellectual, really."

"Was Bolton a scholar?"

"He had bookish interests. He liked having the University of Chicago handy. Now why would a man of his sensibilities endure a violent harridan like Mildred Bolton?"

"In my trade, Doc," I said, "we call that a mystery."

I talked to more people. I talked to a pretty blond legal secretary named Peggy O'Reilly who, in 1933, had been employed by Ocean Accident and Guarantee Company. Joseph Bolton, Jr., had been a business associate there.

"His desk was four feet from mine," she said. "But I never went out with him. There was no social contact whatsoever, but Mrs. Bolton didn't believe that. She came into the office and accused me of—well, called me a 'dirty hussy,' if you must know. I asked her to step out into the hall where we wouldn't attract so much attention, and she did—and proceeded to tear my clothes off me. She tore the clothes off my body, scratched my neck, my face, kicked me, it was horrible. The attention it attracted . . . oh, dear. Several hundred people witnessed the sight—two nice men pulled her off of me. I was badly bruised and out of the office a week. When I came back, Mr. Bolton had been discharged."

A pattern was forming here, one I'd seen before; but usually it was the wife who was battered and yet somehow endured and even encouraged the twisted union. Only Bolton was a battered husband, a strapping man who never turned physically on his abusing wife; his only punishment had been to withhold that money from her, dole it out a few bucks at a time. That was the only satisfaction, the only revenge, he'd been able to extract.

At the Van Buren Hotel I knocked on the door of what had been Bolton's room. 3C.

Young Charles Winston answered. He looked terrible. Pale as milk, only not near as healthy. Eyes bloodshot. He was in a T-shirt and boxer shorts. The other times I'd seen him he'd been fully and even nattily attired.

"Put some clothes on," I said. "We have to talk."

In the saloon below the hotel we did that very thing.

"Joe was a great guy," he said, eyes brimming with tears. He would have cried into his beer, only he was having a mixed drink. I was picking up the tab, so Mildred Bolton was buying it.

"Is your mother still in town?"

He looked up with sharp curiosity. "No. She's back in Woodstock. Why?"

"She was up at the office shortly before Bolton was killed."

"I know. I was there, too."

"Oh?" Now, that was news.

"We went right over, after the hearing."

"To tell him how it came out?"

"Yes, and to thank him. You see, after that incident out in front, last Wednesday, when they took me off to jail, Mother went to see Joe. They met at the Twelfth Street Bus Depot. She asked him if he would take care of my bail—she could have had her brother do it, in the morning, but I'd have had to spend the night in jail first." He smiled fondly. "Joe went right over to the police station with the money and got me out."

"That was white of him."

"Sure was. Then we met Mother over at the taproom of the Auditorium Hotel."

Very posh digs; interesting place for folks who lived at the Van Buren to be hanging out.

"Unfortunately, I'd taken time to stop back at the hotel to pick up some packages my mother had left behind. Mrs. Bolton must've been waiting here for me. She followed me to the Auditorium taproom, where she attacked me with her fists, and told the crowd in no uncertain terms, and in a voice to wake the dead, that my mother was"—he shook his head—"'nothing but a whore' and such. Finally the management ejected her."

"Was your mother in love with Joe?"

He looked at me sharply. "Of course not. They were friendly. That's the extent of it."

"When did you and your mother leave Bolton's office?"

"Yesterday? About one-thirty. Mrs. Bolton was announced as being in the outer office, and we just got the hell out."

"Neither of you lingered."

"No. Are you going to talk to my mother?"

"Probably."

"I wish you wouldn't," he said glumly.

I drank my beer, studying the kid.

"Maybe I won't have to," I said, smiled at him, patted his shoulder, and left.

I met with public defender Backus in a small interrogation room at the First District Station.

"Your client is guilty," I said.

I was sitting. He was standing. Pacing.

"The secretary was in the outer office at all times," I said. "In view of other witnesses. The Winstons left around one-thirty. They were seen leaving by the elevator operator on duty."

"One of them could have sneaked back up the stairs . . ."

"I don't think so. Anyway, this meeting ends my participation, other than a report I'll type up for you. I've used up the hundred."

From my notes I read off summaries of the various interviews I'd conducted. He finally sat, sweat beading his brow, eyes slitted behind the glasses.

"She says she didn't do it," he said.

"She says a lot of things. I think you can get her off, anyway."

He smirked. "Are you a lawyer now?"

"No. Just a guy who's been in the thick of this bizarre fucking case since day one."

"I bow to your experience if not expertise."

"You can plead her insane, Sam."

"A very tough defense to pull off, and besides, she won't hear of it. She wants no psychiatrists, no alienists involved."

"You can still get her off."

"How in hell?"

I let some air out. "I'm going to have to talk to her before I say any more. It's going to have to be up to her."

"You can't tell me?"

"You're not my client."

Mildred Bolton was.

And she was ushered into the interrogation room by a matron who then waited outside the door. She wore the same floral print dress, but the raccoon stole was gone. She smiled faintly upon seeing me, sat across from me.

"You been having fun with the press, Mildred, haven't you?"

"I sure have. They call me 'Marble Mildred.' They think I'm cold."

"They think it's unusual for a widow to joke about her dead husband."

"They're silly people. They asked me the name of my attorney and I said, 'Horsefeathers.'" She laughed. That struck her very funny; she was proud of herself over that witty remark.

"I'm glad you can find something to smile about."

"I'm getting hundreds of letters, you know. Fan mail! They say, 'You should have killed him whether you did or not.' I'm not the only woman wronged in Chicago, you know."

"They've got you dead bang, Mildred. I've seen some of the evidence. I've talked to the witnesses."

"Did you talk to Mrs. Winston? It was her fault, you know. Her and that . . . that boy."

"You went to see Joe after the boy was fined in court."

"Yes! I called him and told him that the little degenerate had been convicted and fined. Then I asked Joe, did he have any money, because I didn't have anything to eat, and he said yes. So I went to the office and when I got there he tried to give me a check for ten dollars. I said, 'I guess you're going to pay that boy's fine and that's why you haven't any money for me.' He said, 'That's all you're going to get.' And I said, 'Do you mean for a whole *week*? To pay rent out of and eat on?' He said, 'Yes, that's all you get.'"

"He was punishing you."

"I suppose. We argued for about an hour and then he said he had business on another floor—that boy's lawyer is on the ninth floor, you know—and I followed him, chased him to the elevator, but he got away. I went back and said to Miss Houyoux, 'He ran away from me.' I waited in his office and in about an hour he came back. I said, 'Joe, I have been your wife for fourteen years and I think I deserve more respect and better treatment than that.' He just leaned back in his chair so cocky and said, 'You know what you are?' And then he said it."

"Said it?"

She swallowed; for the first time, those marble eyes filled with tears. "He said, 'You're just a dirty old bitch.' Then he said it again. Then I said, 'Just a dirty old bitch for fourteen years?' And I pointed the gun at him."

"Where was it?"

"It was on his desk where I put it. It was in a blue box I carried in with me."

"What did you do with it, Mildred?"

"The box?"

"The gun."

"Oh. That. I fired it at him."

I gave her a handkerchief and she dabbed her eyes with it.

"How many times did you fire the gun, Mildred?"

"I don't know. He fell over in his chair and then he got up and came toward me and he said, 'Give me that gun, give me that gun.' I said, 'No, I'm going to finish myself now. Let go of me because my hand is on the trigger!'" Her teeth were clenched. "He struggled with me, and his glasses got knocked off, but he got the gun from my hand and he went out in the hall with it. I followed him, but then I turned and went back in his office. I was going to jump out of the window, but I heard him scream in the hall and I ran to him. The gun was lying beside him and I reached for it, but he reached and got it first. I went back in the office."

"Why?"

"To jump out the window, I told you. But I just couldn't leave him. I started to go back out and when I opened the door some people were around. You were one of them, Mr. Heller."

"Where did you get that gun, Mildred?"

"At a pawn shop in Hammond, Indiana."

"To kill Joe?"

"To kill myself."

"But you didn't."

"I'm sorry I didn't. I had plenty of time to do it at home, but I wanted to do it in his office. I wanted to embarrass him."

"He was shot in the back, Mildred. Twice."

"I don't know about that. Maybe his body turned when I was firing. I don't know. I don't remember."

"You know that the prosecution will not buy your suicide claims."

"They are *not* claims!"

"I know they aren't. But they won't buy them. They'll tell the judge and the jury that all your talk of suicide is just a clever excuse to get around planning Joe's murder. In other words, that you premeditated the killing and supplied yourself with a gun— and a reason for having a gun."

"I don't know about those things."

"Would you like to walk away from this?"

"Well, of course. I'm not crazy."

Right.

"You can, I think. But it's going to be hard on you. They're going to paint you as a shrew. As a brutal woman who battered her husband. They'll suggest that Bolton was too much of a gentleman for his own good, that he should have struck back at you, physically."

She giggled. "He wasn't such a gentleman."

"Really?"

"He wasn't what you think at all. Not at all."

"What do you mean, Mildred?"

"We were married for fourteen years before he tried to get rid of me. That's a long time."

"It sure is. What is it about your husband that we're getting wrong?"

"I haven't said."

"I know that. Tell me."

"I won't tell you. I've never told a living soul. I never will."

"I think you should. I think you need to."

"I won't. I won't now. I won't ever."

"There were no other women, were there, Mildred?"

"There were countless women, countless!"

"Like Marie Winston."

"She was the worst!"

"What about her son?"

"That little . . ." She stopped herself.

"That little degenerate? That's what you seem to always call him."

She nodded, pursing her thin wide lips.

"Joe was living in a fleabag hotel," I said. "A guy with *his* money. Why?"

"It was close to his work."

"Relatively. I think it had to do with who he was living with. A young man."

"A lot of men room together."

"There were no other women, were there, Mildred? Your husband used you to hide behind, didn't he, for many years."

She was crying now. The marble woman was crying now. "I loved him. I loved him."

"I know you did. And I don't know when you discovered it. Maybe you never did, really. Maybe you just suspected, and couldn't bring yourself to admit it. Then, after he left you, after he moved out of the house, you finally decided to find out, really find out. You hired me, springing for a hundred precious bucks you'd scrimped and saved, knowing I might find things out you'd want kept quiet. Knowing I might confirm the suspicions that drove you bughouse for years."

"Stop it . . . please stop it . . ."

"Your refined husband who liked to be near a college campus. You knew there were affairs. And there were. But not with women."

She stood, squeezing my hanky in one fist. "I don't have to listen to this!"

"You do if you want to be a free woman. The unwritten law doesn't seem to apply to women as equally as it does to men. But if you tell the truth about your husband—about just who it was he was seeing behind your back—I guarantee you no jury will convict you."

Her mouth was trembling.

I stood. "It's up to you, Mildred."

"Are you going to tell Mr. Backus?"

"No. You're my client. I'll respect your wishes."

"I wish you would just go. Just go, Mr. Heller."

I went.

I told Backus nothing except that I would suggest he introduce expert testimony from an alienist. He didn't. His client wouldn't hear of it.

The papers continued to have a great time with Marble Mildred. She got to know the boys of the press, became bosom buddies with the sob sisters, warned cameramen not to take a profile pic or she'd break their lens, shouted greetings and wisecracks to one and all. She laughed and talked; being on trial for murder was a lark to her.

Of course, as the trial wore on, she grew less boisterous, even became sullen at times. On the stand she told her story more or less straight, but minus any hint her husband was bent. The prosecution, as I had told her they would, ridiculed her statement that she'd bought the .32 to do herself in. The prosecutor extolled "motherhood and wifehood," but expressed "the utmost comtempt for Mildred Bolton." She was described as "dirt," "filth," "vicious," and more. She was sentenced to die in the electric chair.

She didn't want an appeal, a new trial.

"As far as I am concerned," she told the stunned judge, "I am perfectly satisfied with things as they now stand."

But Cook County was squeamish about electrocuting a woman; just half an hour before the execution was to take place, hair shaved above one ear, wearing special females-only electrocution shorts, Mildred was spared by Governor Horner.

Mildred, who'd been strangely blissful in contemplation of her electrocution, was less pleased with her new sentence of 199 years. Nonetheless she was a model prisoner, until August 29, 1943, when she was found slumped in her cell, wrists slashed. She had managed to smuggle some scissors in. It took her hours to die. Sitting in the darkness, waiting for the blood to empty out of her.

She left a note, stuck to one wall:

> To whom it may concern. In the event of my death do not notify anybody or try to get in touch with family or friends. I wish to die as I have lived, completely alone.

What she said was true, but I wondered if I was the only person alive who knew that it hadn't been by choice.

AUTHOR'S NOTE: I wish to acknowledge the true-crime article "Joseph Bolton, the Almost Indestructible Husband" by Nellise Child. Also helpful was the Mildred Bolton entry in *Find the Woman* by Jay Robert Nash. And my thanks to my research associate George Hagenauer. Most names in the preceding fact-based story have been changed or at least altered (exceptions include the Boltons and Captain Stege); fact, speculation, and fiction are freely mixed therein.

MICHAEL COLLINS

BLACK IN THE SNOW

Michael Collins's first Dan Fortune novel, Act of Fear, *won the Mystery Writers of America Edgar Award for Best First Novel of 1967. In February of 1988 the new Fortune novel,* Red Rosa, *was published by Donald I. Fine. That makes Fortune presently one of the longest continuously running P.I. series.*

Michael Collins is a past president of PWA, and has also written mystery series as John Crowe, Mark Sadler, and William Arden. Under his real name, Dennis Lynds, he has written novels and works of short fiction.

"Black in the Snow" marks Fortune's second appearance in a PWA anthology.

No more than a black spot in the unbroken snow.

The February afternoon sun reflected from the windows of the silent suburban house, and I looked at the small black dog dead in the white expanse of the Ralstons' front yard. On the distant parkway the traffic throbbed in its endless stream, but on the snow, and in the white frame house with the green shutters, nothing moved.

"It ought to be an easy one, Fortune," the lawyer had said. "George Ralston never hurt a fly. A solid man, an executive. Married twenty years. No children, they lived well. Middle-class people with their own home, bank accounts, the works."

"What does Ralston say happened?"

"He hasn't any idea. Too broken up and under sedation to think about it," the lawyer said. "But it has to be robbery, some nut on the loose. They have a lot of burglaries out in Manhasset; Anna Ralston and the dog must have surprised the bastard and he killed them."

"How?"

"Knife." The lawyer shuddered and shook his head. "The dog

had its throat cut, Anna Ralston was stabbed twice. In the stomach and under the ribs. Blood all over the pantry. George Ralston doesn't kill that way, has a wall of guns to use."

"They find the weapon?"

The lawyer nodded. "It was next to the woman. A butcher knife from the kitchen."

"Their kitchen? It was their knife?"

"That's what I mean. Anna Ralston walked in, some junkie burglar panicked. Blood all over and none on George Ralston."

"Any prints?"

"Smudges. You know prints on a wood-handled knife."

"Why are they holding him?"

"Nothing was stolen," the lawyer said. "The house wasn't broken into, no tracks in the snow. Some neighbor heard the Ralstons in a screaming fight the night before, and George's alibi isn't airtight. He was in Great Neck that afternoon, but could have gotten home an hour or two before he did."

"What's Ralston's story?"

"He stopped in a couple of bars, no one saw him. When he got home he found her dead in the pantry. He doesn't remember much after that except he called the police."

Lawyers see what they want to see, believe what they have to believe, tell an investigator just enough so he can find what they want him to find.

"Why the dog, Counsellor? Why kill the dog?"

"Maybe it attacked the killer."

"What kind of dog?"

Even he had the grace to look away. "Pomeranian."

"Some thief."

Lawyers don't give up easily. Without hard evidence, one theory is as good as another.

"Look," the lawyer said, "the wife always had a dog. Four in the twenty years they were married. Small dogs, maybe because she was small herself, Ralston says. He's a big guy, burly, used to work in the factory where he's vice president now. He says she was always with the dog. She carried them around with her everywhere. So when she surprised the thief she had the dog. It got in the way or he had to stop its barking."

And then threw the dead dog out into the snow? Why? The lawyer would have had an answer, but I didn't. I stood in the evening winter light and looked at the silent suburban house and

saw a small black dog dead in the snow without footprints or any
other tracks leading to it.

There were drops of blood in the center of the pale carpeting in
the hallway to the front door, and then no more until the narrow
pantry behind the kitchen. The large, formal living room was
immaculate, with green brocade period furniture, the dining
room furnished in light, delicate woods from what could have
been the same antique period. The silver on the sideboard was
rubbed to a soft glow and probably used every day.

I stood in the doorway between the dining room and kitchen
and imagined the Ralstons eating dinner every night in the
spotless formal room with its perpetually polished silver. Two
middle-aged people alone at the long table. He, from what the
lawyer said, a big, burly man who liked shirtsleeves; she a small,
slender woman still pretty and birdlike, the small black dog at her
feet if not in her lap. It was a picture violence had no place in.
Boredom, maybe, but not violence.

The windowless pantry across the kitchen held a different
picture. Blood black on the walls, the floor, even the ceiling. The
random slashing of a psychotic, or terrified amateur, or drug-
crazed thief? I let my eyes take it in, squatted down to study the
floor. The blanket and basket of the dog's bed were soaked with
blood, and the floor around it was literally coated. The killings
must have happened there, and without much struggle, the
spattered blood thin on the walls and ceiling. Savage, yes, but not
the pattern of a random, senseless slashing.

The kitchen with its flowered curtains was polished but not
immaculate: a dirty cup and saucer in the sink; a plate with a
soggy crust; the coffee maker still with stale coffee; one chair
moved from the kitchen table to the wall telephone. I looked
again at the well-used dining room with everything in its proper
place, at the living room barely dusty even after a week of being
untouched, and then went upstairs.

There were two bedrooms, a small sewing-and-plant room with
a half-greenhouse wall, and a den-office.

The faint sound came from below.

A key turning softly in the front door.

Footsteps of someone trying to be soundless. Inside the den-
office I stood back behind the door. Who had a key beside me,
George Ralston, and the police?

Then she was in the room. A woman with dark hair, slim and more than attractive, but with the hands of over forty.

"George?"

I stepped out. "You often meet George here?"

"Jesus!" She jumped a foot and turned scared. "Who . . . who are you?"

"Did Mrs. Ralston know about you and George?"

Her eyes were brown and confused. "You're the police? Have you found anything? I mean, the man—"

"Private detective," I said. "I've found something now. You want to tell me about you and George?"

The brown eyes blinked. "George and me?" She shook her head. "No, I'm his sister. You thought George—?"

Guns hung all over the den walls: modern military rifles and pistols, even a light machine gun, as the lawyer had said. But he had forgotten to mention, or hadn't known, that they were all inoperative. No matter how violent George Ralston got, they were no more than clubs.

"Private detective?" the sister said.

"His lawyer hired me."

"Then they think George could have—!"

"What do you think, Miss Ralston?"

"Mrs. Deming," she said. "Sarah. I think they're insane."

"Someone killed her and the dog."

The desk was piled with books, pamphlets, letters. There was a TV set, a small refrigerator to save trips downstairs for beer, and a convertible couch that had been used and left open. Someone had slept in the den sometime before the killings, and no one had made the bed.

"George drinks," Sarah Deming said. "Anna wouldn't let him sleep with her when he was drunk."

"Which came first?" I said.

"What?"

"Which came first, not sleeping together or his drinking?"

She flushed. "I wouldn't know. Perhaps a little of both."

Between the guns on the wall above the desk were photographs of men in heavy shoes and work clothes inside a factory. Only one face was in all the photos: a big, heavyset young man with a wide grin and his arms around his buddies.

"George is proud of having worked with his hands," Sarah Deming said. "Down on the factory floor with the real workers.

He's never really gotten used to being an executive, goes out with his old work friends when he drinks."

"He drinks a lot?"

She shrugged. "Enough, mister . . . ?"

"Dan Fortune. Were they having any trouble, Mrs. Deming?"

"Make it Sarah, okay? Deming and I busted a long time ago." She smiled for the first time. It was a nice smile that faded almost at once. "No trouble I know except his drinking. That bothered her a lot. She even had a plan to get him to stop."

"She talked to you about it?"

"To all of us. The Wednesday afternoon coffee club just the day before she . . . died. She started talking about George."

They sit in the green brocade living room. Five ladies around the coffee table eating small cakes, talking.

"I'm not sure when he changed," Anna Ralston says. "He always drank, mostly beer with his friends. I never liked it, but he didn't drink when we were together, so it wasn't that important. But now he's drinking all the time."

Anna holds the small dog in her lap, a black puff of fur. A nervous ball of fur, its eyes fixed on Miss Guilfoyle as she speaks. Anna strokes the tiny dog, soothes, reassures. The dog turns its fox-like face up to her, its small blue tongue out.

"I don't know why men have to drink," Miss Guilfoyle says. She sells a little real estate, inherited a house from her brother, almost married a man named Donald once, and has never forgotten. "Not that Donald drank. That wasn't our problem."

Grace Hill says, "My Fred says George can be very insulting when he's had too much, especially in the executive lounge."

"I'm sorry, Grace. You see, it's even affecting his work now. Something has to be done."

"He's forty-six," Sarah says. "Maybe it's change of life."

Barbara Oliveri giggles. "Men do get moody around fifty."

Anna says, "It's a wife's job to help her husband; my mother always told me, be a jump ahead of him."

"You've got some plan for old George," Sarah says.

Anna nods. "It came to me this morning when I was combing Mitzi."

She smiles down at the dog curled into her lap. The small dog lays back its ears and closes its eyes, oblivious now that its mistress is talking, going to sleep while its body continues to twitch in the nervousness of all small animals.

Anna smiles at her friends. "I've decided to buy George a dog of his own. I suddenly realized how unfair I've been. He's wanted a big dog ever since he had to give that collie away before we were married. Don't you think it's a fine idea?"

"It would certainly give him something to do beside drink," Miss Guilfoyle says.

Grace Hill isn't sure. "Two dogs are a lot of trouble."

"Especially a big dog," Barbara Oliveri says.

"Have you told him?" Sarah asks.

"I'm going to tell him tonight," Anna says, satisfied. "I think it's a wonderful idea. Mitzi means so much to me."

I said, "Did she get him the dog?"

"No," Sarah Deming said.

We had moved on to the front bedroom. It was a large, light bedroom that faced the front lawn with its evening sun glare reflecting off the snow. Outside, the small smudge of black still lay motionless in the expanse of white. Inside, a queen-sized bed had only one side slept in. It was unmade, too.

"Did she make the beds first or last?" I asked.

"In the morning," Sarah Deming said. "Always. She cleaned like a temple every day, beds first."

The bedroom had a feminine, girlish aura: pastel pinks and yellows; ruffles and skirts on the chairs and vanity; dried corsages, old programs, high school pennants; yellowed photos on the walls. In the photos a girl in longish fifties dresses, and an older couple in dark, reserved clothes, mingled with small Oriental people in Japanese kimonos and polyglot Western garb.

"Anna and her parents," Sarah Deming said. "Missionaries in Japan all through the war and after. Anna was born over there."

"Where are they now?"

"Dead. Her father died soon after they came back in the late fifties, her mother only five years ago. I met her a few times when she came to visit, didn't like her much. A real sour type full of pronouncements and wise sayings. A chip on her shoulder about something, probably the wicked world."

"Where did they go after Japan?"

"Nowhere. There was some trouble. They retired as missionaries when they got back. Anna didn't like to talk about it."

Nothing on the second floor showed evidence of an intruder as far as I could tell, and we went downstairs. Nothing in the whole house indicated an intruder. We stood in the kitchen.

"Was your brother messing around, Sarah? Another woman?"

"So they do think George killed her!"

"They don't know who killed her. Or why."

She shook her head, angry. "He just drank. Most people don't go to the effort of breaking out when they're comfortable, do they? Anna's mother said it: 'Give a man a home, take care of him, that's all he really needs.' Anna was good at that."

"Then he had a reason to break out?"

"He had a reason to drink." She shook her head. "He wasn't happy, hadn't been for years, but he wasn't the type to go to another woman."

"What about her? His drinking bothered her a lot."

"Anna? God no! She had her house, her duties, and her dogs. She always had her dogs. Mitzi was the fourth since they were married. She got the first one while George was still on the factory floor and they had a small apartment in Queens."

"Any enemies? Maybe from the past? In Japan? Something to do with her parents? With their work?"

She shook her head. "I wouldn't know about that." She looked at me. "I just know George didn't kill her."

I wished I knew as much. Lawyers don't hire a detective to prove their client guilty. I wanted to talk to the neighbors, but it was dinnertime in the suburbs, the men coming home. No one would want to talk now, and I needed a beer.

"Buy you a drink?"

Sarah Deming smiled. "Why not. As long as you're on our side. You are on our side?"

"I'll do my best."

The tavern was on the water overlooking Manhasset Bay. We both had Amstel Lights. She hadn't even asked about my missing arm.

"Why didn't she buy the dog for George?"

"He didn't want it." She poured the last of her beer. "You always knew George was home because her dog started barking. That evening Mitzi barked even before we heard the garage door open. He always came in and sat in his big armchair, his suitcoat off, his feet up on another chair. Anna hated that, but she never said anything because her mother told her you had to put up with things men did, make allowances. That was one of the mother's favorite sayings. Anna didn't always follow it with George, but that night she was eager to tell him her big idea."

"Two dogs are too much trouble, Anna."

"You always wanted your own dog, George. A nice big one. You can fence in the backyard, even build a doghouse."

"The yard for my dog, eh?"

"A house is no place for a big dog. Certainly not a male."

George begins to laugh. "We could mate him to Mitzi. God, can you see the pups? Mitzi and a Great Dane?"

Sarah laughs, too. Anna doesn't laugh. The small dog raises its head on Anna's lap, its eyes watchful, alert. Anna holds the dog with both hands.

George shrugs. "I don't need a dog, Anna."

"You've always said you'd like a big dog."

"I don't need another damned dog!" George is up, walks to the liquor cabinet, pours a whiskey. "Anyone else?"

"I'll have a beer," Sarah says.

Anna says nothing; the dog only watches, its lips skinned back from small, pointed teeth as it senses George Ralston's anger. George brings beer in a glass from the kitchen for Sarah, sits down again in his chair, and stares moodily at his whiskey.

"A real dog'd be nice. One you can tell what it is. With those little ones of yours I forget which was which. Never could tell one of the damned things from another."

"That's ridiculous!" Anna snaps. "Mitzi's a Pom. Mrs. Ching was a Peke and so was Dodo. Suzy Q was a King Charles."

"Remember the collie I had when we met? Admiral? We mated him once, got half the litter. I think Ed Riley had one, dead now, of course. I saw Ed the other day down on the plant floor."

"I don't see how you could possibly confuse a Pom with a Peke or a King Charles."

"Sometimes I wish I'd stayed in the plant. Work hard all week, booze and whore on the weekend."

"I don't allow words like that, George!"

He drinks. "It's just a word, Anna."

"Sometimes I wish I'd never married you!"

He stands, drains his glass. "So do I."

"Go and drink!" Her voice is shrill. "Go and get drunk!"

The small dog barks, teeth bared in Anna's lap, its high, yapping bark as shrill as her voice.

"Why not? Falling-down drunk."

The dog goes on barking until the back door slams shut. Then it stops, looks alertly up at its mistress for approval. Anna strokes it.

Sarah Deming swirled her second Amstel. "The dog stopped the moment George was gone, and Anna got up and started to wash the glasses, straighten up, and get ready for the Girls' Club meeting she was having later. As if nothing had happened."

"Or as if it had happened a lot of times before."

She drank. "I suppose."

"What did you do?"

"Helped Anna, then went home."

"Where's home?"

"A few blocks from here. Deming at least left me a house."

"I'll escort you home after some dinner."

She smiled. "Not tonight, Dan. I'm . . . I'm still upset. You can't think George . . . ? Not George."

"No," I said, "not George."

It was never George. I paid for the drinks, watched her drive off, then headed for the parkway into the city.

Next morning I lay in bed in my loft and thought. Then I got dressed, put a long scarf under my duffel against the wind that blew the old snow river to river, went out and had some breakfast at the diner on Eighth Avenue, and called on my client.

"No evidence of a burglar around the house." I took the chair facing his desk. "I don't think there was an intruder."

"You talk to the neighbors? Any other burglaries around?"

A lawyer's job is get his client off. Innocent or guilty.

"The cops'll have done that."

"The cops aren't talking to me," the lawyer said, "but they must have something. They released George Ralston this morning."

"They make an arrest?"

"Not that I heard. I'm paying you to find out what the cops have and maybe more, not make guesses."

I went up to the main library and checked old newspapers from the late fifties, the publications of missionary societies. Then I drove my rental car out to the Nassau County Medical Center in East Meadow. The pathologist on duty read my credentials and the papers from the lawyer.

"What do you want to know about Anna Ralston?"

"Time of death first."

He opened a file. "Between four or five P.M. the afternoon she was found."

"Did she have scratches on her hands? Maybe her face? Rips in her clothes besides the knife wounds?"

He looked up at me. "You know something the police don't?"

"Then there are scratches?"

"Deep ones on both hands, even her face. Rips on the top of her dress that probably weren't the knife."

"Thanks."

If they'd released George Ralston the case probably hadn't gone to Mineola Homicide yet, so I drove to the Sixth Precinct in Manhasset. Frank Domenici was on the case. We'd worked together maybe three years ago.

"You don't buy the burglar theory?" I asked.

"Nothing to back it up yet."

"But you let George Ralston go."

"Only as far as home. He's got a so-so alibi, psychiatrist says he's really broken up, and we can't figure a motive."

"Not enough to hold him, but he's still your best bet?"

"Until somebody hands us the crazy burglar, or a stoned vagrant with red hands."

"Tell me about the screaming fight made you hold Ralston in the first place."

Domenici shrugged. "The next-door neighbor couldn't sleep the night before the killing, went out for a walk in the snow with his dog. He was right out front when he saw the light go on in the bedroom. He noticed because it was after two A.M., and he'd never known Anna Ralston to be up past eleven tops."

"Which bedroom?"

"The front," Domenici said. "The neighbor hears Ralston laugh, drunk and slurring which wasn't unusual, and say Anna gave him an idea. The neighbor hears her say, 'Go to bed, George.'"

"She made him sleep in his office when he was drunk."

"What else is new?" Domenici said. "Only he won't go to bed, says something about old Mitzi earning her keep. She tells him to look at the time. The neighbor can see his shadow weaving around while he talks about money, and she's starting to yell."

"What about the dog?"

"It's up there, the neighbor hears it growling and yapping. Ralston's voice turns nasty, says something about 'upside down,' and the wife flips out. She's yelling 'animal,' and 'pig,' and the dog's barking like crazy, and Ralston's staggering around and laughing loud and nasty, and the wife screams not to touch her and get out, and finally Ralston leaves after yelling about tomorrow, and damned bitch, and like that."

"The neighbor didn't hear what about tomorrow?"

Domenici shook his head. "It's all silent after that, the neighbor goes on walking his dog. When he comes back the light's still on in the bedroom; he can hear her sort of singing real soft but can't hear the words. He goes home to bed, but he wakes up again around dawn and the light's still on. He doesn't hear anything more until Ralston starts bumping things in the kitchen and finally goes to work. He swears the light looked still on in the bedroom, but he didn't hear the wife moving around the way she usually did before he had to leave himself. He got back late, we were already there, and Anna Ralston was dead."

"Can I make a phone call?"

"Is it about the case?"

"Yes. You have Ralston's office number?"

He gave it to me. I dialed, told Ralston's secretary, Miss Kerry, who I was and what I wanted. I heard the protectiveness in her voice. She wanted to help Ralston's lawyer, but she didn't want to say anything that might make Ralston look bad.

"He left about three that afternoon, was going to a kennel in Great Neck. That's all I know, Mr. Fortune."

"When did Anna Ralston call?"

There was a silence. "About four. How did you know she called?"

"What did she want, Miss Kerry?"

"To talk to Mr. Ralston. It wasn't unusual."

"I'm sure it wasn't. What did you tell her?"

"That he'd already left."

"What did she say?"

"She asked where he'd gone."

"Did you tell her?"

"Yes."

"What did she say then?"

"She thanked me and hung up."

I thanked her, hung up, and stood up. Domenici watched me.

"Let's go talk to George Ralston," I said.

"Am I going to like what we talk about?"

"I don't know," I said.

George Ralston sat in the immaculate, green antique living room that wasn't so immaculate now, dust already on the brocade.

"There wasn't any burglar, Mr. Ralston," I said. "No dope addict, no psycho or punk vagrant."

"Yes," Ralston said. "He came in and killed Anna."

I said, "You want me to tell what happened the night before and when you got home, or do you want to tell us?"

I had his attention, but he said nothing.

"A neighbor heard the fight," I said. "Not all the words, but I think I can fill in most of them. When I get it wrong, you correct me. You'd argued about her getting you a big dog, a yard dog, a male dog, and you went out and got pretty plastered and staggered home late. She was asleep, but you turned on the light, woke her up. You had this idea of your own."

Anna Ralston looks up at George's red face grinning down at her. He's drunk. Mitzi growls on the bed beside her. She only slowly becomes aware of what he is saying.

". . . got a great idea. Yessir. Know what gave me the idea? You did, with your big male dog."

"Go to bed, George."

"I'm in this bar, told this guy about you having all these damned little bitches and wanting to get me a big one and he said there was more money in little dogs than big ones. He says everyone wants small dog pups for apartments and that's when it hit me. Real pedigree pups're worth plenty. About time that Mitzi earned her damned keep."

"You're drunk! Look at the time."

George sits heavily on the bed. Anna shrinks, holds the covers to her chin.

George grins. "Mate her with a real good stud and the pups'll be worth a hell of a lot of money."

Anna is pale. "Mitzi's much too small. Go to bed now."

"Supposed to be small. Smaller they are, more the pups're worth. Use a small stud. Feisty little stud shove it to her good." *George laughs.* "Guy says the bitches get so scared they try 'n hide with the damn little hard stud after 'em."

Anna's voice in a rage of anger. "Go to bed, George!"

Mitzi, curled against her mistress on the bed, growls. Anna holds the covers tight, her voice angry, almost violent, with a trembling violence that alarms the dog, its neck fur bristling. Its lips skin back over sharp teeth. George still laughs.

"After they get it you got to hold them upside down so the stuff doesn't run out. Can you see it? Old Mitzi fucked good and upside down?"

Then Anna is shouting, screaming in the pink and lace late-night bedroom. The small dog barks, snarling and barking and shrinking against its mistress. Anna drops the covers, holds the dog against her. "You leave my baby alone! You animal! No one is going to hurt my little Mitzi. Get away. Animal! Pig! Don't you touch my baby! Never! Animal!"

George gets to his feet, sways. "Tomorrow. Some damn good out of her."

Anna is trembling and shaking. She holds the dog, croons, "My poor Mitzi. Poor helpless little girl. He won't touch you, no. My little girl."

George glares at the small woman in the thin nightgown, and the small black dog held against her. "Damned little bitch."

He blinks at them, turns and staggers out and down the hall to fall onto the already opened sofa bed in his office-den. The house becomes silent except for the low snarls of the frightened dog and the thin, soothing voice of Anna as she croons to the little dog. The light does not go out.

Anna Ralston sits in the neat bed barely disturbed by her small body and holds the dog until it stops shivering and goes to sleep against her. She still doesn't turn out the light, sits the rest of the night holding the dog and watching the half-open door of her bedroom and the unseen office-den along the hall where the faint snores of George Ralston go on and on. Until the sky outside lightens into a morning gray. Until the alarm she had set in George's den last night to wake him for work goes off. Until George staggers up, swearing and groaning, bumps down stairs, crashes around the kitchen, goes out and drives off. Until the sun is up and long after.

She sits in the bed holding the dog until the morning is half gone. Then she turns off the light, dresses, goes down and feeds the small dog. After that she sits by the kitchen telephone and waits. She does not make the beds, dust, run the vacuum, clean George's breakfast dishes from the kitchen, put her polished house in order. She waits by the telephone. Because George will call to apologize. She knows he will call. But he doesn't, and at four P.M. she calls his office. She talks to his secretary. She hangs up. She calls Mitzi to her.

"Come here, little girl. Come to mother, little girl."

Then she takes the butcher knife from the drawer.

"You didn't call," I said to George Ralston where he sat in the antique brocade chair. "You always called after a fight to apologize, say you were sorry. This time you didn't. You went to a kennel in Great Neck."

Ralston looked at his thick, heavy hands. "I was still mad. I went to the kennel, but only to ask about a dog for me. Then I changed my mind, didn't want a damned dog, stopped in some bars."

"She'd grown up in Japan," I said. "Her father was accused of chasing girls. It was hushed up, but they were forced to leave Japan. Her mother probably never let him forget it. Or Anna. She took the knife and the dog into the pantry. She cut the dog's throat. It struggled and clawed and bit. There were scratches all over her hands, her face. Then she used the knife on herself."

George Ralston's voice was flat and empty. "They were in the pantry. On the floor as if they were asleep. She was still holding the knife in her. I took her dress and pulled the knife out. I picked up the dog. It was stiff, not much blood. I suppose I carried it all the way to the front door. I don't remember that part. I threw it out into the snow. I remember that. I threw that goddamned little bitch of a dog that had killed my wife out into the goddamned snow!"

Domenici and I waited, but Ralston said nothing more. Just sat there and stared at his hands and at nothing.

"You didn't want anyone to know she'd killed herself," I said. "Maybe you didn't want to believe it yourself."

Ralston still looked only at his hands. "She never wanted me, sex, not from the start. I don't know why she married me."

"Because she was supposed to marry," I said. "She had to get married to someone. Her mother would have told her that."

He looked up at us. "The last few years there was nothing. I stank, I was coarse, I drank too much, I was an animal." An expression almost of surprise. "Married twenty years, I never saw her naked."

Domenici asked him to go to the precinct to make a statement. I rode with them to my rented car, called Sarah Deming, and asked her to dinner. Over coffee I told her. She cried. We went home to her place. Neither of us wanted to be alone.

WAYNE D. DUNDEE

THE JUDAS TARGET

Wayne Dundee's Joe Hannibal appeared in the second PWA anthology, Mean Streets, *in a story called "Body Count." It collected nominations for an Edgar, a Shamus, and an Anthony (the award presented by crime-fiction fans). In 1988 the first Hannibal novel,* Burning Season, *will be published by St. Martin's Press. Wayne is also the publisher and editor of* Hardboiled, *a small-press fiction magazine specializing in tough, hard fiction written by established pros and newcomers alike. In fact, Hardboiled is one of the few training grounds there are for new writers, which was Wayne's intention from the beginning. At the present time, he is serving as a member of the Board of Directors of PWA.*

In a relatively short time Wayne has established himself as a writer to watch. We feel that "The Judas Target" will only add to his growing reputation.

"**E**ver see one of those el cheapo kung fu movies?" The Bomber asked rhetorically. "You know, the kind where every time somebody gets hit, it sounds like a five-pound T-bone landing on the sidewalk after being dropped out of an upstairs window? Well, that's how it sounded when the bullet smacked into the brick wall beside my head. Like a loud slap. The report of the gun came a fraction of a second later and then brick fragments were stinging the side of my face and that's when it finally dawned on me that somebody had taken a shot at me."

"Just one shot?" I said.

He shrugged his massive shoulders. "Far as I could tell. I didn't exactly stand around counting, you know? I got the hell off those steps, did a swan dive down behind a row of garbage cans. All the clanging and banging I did when I landed, I probably wouldn't have heard if they'd fired a dozen more times. But the police only found evidence of one slug, the one that hit the wall where I'd been standing."

"Those lab boys don't miss too damn much," I allowed. "If there'd been more than one shot, they would have found some indication. Funny, though, that whoever opened up on you only fired the once."

"So what are you—disappointed he didn't make Swiss cheese out of me?"

"Of course not. It just seems strange that somebody would go to all the trouble of setting up an ambush and then spend only one bullet. Let's face it, those garbage cans didn't offer much protection. Almost anything bigger than a BB gun can penetrate that cheap galvanized steel. Why not at least throw a few random rounds into them in hopes of scoring a lucky hit?"

The Bomber screwed up his face and thought about it. "Maybe when they saw me dive off those steps," he suggested, "they thought they'd hit me and I fell."

"Or maybe," Liz offered from her side of the bar, "they mistook Bomber for somebody else and didn't realize their mistake until after they'd taken that first shot."

"Come on," I said. "How the hell could you mistake The Bomber for somebody else? You see that many guys walking around who stand six-six and weigh over three hundred pounds? Besides, what about the car that tried to run him down the other day? Were they after somebody else, too?"

Liz's pretty face reddened—first with embarrassment, then with defensive anger. "You can just climb down off your high horse, Joe Hannibal," she snapped. "If I'm not making any sense, it's because this whole business has me scared half to death. You're supposed to be the hotshot private eye, *you* tell *me* what's going on then."

It was quarter of ten in the morning and the three of us were huddled in the preopening hour stillness of The Bomb Shelter, the State Street bar owned and operated by my mountainous pal. If the name Bomber Brannigan is familiar to you, you're showing your age as a sports fan. Before retiring from the ring wars to turn The Bomb Shelter into one of Rockford's most popular watering holes, The Bomber spent several years as a top-ranked heavyweight boxer and then nearly two decades as one of the biggest draws on the pro wrestling circuit.

Liz is Liz Grimaldi, Bomber's gal Friday and a special kind of friend to me. It had been a phone call from her that had awakened me earlier that morning and informed me that another attempt had been made on The Bomber's life, this time a shooting in the side alley adjacent to the bar after he'd closed up last night and was leaving to go home. Less than forty-eight hours before that, a late-model sedan (reported stolen and later found abandoned) had tried to run him down in a shopping center parking lot. I'd already known about the parking lot incident, but like everyone else (including The Bomber) had managed to convince myself that it was just one of those freaky things that sometimes happen and not really a deliberate attack. But this time they'd left no room for doubt. They were playing with guns, and that's about as deliberate as you can get.

"What's going on," I replied to Liz, "is that somebody's apparently trying to kill Bomber here. The question is, why? And—ultimately—who?"

The Bomber grunted. "You sound just like the cops. 'Any idea *why* someone wants you dead, Mr. Brannigan? Any idea *who* dislikes you enough to try and kill you, Mr. Brannigan?' Christ, their questions can get on your nerves almost as bad as the thought of some whacko running around out there with your name at the top of his hit list."

"They're only trying to do their jobs and—just incidentally— save your ass," I pointed out. "I hope you had sense enough to cooperate and not get sore and clam up on them?"

"Yeah, yeah, of course I cooperated. You think I like any of this? It's just that I didn't have any answers for them because I don't know of anybody who'd want to kill me. Christ knows you don't get to be my age without making a few enemies. But not the kind who'd run you down with a car or blow your brains out in an alley, for crying out loud. Besides, most of the enemies I made— and *enemies* is really too strong a word—were back when I was making my living in the ring."

"You may have to go back that far," I told him. "Sometimes hatred can build up inside a person for years before it builds up enough pressure to drive them to murder."

Bomber and I were perched on stools, sipping coffee from thick, old-fashioned mugs, while Liz was behind the bar, rattling around in glassware between contributions to the conversation. She stopped rattling now and said, "Anyway, what you said isn't entirely the truth, Bomber. I can think of at least two run-ins you've had in the past six months with guys I certainly wouldn't consider incapable of murder."

The Bomber made a face. "Aw, Liz, you know you overreact. Jeez, I can't sic the cops on everybody I've had a barroom argument with."

"Why not? Haven't you ever heard the expression 'Better safe than sorry'? We're talking about your life here, you stubborn mule. And the way I remember it, those were a little more than simple barroom arguments."

I said, "Somebody mind telling me just what it is you're talking about?"

Bomber and Liz glared at each other. After several seconds, he made a condescending gesture with his hand. "Go ahead, you're the one who started it."

It turned out that a few months back The Bomber had butted heads with a local pimp who called himself Sweet Thomas. Sweet had decided to expand his territory that spring and had started dropping off girls to work the bars along this previously unclaimed stretch of State Street. After Bomber had run the girls out of his place three nights in a row, the pimp stopped by one afternoon to try and grease the way. First he offered money, then he made thinly veiled threats. Bomber's response had been classic Bomber: Without saying a word he'd reached out and gently but firmly removed Sweet's trademark hundred-dollar hat, taken a huge bite out of the brim, than spat the chewed remains in the gaping pimp's face. The Bomb Shelter hadn't been visited by Sweet Thomas or any of his girls since. But they continued to work the surrounding blocks and rumor had it that Sweet on more than one occasion had vowed to make Bomber "spit his own damn honky blood the way he spit my hat, man."

More recently, there'd been some trouble with a guy named Mallory, the estranged boyfriend of a young woman The Bomber had employed briefly as a dancer. When the dancer ditched him and moved on, Mallory had continued to hang around, bitter, heartbroken, unshakably convinced that Bomber knew something of his errant girlfriend's whereabouts. There had been a number of drunken accusations and arguments before he was finally barred from The Bomb Shelter. But Mallory had a reputation for being a hothead and a bully and he, too, had been heard threatening to "get" The Bomber.

As I listened to Liz recount the two incidents, I remembered hearing about them back when they occurred. There'd been no reason to stick my nose in, either time. Bomber is a big boy and he seemed to have things under control. In the wake of the recent murder attempts, however—and particularly with no other murder suspects at hand—I found myself agreeing with Liz that Sweet Thomas and Mallory rated a closer look.

"Hell, Joe," Bomber protested. "They're just a couple punks who like to hear themselves blow. The two of them put together wouldn't have enough balls to actually come after me."

"Not head-on maybe," I said. "But they sound exactly like the kind who wouldn't be above staging an ambush in an alley. Besides, you got any better leads?"

He shook his head sullenly. "I already told you I don't."

"All right then. If it'll make you feel any better, we can leave the cops out of it for the time being. I got nothing much going right now; I'll do some poking around myself." I drained my coffee mug, stood, jabbed an admonishing finger. "In the meantime, you keep a low profile and rack your brain for any more possibilities. I don't care how far back you have to go or how trivial it might seem, I want the names of everybody you've had any kind of serious conflict with and/or who's threatened you in any way. It wouldn't be a bad idea to write them down. Don't make faces, just do it. I'll check back later."

By six o'clock that evening, I was back to square one. Sweet Thomas and Mallory had both checked out clean—well, clean as far as having anything to do with the attempts on Bomber's life.

Mallory had been in the county lockup for the past week and would remain there for quite a while longer, serving time on a DUI charge he couldn't post bail for. And Sweet Thomas had just been released from a three-day stint in Swedish American with seventy-odd stitches adorning his chest and one forearm, the result of one of his girls turning on him when he tried batting her around for not bringing in enough money.

I'd considered the possibility of one of them having hired somebody to hit The Bomber. In Mallory's case it seemed laughable. And when I suggested the idea to Sweet Thomas, he denied it vehemently. Inasmuch as I'd threatened to reopen his stitches one at a time if I thought he even *might* be lying, his denial had sounded sincere.

So, despite my earlier stated intentions, the end of the day found me seated in a little coffee shop around the corner from police headquarters, hashing over the whole thing with Lieutenant of Detectives Ed Terry. Terry is my best contact with the RPD and, though I wouldn't go so far as to call him a friend, over the years we've developed a working relationship we can both live with. He knew The Bomber and knew of our friendship, so while he couldn't officially condone my involvement, he at least understood my interest in the matter.

"What you ought to do," he said as he stirred a second heaping teaspoon of sugar into his coffee, "is get Bomber out of the city for a while. Whoever's behind this thing is keyed up, anxious, pissed off because he's failed twice already. If you suddenly take away his target it'll increase the pressure on him, maybe make him do something to show his hand. At the same time, it would give us some breathing room, more opportunity to work the streets, lean on our snitches, until we turn up some kind of lead. With no suspects—hell, we didn't even have Sweet Thomas and this Mallory—that's the only way we've got to play it."

"What's to prevent the guy from just laying low until The Bomber returns?" I asked.

The lieutenant shrugged. "It could happen that way, I suppose. But I don't see this character as being that cool. First he tries to be a little tricky by using an automobile; when that doesn't work, he resorts pretty quickly to a gun. I read that as a kind of growing desperation. Plus he's got to know his quarry is alerted now; that should make him even more desperate."

"The Bomber's been after me to go up into Wisconsin with him and do some fishing before cold weather sets in," I mused. "Might not be a bad time to take him up on it. I'm damn sure not tied down by a heavy caseload right now. We could rent a cabin on some out-of-the-way little lake for a week or so and give this whole mess down here a chance to come to a head."

Terry nodded. "Sounds like just the ticket to me. You'd even be along to act as bodyguard in case the trouble somehow followed him up there."

* * *

To say that Bomber wasn't very receptive to the idea when I tried it on him a couple hours later would be something of an understatement.

"I never ran away from a fight in my life," he exploded, "and I'm damn sure not going to start now!"

"You wouldn't be running away," I tried to explain. "You'd be turning the tables on whoever's out to get you by taking control of the situation away from them. The way it is now, they can keep trying for you whenever and wherever they want—until they get the job done."

"I'm not running and that's that," he said stubbornly, then turned and stalked away to busy himself elsewhere.

The Bomb Shelter was doing exceptionally good business for a weeknight. Cindy, one of the most popular dancers, was gyrating energetically up on the go-go stage and the predominately male crowd seemed duly appreciative. I noticed Liz was still on hand, sharing bartending duties with Bomber and Old Charley. She normally opened up in the morning, took care of the lunch-hour crowd, and was gone by six. It was obvious she was hanging around tonight to keep an eye on The Bomber. Despite his hulking size, he brings out the mother hen in her. Of course, I do, too, but that's another story.

I brooded through the rest of my beer, didn't order another. I decided there was no sense badgering Bomber anymore tonight. I knew him too well for that. In the morning, I'd put a bug in Liz's ear. She had a knack for being able to get him to do things when no one else could.

I left around nine. I drove to Dan's Dog House on Broadway and ordered two kraut dogs with the works. Dan Modesto and his wife, Sunshine, are the last of the original hippies. Dan is a bearded, wiry little runt who looks for all the world like Charles Manson, while Sunshine is a shapely, stunning blond Amazon who hasn't aged a minute since the middle 1960s. Ironically, despite the success of their unpretentious little hot dog stand, both are staunch vegetarians who wouldn't eat their own fare on a bet. But somehow that doesn't prevent them from preparing and serving the best red-hots on the planet. As a lifelong aficionado of the vastly underrated, much maligned, generally ill-treated great American hot dog, it took me about three seconds to

sniff out the Dog House after it opened, and I've been going back
several times a week ever since.

Business was slow this night so Dan and Sunshine had a
Scrabble board set up in one of the corner booths. After I'd
finished my kraut dogs, I surprised myself by accepting their
invitation to join in. I quickly discovered that my usually mellow,
laid-back hosts took their board games very seriously. The play
was intense. We won a game each and it was sometime after
midnight when we were going to the wire on the tie breaker. I
managed to pull it out by adding *I-O-N* to DIVERS and ending up
on a double-word-value square with DIVERSION for twenty-six
points.

It was only later that I would look back and recognize the
omenlike significance of the word.

Half past one found me parked across the street and down
slightly from The Bomb Shelter. I could see any comings and
goings through the establishment's front door and I also had a
good view down the length of the alley where the shooting had
taken place last night. Tonight—well, it was morning now if you
want to be technical—The Bomber's big Buick was parked at the
curb near the mouth of the alley instead of in the back where he
usually kept it. So at least he was showing enough good sense not
to invite trouble.

The September night was cool, with a gusting wind that rocked
my old Mustang on its worn springs. I sat and smoked, watching,
taking occasional hits from the glove compartment flask, rumi-
nating.

Bomber Brannigan. Big, gregarious bear. Sucker for dewy-eyed
blondes and hard-luck stories. Always willing to loan you a few
bucks even when he really couldn't spare it, or to extend your bar
tab for another day or another week. Wouldn't hesitate to bust
your head if you caused trouble in his place, then turn around
and offer to help pay the emergency room fees or go your bail if
the cops threw you in the clink over it. Who the hell would want
to murder a guy like that? It just didn't figure.

Any way I looked at it, it had to go back to Bomber's past.
Someone from some incident he either wasn't admitting to or
didn't recognize as a danger. I had to believe it was the latter—I
couldn't picture him keeping something from both me and Liz,

especially not under the circumstances. The problem, then, was getting him to realize who it might be.

By two o'clock my rear end was falling asleep and I had gas from the additional kraut dog I'd eaten before leaving Dan's. If I hadn't had the bourbon to comfort me, I might have decided this stakeout wasn't necessary after all.

I'd figured Bomber was safe enough in the midst of The Bomb Shelter's crowd, but I wanted to be around when he closed up tonight to make sure there were no repeats of last night's incident. I hadn't bothered mentioning this to him because he was already in a funk and undoubtedly would have objected. So if he caught me at it, he'd be sore as hell. But I could live with that. And, more to the point, so could he.

Twice I spotted police squad cars circling the block and one of them even made a pass down through the alley. I had a feeling Ed Terry had something to do with that. He maybe couldn't assign a man full time to The Bomber, but at least he could see to it that there was some extra attention given.

At two-thirty, with the last of the drinking crowd herded out ahead of them, the lights inside The Bomb Shelter winked off and Liz, Old Charley, and Bomber emerged together from the front door. They stood talking for a minute or so, then Liz and Old Charley headed east down the sidewalk. I could see Liz's VW Bug parked in the block and knew that Old Charley's hotel was just a couple blocks farther.

Bomber stood watching until Liz reached her car before turning and heading for his own. He paused at the mouth of the alley for a moment and glared into it as if daring it to cause him some trouble this night. Then he continued on to the Buick, unlocked the driver's door, pulled it open. Instead of getting in, however, he froze suddenly and craned his neck to peer back at the alley as if he'd heard something there. He stood like that for maybe five seconds, listening intently, then eased the door shut and started toward the alley.

I felt the short hairs on the back of my neck stand up. My left hand reached for the door handle, my right snaked inside my jacket and closed around the butt of the .45 nestled there in its shoulder holster. I don't always carry the big gun. My everyday walkaround piece is a two-shot .22 magnum derringer clipped inside my right boot. But when I know in advance I could be walking into a hard scene, I'll drag out the manstopper.

Because I had the car windows rolled up against the cool night air, whatever The Bomber had heard hadn't reached my ears. But whatever it was, I didn't like it.

I shouldered open the door and piled out of the Mustang. I'd just opened my mouth to call out when the night split wide open. A ball of brilliant light seemed to fill the inside of Bomber's Buick and then grow to envelop the entire vehicle. A dull, jarring boom hammered my ears and shook the macadam underneath my feet. And out of the brilliant light shot a gigantic, orange-gold, fiery hot fist that knocked me down and sent me rolling into unconsciousness.

"The explosives were fastened underneath the car, directly below the driver's seat, and rigged to the doorlatch mechanism," Ed Terry explained. "When the door was opened, a timer was activated and twenty seconds later—ka-blooey!"

"Twenty seconds," I said. "About the average amount of time it would take someone to get in their car, get settled, maybe even fasten their seat belt so they'd feel nice and secure."

"Exactly. If The Bomber hadn't heard that noise in the alley after he opened his door and started over to investigate . . . well, we'd probably be talking about so much burnt meat in the morgue right now."

"What did he hear anyway? Did he ever say?"

"The sound of breaking glass. When my men checked, they found a freshly broken beer bottle beside one of the garbage cans. The can was pretty full, it could have rolled out on its own or maybe been knocked out by a cat or rat or something."

I nodded. "It would've had to have been something like that. There was no person in that alley, I'm sure of that. I had it under surveillance for over an hour." I sat on the edge of the hospital bed and began pulling on my socks. "The Bomber's being released this morning, too, right?"

"Uh-huh. They kept him overnight for observation, same as you. You two were both damn lucky to get away with only your pinfeathers singed and your eardrums rattled."

"Pinfeathers singed. That's real cute." I reached up and gently touched my left cheek. It smarted like hell and I knew from looking in the mirror that it was as red as a scalded lobster. "I won't be able to shave for a week."

"Shouldn't be a problem. You take Bomber up to that fishing

lake like we talked about and the both of you can let your beards grow, pretend you're regular mountain men or something."

I grunted. "He hasn't agreed to go yet. But I've got Liz working on him right now. She was here a little while ago and I told her your idea, how getting Bomber out of town might help."

Twenty minutes later, after I'd fought off a hatchet-faced old nurse armed with a wheelchair she was bound and determined I was going to let her push me away in, the elevator doors opened and Terry and I emerged into the hospital's main lobby. Liz and The Bomber were waiting for us. Terry went over and stood with them while I went to the front desk and made arrangements on my bill.

When I joined the others, Bomber regarded me with a skeptically arched brow. The back of his head and neck were lumpy with bandages.

"You look like a boiled tomato," he observed.

"Thanks," I replied. "You, you sort of resemble a giant Q-Tip."

"That's what you get for poking your nose in where you weren't invited, you know."

I shrugged. "Just looking out for my interests. You're the only bartender in town lets me run a tab. Anything happened to you, I might have to start drinking water part of the time."

"Why don't you two save the Frick and Frack routine," Liz suggested, "until you're up in the middle of some Wisconsin lake where no one else has to suffer through it?"

I glanced at her, then back at Bomber. "The Lone Ranger here finally agree to go?" I asked.

"That's exactly *why* he agreed to go," Liz said. "I pointed out to him that he's *not* the Lone Ranger. He's surrounded by a lot of friends. As crazy as this thing is getting, the next explosion might go off *inside* The Bomb Shelter and hurt—maybe kill—dozens of innocent people."

The Bomber looked at a spot on the floor, said nothing. I saw his jaw muscles clench and unclench.

"It really is a smart move," Ed Terry said. "It's just a matter of time before we get a line on this asshole. The bombing was a big mistake. It's pretty hard to cover your tracks once you start messing with explosives."

The fishing lodge we selected was on Dogleg Lake, about two hundred and fifty miles up into Wisconsin. Since it was the off-season, we had no trouble getting reservations on short notice. Less than three hours after being released from the hospital—the backseat of my Mustang piled with beer and gear—we'd put Rockford behind us and were across the state line. "Let's do it," The Bomber had said, "before I change my mind."

The last sliver of sunlight was sinking behind the jack pines when we arrived at the lodge. The manager, a guy named Hogan, showed us to our cabin, explaining the camp's simple setup and its rules and regs as we climbed a grassy incline that sloped up from the gravel parking lot.

"That pier down there," he said, pointing, "goes with your cabin. I'll have a boat brought around and tied there, motor all gassed up and ready, so you can get as early a start as you want in the morning. The walleyes have been hitting real good on live minnows all week. I've got plenty of those at the bait shop, any time you want to stop and get some."

The cabin was a low-ceilinged, single-room affair with kitchen facilities at one end and a broad fireplace flanked by sturdy bunk beds at the other. When Hogan was ready to leave us to our own devices, he paused in the doorway and said, "Oh, yeah, one more thing. About the lake. I was out just a little while ago and saw that some of the warning buoys are gone again. Damn kids keep cutting them loose, think it's real cute I guess. I'd like to catch 'em at it one of these times, show 'em how cute a boot in the ass is. But anyway, stay clear of the north end of the lake. Too many shallow spots there, especially after a dry summer like we've just had. The whole section is ribbed with sand and gravel bars just under the surface of the water. Hard to see, but pure hell on boat bottoms and propellers, take my word for it. I'll get the buoys back in place sometime tomorrow."

After Hogan had gone, while The Bomber set to work making a batch of his "world-famous, gonad-grabbing, high-tech, industrial-strength" chili for supper, I lugged the rest of our gear up from the car. On my last trip, I stopped at the old-fashioned, booth-type pay phone outside the bait shop and called Liz at The Bomb Shelter. I told her we'd arrived okay, that the lodge appeared rustic but comfortable, and suggested boastfully that she bone up on her fish-cleaning skills because we'd probably have to rent a U-Haul to carry home our catch. Before ringing off, she made me promise to call frequently and said she'd let us know if Lieutenant Terry came up with anything on their end.

Bomber's chili lived up to its high standards. I demonstrated my appreciation by eating three bowlfuls. I washed it down with twice that many cans of cold Michelob mined from the depths of one of the ice-filled coolers.

Later, before nodding off, I lay for a time in the dark and tried to fit some of the pieces of this potentially deadly puzzle together in my mind. A part of me, too, felt as if we were running away from the problem, and yet everything Ed Terry said had made sense. But who would want to kill Bomber in the first place? That's what it all kept coming back to, and that's where it all fell apart. Sleep finally nudged aside the scattered pieces and unanswered questions and, for a while at least, made them go away.

Armed with Thermoses of coffee, fishing poles, and a bucket of minnows, we were out on the lake before dawn the next morning. A storm had blown through during the night, leaving in its wake an overcast sky and a stiff breeze that churned the gunmetal-gray water into shifting sheets of corrugated steel.

Wherever those hard-hitting walleyes Hogan had told us about were, we never found them. After nearly four hours, out of patience and out of coffee, bellies growling for breakfast, we were ready to head in.

Bomber fired up the outboard with one pull of the starter cord. But then, before it had taken us more than twenty yards, the motor abruptly coughed a couple times and died. A dozen more yanks failed to revive it.

"Damn!" The Bomber muttered after unscrewing the cap and peering into the gas tank. "Dry as a bone. Looks like our friend Hogan forgot about the 'gassed up and ready' part when he brought this baby around last night."

"Swell," I said.

I looked around us. The lake, as its name implied, was a rectangularish body of water bent more or less in the middle like a dog's leg. It was three, three-and-a-half-miles long and about two miles at its widest. We were above the point of the inner bend, well out of sight of our lodge and nearly three-quarters of a mile from the nearest shore. I could see a couple cabins on the shoreline, but there were no signs of activity around them. We hadn't seen another boat on the water all morning.

"Only one thing to do," Bomber said matter-of-factly. "That's break out the oars and make for shore the hard way."

"Swell," I said again.

We dragged the oars out from under the seats, fastened them into their locks, flipped a coin to see who took first turn. I lost.

Given my inexperience and the roughness of the water, I hardly sent us streaking on our way. After fifteen minutes of tugging and puffing, I'd maybe equaled the distance the motor had propelled us in a matter of seconds.

Just as he was getting ready to spell me, The Bomber suddenly leaned out to gaze past my shoulder. "Don't look now," he said, "but I think I'm about to get beat out of my turn."

I twisted around in my seat. Another boat, a twelve-footer almost identical to ours, was cutting across the water toward us.

"Swell," I panted.

The craft's single occupant was a guy in his middle thirties, tall, slightly built, with a rust-colored beard and a baseball cap pulled low over his eyes. He guided his boat alongside ours, cut the motor to idle, regarded us from under the long bill of his cap.

"Trouble, fellas?"

"Out of gas," The Bomber answered. "Guy at the lodge where we're staying was supposed to've filled it for us. We never thought to check."

The guy in the cap nodded. "Happens. Hate to admit how many times I've been in the same pickle. Let me maneuver up in front of you, then you can tie on with your anchor line there and I'll tow you in. You'll row your guts out trying to get anywhere in this chop."

"Tell me about it," I muttered.

He had us secured in a matter of minutes. All the while his boat's motor gurgled reassuringly.

"There now," our rescuer said. "Looks like we can be on our way."

"Sounds good to me," The Bomber replied, grinning.

As Bomber and I settled back in our boat, the guy in the cap leaned forward in his and busied himself for a moment with the tarp roll at his feet. When he straightened up and turned back toward us, he held a sawed-off shotgun leveled calmly, menacingly in our direction. He said, "But there is one more little thing."

The grin froze on Bomber's face. I felt my guts jump into a knot and Ed Terry's words echoed hauntingly through my mind: "You'd even be along to act as bodyguard in case the trouble somehow followed Bomber up there."

When I found my voice, it was a sandpapery rasp. I said, "What the hell is this? Somebody's sick idea of a joke?"

The guy in the cap shook his head. "No joke, Hannibal. No joke at all."

"How do you know my name?" I demanded.

"Oh, I know a lot of things about you, Hannibal. I know, for instance, about the derringer you always carry in your boot, and I know how you sometimes back it up with a heavier piece. Judging from the bulge under your jacket, I'd say this is one of those times. I guess I should be flattered, since the extra firepower is probably in honor of me. I think you can understand, though, how I'd feel better if you were unarmed. So, one at a time, very slowly, using only the thumb and forefinger of your left hand, I want you to take the pieces out and drop them over the side."

There's no arguing with a shotgun. I did as he said.

After my weapons had disappeared into the gray water, he said, "You still don't see it, do you? You still don't recognize me. But you recognized me okay seven years ago, you bastard. Think back. It was your testimony that put me away, and I swore then that I'd get even. Maybe you forgot over the years, but I never did. Never for a fucking minute!"

He swept his cap off with a dramatic gesture and suddenly I knew who the hell he was. He'd lost some weight in seven years, turned harder around the eyes and mouth. The beard was new and so was the rusty brown color it and his hair had been dyed. It had been his hair as a matter of fact—so pale and so fine that the pinkish color of his scalp showed through—that had earned him his nickname, the only name I ever knew him by.

I said it out loud now. "Pinky Bascomb."

"Jackpot, shamus," he confirmed with a cold smile.

My brain was reeling. This was crazy. Had we come all this way, gone to all this trouble to avoid Bomber's would-be murderer—only to be cornered by a vengeance-crazed killer from *my* past?

Bascomb produced a pair of silvery handcuffs and tossed them to me. I made the catch out of reflex.

"Link up with your oversized buddy there. Now!" He made a jabbing motion with the sawed-off to emphasize the command.

As I cuffed his right wrist to my left, Bomber said, "Who is this guy, Joe? What the hell's going on?"

"What's going on," Bascomb answered him, "is revenge. Your

friend there is about to pay for sticking his nose in my business seven long years ago."

"Yeah," I said. "Pinky and one of his punk cohorts had a real sweet 'business,' Bomber. Think back, you ought to remember. Whenever they needed a little extra spending money they'd knock over an all-night convenience store and, just for kicks, pistol-whip the clerk. Two of those clerks died. One of the stores that hadn't been hit yet hired me to provide some extra security, and when Pinky and his pal finally got around to us, I was there waiting. I blew his partner away with my first shot because he had guts enough to stand his ground. But I only managed to wound Pinky in his yellow streak as he was running away. The police dragnet got him a couple hours later, though, and, like he said, my testimony put him away. It's just too damn bad my aim was a little off that night."

"Too bad, all right," Bascomb agreed icily. "Too bad for *you*. The only thing that kept me going all that time in the joint—kept me on my best behavior so I could make early release—was the thought of you and how I was going to make my payback. In case you're interested, I'm loving every fucking second of it so far. Revenge truly is sweet. And the fact that I'm going to take your friend down with you—just the way you took my friend down— makes it even sweeter."

"Why? The score you have to settle is with me. Bomber's no part of it."

"But of course he's part of it. He's a very important part. After all, he was my Judas goat. Or, more accurately, I guess I should call him my Judas target. At any rate, he's the one who led you here . . . to your slaughter."

I saw it then. All of it. The pieces of the puzzle came together with a mind-jarring snap and the insane brilliance of the completed picture they made was a frightening thing to comprehend.

"So it was you," I said. "All along it's been you. Those attempts on The Bomber's life were never meant to succeed—they were only staged to draw me into the picture. Because of our friendship, you knew that sooner or later I'd get involved. It was your intention all along to kill us both, knowing everyone had been misled and would assume Bomber was the primary target and I was just unlucky enough to get caught in the crunch."

Bascomb actually beamed. "Exactly. If I'd gone directly after you, how long do you think it would have taken before some enterprising cop or newspaper reporter would have remembered me and my courtroom threats? A man in your business has plenty of enemies, and I would have been on the list. When they checked and found I'd recently made parole, I would have shot right to the top. No matter what kind of alibi I rigged up, the fucking pigs would have stayed on my ass. There's nothing those bastards like better than hassling ex-cons."

"The attempted rundown with the car and the shooting would've been easy enough to stage," I said. "But how did you know how to rig the bomb? How could you be sure Bomber would walk away from his car before it went off?"

"Because you big macho types are all alike. Predictable. I knew if he heard a noise in that alley he'd feel obligated to go check it out. As far as the bomb, well, if you just keep your mouth shut and your ears open, it's amazing what you can learn in the joint."

"But you weren't in that alley," I insisted. "I was watching."

"I was watching, too, from the roof of The Bomb Shelter. When I saw Brannigan open his car door, I dropped the beer bottle down beside the garbage cans. Simple as that. The only hard part was restraining myself from putting a bullet in you right then and there. You made such a perfect target, sitting across the street so conveniently framed in your car window."

"This your doing, too?" The Bomber asked, indicating our outboard's empty gas tank with a jerk of his head.

Bascomb nodded. "That it is. So you see, your man Hogan was dependable after all. You can die with your faith in mankind restored."

"How did you find us up here?" I said, remembering the various checks I'd made and the driving tricks I'd pulled to make certain we weren't followed.

"Ah, yes. Have to admit you did catch me by surprise when you left the city the way you did. Very unmacho, that. As I saw it, the only move I had left then was to pry your whereabouts out of your lady friend at The Bomb Shelter. I was working my way up to that when you obligingly made your phone call last night, Hannibal. I happened to be sitting at the bar nearby and overheard her end of the conversation. Afterwards, I heard her telling one of the dancers about it and she mentioned Dogleg Lake. She had no way of knowing, of course, but she saved herself a good deal of unpleasantness with that. On the other hand, she denied me a bit of pleasure. Maybe when we're finished here, I'll go back and look her up again . . . just for the hell of it."

Bomber tensed like a steel cable beside me. "You sick son of a bitch."

Bascomb's face tightened above the lethal black mouths of the shotgun. "Enough talk. We'll get to shore and finish this. Chained together like you are, you gotta know you have no chance of rushing me or jumping over the side and escaping. One wrong move from either of you and I let go with both barrels. You'd be two piles of hamburger. If you're smart, you'll sit still and live as long as you can."

Like I said, there's no arguing with a shotgun.

Bascomb nudged open the throttle and we began moving across the lake . . . toward whatever end he had in mind for Bomber and me. He swung north, taking us further away from the lodge and away from the cabins I'd spotted earlier. In the distance I could see a heavily wooded shoreline at the end of the lake, with no cabins or piers anywhere in sight.

My mind raced, trying to figure some way around that damned sawed-off. The wind blew cold and bitter against my face, yet under my jacket I was dripping sweat. In the final analysis, I knew, there was no way I was going to let Bascomb pump a slug in me without putting up a fight, no matter how hopeless the odds. And I knew Bomber well enough to know he'd feel the same way. Big macho types, Bascomb had called us. Predictable. Yeah, well, fuck that. If you're going to go down it's a hell of a lot better to go down swinging, that's all. So when the time came—

And then it hit me. What Hogan had said about the north end of the lake. Warning buoys down. Sand and gravel bars just under the surface of the water. Stay away from there.

That was exactly where Bascomb was taking us. Wherever he had gotten his boat, he had not received the same warning.

I glanced at The Bomber. If he shared my realization, he showed no sign. I tensed myself and tried to think of a way to warn him. Bascomb sat sideways in his seat, taking his eyes off us very seldom, steering mainly by peripheral vision. The shoreline loomed ever closer.

Even though I was scanning the water intently, I missed the gravel bar that nailed us. Bascomb's boat bottomed out with a sharp scratching sound followed instantly by the metallic *whang!*

of the propeller impacting. Our craft, weighted down by two bigger men and thus riding lower in the water, hit harder still.

We pitched forward, somersaulting, spinning wildly through the air. Fishing gear and minnow bait swirled around us like shrapnel. Hitting the water was like hitting a wall. My wrist and shoulder shrieked with agony as Bomber's weight—on the other end of the handcuff chain—twisted savagely away from me.

Everything was upside down and crazy for several seconds. Cold black water. Bubbles. Pain. Panic.

My head and shoulders broke to the surface. I sucked in great mouthfuls of air and found that if I just put my feet down I was in water barely chest high. Bomber surfaced beside me, coughing and cursing. When he lifted his face, it was chalky white and his eyes were pain-dulled. Red tendrils of blood began rising up, clouding the water around him.

I clutched him to me. Through clenched teeth he said, "Damn propeller caught me just before we hit the water. Pretty bad I think; I can hardly move my left leg."

The propeller. I could still hear its irritating buzz. I looked around.

Bascomb's boat, tilted onto one side, was lodged on the gravel bar. The motor had flipped up on its hinges from the impact, but was still running at three-quarter throttle, the propeller blades chewing the air. The towline had snapped and our boat had ended up several yards beyond, upside down, split open, sinking fast.

And then I saw Bascomb. He came around the end of his boat. He had a gash above one eye that left a watery smear of blood across his forehead. There was no sign of the shotgun. Instead, he carried one of the oars like a baseball bat.

"You're still mine, Hannibal," he crowed maniacally. "Damn you to hell, you're still mine!"

He moved toward me, the oar raised to swing.

With my left arm badly wrenched and chained to Bomber's injured bulk, I was one-handed and practically immobile. I looked around wildly for some sort of weapon to defend myself with, but there was none to be had.

"I'm going to club you, Hannibal," Bascomb jeered. "I'm going to club you to death like a gaffed mackerel."

He swung, a vicious downward chop with the edge of the oar's paddle end. Somehow, I got out of the way. He swung again almost immediately, this time a swooping blow that skimmed the surface of the water. He caught a piece of my good shoulder with that one, but nothing serious.

I backpedaled frantically, dragging Bomber along with me.

Bascomb circled. He moved into slightly shallower water and poised to strike again.

The Bomber sagged against me, seemingly on the verge of passing out. I shook him and swore at him, shouting for him to hang on. If he blacked out, became totally dead weight on the other end of that chain, neither of us had a prayer.

Bascomb swung again, and again I somehow managed to dodge it. But my breath was starting to come in ragged gasps and the water running down my face was as much from sweat as it was from being dunked in the lake. This deadly game of cat and mouse was incredibly exhausting, and I wouldn't be able to keep it up for very long.

And then, on the other side of Bascomb, something caught my eye. His boat moved! The vibrations from the still-running motor were causing it to shift on the gravel bar.

As Bascomb's shoulder muscles bunched for a fourth swing, the craft abruptly slid down off the crown of the bar and righted itself in the water with a wet slap. This last movement caused the motor to drop back down. The propeller bit deep into the wind-whipped waves and the boat shot forward.

Even if I'd wanted to, I never had a chance to warn him.

The prow caught Bascomb square between the shoulder blades. I heard his spine snap above the growl of the motor and saw him go down like a wrecking-balled wall. The boat veered away at impact and began moving parallel with the shoreline. It traveled only a couple dozen yards before striking another gravel bar. This time the motor stalled.

The silence was a sudden, overwhelming thing.

They didn't find Pinky Bascomb's body until the following spring. I had a few bad nights that winter, waking from cold-sweat dreams with chilling visions of Pinky rising up through the ice, clutching a frost-covered shotgun, eyes still burning red with vengeance. I was through the worst of it by the time his remains finally washed up.

After I'd gotten The Bomber to shore, I'd been able to stanch the bleeding of his wound pretty effectively with strips torn from my shirt. The propeller blades had caught him low on the hip and back slightly, toward the buttock, an area of the body where there are no big blood vessels.

I'd broken our handcuff chain between two rocks, then fashioned Bomber a crutch from the oar Bascomb had tried to split my skull with. With me supporting him on one side and the oar crutch on the other, we'd made our way along the shoreline until we reached a cabin where we were able to phone for medical assistance and the police.

I guess the bottom line on the whole thing is the pact Bomber and I made shortly after his release from the hospital. You should probably know about it in case you ever stop by The Bomb Shelter for a couple cold ones. It goes simply like this: The next time we hear somebody blowing about what a great Wisconsin fishing trip they've had, we vowed that one of us is going to march over and belt that person right in the mouth.

LOREN D. ESTLEMAN

STATE OF GRACE

*Loren D. Estleman is one of today's finest practitioners of the
P.I. form. This is a belief widely held, and reinforced by novels
like* Every Brilliant Eye *(1986),* Lady Yesterday *(1987),
and his Shamus Award–winning* Sugartown *(1985). All of
these novels featured his Detroit-based P.I. Amos Walker.
"State of Grace," however, introduces a new—and quite
"different"—character. We think you'll find Ralph Poteet gives
Walker a run for his money in his first appearance, anywhere.*

"Ralph? This is Lyla."

"Who the hell is Lyla?"

"Lyla Dane. I live in the apartment above you, for chrissake. We
see each other every day."

"The hooker."

"You live over a dirty bookstore. What do you want for a
neighbor, a freaking rocket scientist?"

Ralph Poteet sat up in bed and rumpled his mouse-colored hair.
He fumbled the alarm clock off the night table and held it very
close to his good eye. He laid it facedown and scowled at the
receiver in his hand. "It's two-thirty ayem."

"Thanks. My watch stopped and I knew if I called you you'd
tell me what time it is. Listen, you're like a cop, right?"

"Not at two-thirty ayem."

"I'll give you a hundred dollars to come up here now."

He blew his nose on the sheet. "Ain't that supposed to be the
other way around?"

"You coming up or not? You're not the only dick in town. I just
called you because you're handy."

"What's the squeal?"

"I got a dead priest in my bed."

He said he was on his way and hung up. A square gin bottle
slid off the blanket. He caught it before it hit the floor, but it was

empty and he dropped it. He put on his Tyrolean hat with a feather in the band, found his suitpants on the floor half under the bed, and pulled them on over his pajamas. He stuck bare feet into his loafers and because it was October he pulled on his suitcoat, grunting with the effort. He was forty-three years old and forty pounds overweight. He looked for his gun just because it was 2:30 A.M., couldn't find it, and went out.

Lyla Dane was just five feet and ninety pounds in a pink kimono and slippers with carnations on the toes. She wore her black hair in a pageboy like Anna May Wong, but the Oriental effect fell short of her round Occidental face. "You look like crap," she told Ralph at the door.

"That's what two hours' sleep will do for you. Where's the hundred?"

"Don't you want to see the stiff first?"

"What do I look like, a pervert?"

"Yes." She opened a drawer in the telephone stand and counted a hundred in twenties and tens into his palm.

He stuck the money in a pocket and followed her through a small living room decorated by K-Mart into a smaller bedroom containing a Queen Anne bed that had cost twice as much as all the other furniture combined and took up most of the space in the room. The rest of the space was taken up by Monsignor John Breame, pastor of St. Boniface, a cathedral Ralph sometimes used to exchange pictures for money, although not so much lately because the divorce business was on the slide. He recognized the monsignor's pontifical belly under the flesh-colored satin sheet that barely covered it. The monsignor's face was purple.

"He a regular?" Ralph found a Diamond matchstick in his suitcoat pocket and stuck the end between his teeth.

"Couple of times a month. Tonight I thought he was breathing a little hard after. Then he wasn't."

"What do you want me to do?"

"Get rid of him, what else? Cops find him here the Christers'll run me out on a cross. I got a business to run."

"Cost you another hundred."

"I just gave you a hundred."

"You're lucky I don't charge by the pound. Look at that gut."

"*You* look at it. He liked the missionary position."

"What else would he?"

She got the hundred and gave it to him. He told her to leave. "Where'll I go?"

"There's beds all over town. You probably been in half of them. Or go find an all-night movie if you don't feel like working. Don't come back before dawn."

She dressed and went out after emptying the money drawer into a shoulder bag she took with her. When she was gone Ralph helped himself to a Budweiser from her refrigerator and looked up a number in the city directory and called it from the telephone in the living room. A voice like ground glass answered.

"Bishop Stoneman?" Ralph asked.

"It's three ayem," said the voice.

"Thank you. My name is Ralph Poteet. I'm a private detective. I'm sorry to have to inform you Monsignor Breame is dead."

"Mary Mother of God! What happened?"

"I'm no expert. It looks like a heart attack."

"Mary Mother of God. In bed?"

"Yeah."

"Was he—do you know if he was in a state of grace?"

"That's what I wanted to talk to you about," Ralph said.

The man Bishop Stoneman sent was tall and gaunt, with a complexion like wet pulp and colorless hair cropped down to stubble. He had on a black coat buttoned to the neck and looked like an early martyr. He said his name was Morgan. Together they wrapped the monsignor in the soiled bedding and carried him down three flights of stairs, stopping a dozen times to rest, and laid him on the backseat of a big Buick Electra parked between streetlamps. Ralph stood guard at the car while Morgan went back up for the monsignor's clothes. It was nearly 4:00 A.M. and their only witness was a skinny cat who lost interest after a few minutes and stuck one leg up in the air to lick itself.

After a long time Morgan came down and threw the bundle onto the front seat and gave Ralph an envelope containing a hundred dollars. He said he'd handle it from there. Ralph watched him drive off and went back up to bed. He was very tired and didn't wake up until the fire sirens were grinding down in front of the building. He hadn't even heard the explosion when Lyla Dane returned to her apartment at dawn.

"Go away."

"That's no way to talk to your partner," Ralph said.

"Ex-partner. You got the boot and I did, too. Now I'm giving it to you. Go away."

Dale English was a special investigator with the sheriff's department who kept his office in the City-County Building. He had a monolithic face and fierce black eyebrows like Lincoln's, creating an effect he tried to soften with pink shirts and knobby knitted ties. He and Ralph had shared a city prowl car for two years, until some evidence turned up missing from the property room. Both had been dismissed, English without prejudice because unlike the case with Ralph, none of the incriminating items had been found in English's possession.

"The boot didn't hurt you none," Ralph said.

"No, it just cost me my wife and my kid and seven years' seniority. I'd be a lieutenant now."

Ralph lowered his bulk onto the vinyl-and-aluminum chair in front of English's desk. "I wouldn't hang this on you if I could go to the city cops. Somebody's out to kill me."

"Tell whoever it is I said good luck."

"I ain't kidding."

"Me neither."

"You know that hooker got blown up this morning?"

"The gas explosion? I read about it."

"Yeah, well, it wasn't no accident. I'm betting the arson boys find a circuit breaker in the wall switch. You know what that means."

"Sure. Somebody lets himself in and turns on the gas and puts a breaker in the switch so when the guy comes home the spark blows him to hell. What was the hooker into and what was your angle?"

"It's more like who was into the hooker." Ralph told him the rest.

"This the same Monsignor Breame was found by an altar boy counting angels in his bed at the St. Boniface rectory this morning?" English asked.

"Thanks to me and this bug Morgan."

"So what do you want?"

"Hell, protection. The blowup was meant for me. Morgan thought I'd be going back to that same apartment and set it up while I was waiting for him to come down with Breame's clothes."

"Bishops don't kill people over priests that can't keep their vows in their pants."

Ralph screwed up his good eye. Its mate looked like a sour ball someone had spat out. "What world you living in? Shape the Church is in, he'd do just that to keep it quiet."

"Go away, Ralph."

"Well, pick up Morgan at least. He can't be hard to find. He looks like one of those devout creeps you see skulking around in paintings of the Crucifixion."

"I don't have jurisdiction in the city."

"That ain't why you won't do it. Hey, I told IAD you didn't have nothing to do with what went down in Property."

"It would've carried more weight if you'd submitted to a lie detector test. Mine was inconclusive." He paged through a report on his desk without looking at it. "I'll run the name Morgan and the description you gave me through the computer and see what it coughs up. There won't be anything."

"Thanks, buddy."

"You sure you didn't take pictures? It'd be your style to try and put the squeeze on a bishop."

"I thought about it, but my camera's in hock." Ralph got up. "You can get me at my place. They got the fire out before it reached my floor."

"That was lucky. Gin flames are the hardest to put out."

He was driving a brand-new red Riviera he had promised to sell for a lawyer friend who was serving two years for suborning to commit perjury, only he hadn't gotten around to it yet. He parked in a handicapped zone near his building and climbed stairs smelling of smoke and firemen's rubber boots. Inside his apartment, which was also his office, he rewound the tape on his answering machine and played back a threatening call from a loan shark named Zwingman, a reminder from a dentist's receptionist with a Nutra-Sweet voice that last month's root canal was still unpaid for, and a message from a heavy breather that he had to play back three times before deciding it was a man. He was staring toward the door, his attention on the tape, when a square of white paper slithered over the threshold.

That day he was wearing his legal gun, a short-nosed .38 Colt, in a clip on his belt, and an orphan High Standard .22 magnum derringer in an ankle holster. Drawing the Colt, he lunged and tore open the door just in time to hear the street door closing below. He swung around and crossed to the street window. Through it he saw a narrow figure in a long black coat and the back of a close-cropped head crossing against traffic to the other side. The man rounded the corner and vanished.

Ralph holstered the revolver and picked up the note. It was addressed to him in a round, shaped hand.

> Mr. Poteet:
>   If it is not inconvenient, your presence at my home could prove to your advantage and mine.
>
>   Cordially,
>   Philip Stoneman,
>   Bishop-in-Ordinary

Clipped to it was a hundred-dollar bill.

Bishop Stoneman lived in a refurbished brownstone in a neighborhood that the city had reclaimed from slum by evicting its residents and sandblasting graffiti off the buildings. The bell was answered by a youngish bald man in a dark suit and clerical collar who introduced himself as Brother Edwards and directed Ralph to a curving staircase, then retired to be seen no more. Ralph didn't hear Morgan climbing behind him until something hard probed his right kidney. A hand patted him down and removed the Colt from its clip. "End of the hall."

The bishop was a tall old man, nearly as thin as Morgan, with iron-gray hair and a face that fell away to the white shackle of his collar. He rose from behind a redwood desk to greet his visitor in an old-fashioned black frock that made him look like a crow. The room was large and square and smelled of leather from the books on the built-in shelves and pipe tobacco. Morgan entered behind Ralph and closed the door.

"Thank you for coming, Mr. Poteet. Please sit down."

"Thank Ben Franklin." But he settled into a deep leather chair that gripped his buttocks like a big hand in a soft glove.

"I'm grateful for this chance to thank you in person," Stoneman said, sitting in his big swivel. "I'm very disappointed in Monsignor Breame. I'd hoped that he would take my place at the head of the diocese."

"You bucking for cardinal?"

He smiled. "I suppose you've shown yourself worthy of confidence. Yes, His Holiness has offered me the red hat. The appointment will be announced next month."

"That why you tried to croak me? I guess your right bower cashing in in a hooker's bed would look bad in Rome."

One corner of the desk supported a silver tray containing two long-stemmed glasses and a cut-crystal decanter half full of ruby liquid. Stoneman removed the stopper and filled both glasses. "This is an excellent Madeira. I confess that the austere life allows me two mild vices. The other is tobacco."

"What are we celebrating?" Ralph didn't pick up his glass.

"Your new appointment as chief of diocesan security. The position pays well and the hours are regular."

"In return for which I forget about Monsignor Breame?"

"And entrust all related material to me. You took pictures, of course." Stoneman sipped from his glass.

Ralph lifted his. "I'd be pretty stupid not to, considering what happened to Lyla Dane."

"I heard about the tragedy. That child's soul could have been saved."

"You should've thought about that before your boy Morgan croaked her." Ralph gulped off half his wine. It tasted bitter.

The bishop laid a bony hand atop an ancient ornate Bible on the desk. His guest thought he was about to swear his innocence. "This belonged to St. Thomas. More, not Aquinas. I have a weakness for religious antiques."

"Thought you only had two vices." The air in the room stirred slightly. Ralph turned to see who had entered, but his vision was thickening. Morgan was a shimmering shadow. The glass dropped from Ralph's hand. He bent to retrieve it and came up with the derringer. Stoneman's shout echoed. Ralph fired twice at the shadow and pitched headfirst into its depths.

He awoke feeling pretty much the way he did most mornings, with his head throbbing and his stomach turning over. He wanted to turn over with it, but he was stretched out on a hard, flat surface with his ankles strapped down and his arms tied above his head. He was looking up at water-stained tile. His joints ached.

"The sedative was in the stem of your glass," Stoneman was saying. He was out of Ralph's sight and Ralph had the impression he'd been talking for a while. "You've been out for two hours. The unpleasant effect is temporary, rather like a hangover."

"Did I get him?" Ralph's tongue moved sluggishly.

"No, you missed rather badly. It required persuasion to get

Morgan to carry you down here to the basement instead of killing you on the spot. He was quite upset."

Ralph squirmed. There was something familiar about the position he was tied in. For some reason he thought of Mrs. Thornton, his ninth-grade American Lit. teacher. *What is the significance of Poe's "Pit and the Pendulum" to the transcendentalist movement?* His organs shriveled.

"Another antique," said the bishop. "The Inquisition did not end when General Lasalle entered Madrid, but went on for several years in the provinces. This particular rack was still in use after Torquemada's death. The gears are original. The wheel is new, and of course I had to replace the ropes. Morgan?"

A shoe scraped the floor and a spoked shadow fluttered across Ralph's vision. His arms tightened. He gasped.

"That's enough. We don't want to put Mr. Poteet back under." To Ralph: "Morgan just returned from your apartment. He found neither pictures nor film nor even a camera. Where are they?"

"I was lying. I didn't take no pictures."

"Morgan."

Ralph shrieked.

"Enough! His Holiness is sensitive about scandal, Mr. Poteet. I won't have Monsignor Breame's indiscretions bar me from the Vatican. Who is keeping the pictures for you?"

"There ain't no pictures, honest."

"Morgan!"

A socket started to slip. Ralph screamed and blubbered.

"Enough!" Stoneman's fallen-away face moved into Ralph's vision. His eyes were fanatic. "A few more turns will sever your spine. You could be spoon-fed for the rest of your life. Do you think that after failing to kill you in that apartment I would hesitate to cripple you? Where are the pictures?"

"I didn't take none!"

"Morgan!"

"*No!*" It ended in a howl. His armpits were on fire. The ropes creaked.

"Police! Don't move!"

The bishop's face jerked away. The spoked shadow fluttered. The tension went out of Ralph's arms suddenly, and relief poured into his joints. A shot flattened the air. Two more answered it. Something struck the bench Ralph was lying on and drove a splinter into his back. He thought at first he was shot, but the pain was nothing; he'd just been through worse. He squirmed onto his hip and saw Morgan, one black-clad arm stained and glistening, leveling a heavy automatic at a target behind Ralph's back. Scrambling out of the line of fire, Ralph jerked his bound hands and the rack's wheel, six feet in diameter with handles bristling from it like a ship's helm, spun around. One of the handles slapped the gun from Morgan's hand. Something cracked past Ralph's left ear and Morgan fell back against the tile wall and slid down it. The shooting stopped.

Ralph wriggled onto his other hip. A man he didn't know in a houndstooth coat with a revolver in his hand had Bishop Stoneman spread-eagled against a wall and was groping in his robes for weapons. Dale English came off the stairs with the Ruger he had been carrying since Ralph was his partner. He bent over Morgan on the floor, then straightened and holstered the gun. He looked at Ralph. "I guess you're okay."

"I am if you got a pocketknife."

"Arson boys found the circuit breaker in the wall switch just like you said." He cut Ralph's arms free and sawed through the straps on his ankles. "When you didn't answer your telephone I went to your place and found Stoneman's note."

"He confessed to the hooker's murder."

"I know. I heard him."

"How the hell long were you listening?"

"We had to have enough to pin him to it, didn't we?"

"You son of a bitch. You just wanted to hear me holler."

"Couldn't help it. You sure got lungs."

"I got to go to the toilet."

"Stick around after," English said. "I need a statement to hand to the city boys. They won't like County sticking its face in this."

Ralph hobbled upstairs. When he was through in the bathroom he found his hat and coat and headed out. At the front door he turned around and went back into the bishop's study, where he hoisted Thomas More's Bible under one arm. He knew a bookseller who would probably give him at least a hundred for it.

SUE GRAFTON

NON SUNG SMOKE

*With four novels in her alphabetized Kinsey Millhone series
(and several short stories), Sue Grafton has racked up a
Shamus Award ("B" Is for Burglar, Best Novel of 1985), and
three Anthony Awards ("B" Is for Burglar, Best Novel of
1985; "C" Is for Corpse, Best Novel of 1986; and "The
Parker Shotgun," Best Short Story of 1986). "The Parker
Shotgun" appeared in* Mean Streets.

*"Non Sung Smoke" makes her a strong contender for
awards next year, as well.*

The day was an odd one, brooding and chill, sunlight alternating
with an erratic wind that was being pushed toward California
in advance of a tropical storm called Bo. It was late September in
Santa Teresa. Instead of the usual Indian summer, we were
caught up in vague presentiments of the long, gray winter to
come. I found myself pulling sweaters out of my bottom drawer
and I went to the office smelling of moth balls and last year's
cologne.

I spent the morning caught up in routine paperwork which
usually leaves me feeling productive, but this was the end of a
dull week and I was so bored I would have taken on just about
anything. The young woman showed up just before lunch,
announcing herself with a tentative tap on my office door. She
couldn't have been more than twenty, with a sultry, porno-
graphic face and a tumble of long dark hair. She was wearing an
outfit that suggested she hadn't gone home the night before
unless, of course, she simply favored low-cut sequined cocktail
dresses at noon. Her spike heels were a dyed-to-match green and

her legs were bare. She moved over to my desk with an air of uncertainty, like someone just learning to roller skate.

"Hi, how are you? Have a seat," I said.

She sank into a chair. "Thanks. I'm Mona Starling. I guess you're Kinsey Millhone, huh."

"Yes, that's right."

"Are you really a private detective?"

"Licensed and bonded," I said.

"Are you single?"

I did a combination nod and shrug which I hoped would cover two divorces and my current happily *un*married state.

"Great," she said, "then you'll understand. God, I can't believe I'm really doing this. I've never hired a detective, but I don't know what else to do."

"What's going on?"

She blushed, maybe from nervousness, maybe from embarrassment, but the heightened coloring only made her green eyes more vivid. She shifted in her seat, the sequins on her dress winking merrily. Something about her posture made me downgrade her age. She looked barely old enough to drive.

"I hope you don't think this is dumb. I . . . uh, ran into this guy last night and we really hit it off. He told me his name was Gage. I don't know if that's true or not. Sometimes guys make up names, you know, like if they're married or maybe not sure they want to see you again. Anyway, we had a terrific time, only he left without telling me how to get in touch. I was just wondering how much it might cost to find out who he is."

"How do you know he won't get in touch with you?"

"Well, he might. I mean, I'll give him a couple of days of course. All I'm asking for is his name and address. Just in case."

"I take it you'll want his phone number, too."

She laughed uneasily. "Well, yeah."

"What if he doesn't want to renew the acquaintance?"

"Oh, I wouldn't bother him if he felt that way. I know it looks like a pickup, but it really wasn't. For me, at any rate. I don't want him to think it was casual on my part."

"I take it you were . . . ah, *intimate*," I said.

"Un-uh, we just balled, but it was incredible and I'd really like to see him again."

Reluctantly, I pulled out a legal pad and made a note. "Where'd you meet this man?"

"I ran into him at Mooter's. He talked like he hung out there a lot. The music was so loud we were having to shout, so after a while we went to the bar next door where it was quiet. We talked for hours. I know what you're going to say. Like why don't I let well enough alone or something, but I just can't."

"Why not go back to Mooter's and ask around?"

"Well, I would, but I, uh, have this boyfriend who's really jealous and he'd figure it out. If I even look at another guy, he has this incredible ESP reaction. He's spooky sometimes."

"How'd you get away with it last night?"

"He was working, so I was on my own," she said. "Say you'll help me, okay? Please? I've been cruising around all night looking for his car. He lives somewhere in Montebello, I'm almost sure."

"I can probably find him, Mona, but my services aren't cheap."

"I don't care," she said. "That's fine. I have money. Just tell me how much."

I debated briefly and finally asked her for fifty bucks. I didn't have the heart to charge my usual rates. I didn't really want her business, but it was better than typing up file notes for the case I'd just done. She put a fifty-dollar bill on my desk and I wrote out a receipt, bypassing my standard contract. As young as she was, I wasn't sure it'd be binding anyway.

I jotted down a description of the man named Gage. He sounded like every stud on the prowl I've ever seen. Early thirties, five foot ten, good build, dark hair, dark moustache, great smile, and a dimple in his chin. I was prepared to keep writing, but that was the extent of it. For all of their alleged hours of conversation, she knew precious little about him. I quizzed her at length about hobbies, interests, what sort of work he did. The only real information she could give me was that he drove an old silver Jaguar which is where they "got it on" (her parlance, not mine) the first time. The second time was at her place. After that, he apparently disappeared like a puff of smoke. Real soul mates, these two. I didn't want to tell her what an old story it was. In Santa Teresa, the eligible men are so much in demand they can do anything they want. I took her address and telephone number and said I'd get back to her. As soon as she left, I picked up my handbag and car keys. I had a few personal errands to run and figured I'd tuck her business in when I was finished with my own.

Mooter's is one of a number of bars on the Santa Teresa singles' circuit. By night, it's crowded and impossibly noisy. Happy Hour features well drinks for fifty cents and the bartender rings a gong for every five-dollar tip. The tables are small, jammed together around a dance floor the size of a boxing ring. The walls are covered with caricatures of celebrities, possibly purchased from some other bar, as they seem to be signed and dedicated to someone named Stan whom nobody's ever heard of. An ex-husband of mine played jazz piano there once upon a time, but I hadn't been in for years.

I arrived that afternoon at two, just in time to watch the place being opened up. Two men, day drinkers by the look of them, edged in ahead of me and took up what I surmised were habitual perches at one end of the bar. They were exchanging the kind of pleasantries that suggest daily contact of no particular depth. The man who let us in apparently doubled as bartender and bouncer. He was in his thirties, with curly blond hair, and a T-shirt reading BOUNCER stretched across an impressively muscular chest. His arms were so big I thought he might rip his sleeves out when he flexed.

I found an empty stool at the far end of the bar and waited while he made a couple of martinis for the two men who'd come in with me. A waitress appeared for work, taking off her coat as she moved through the bar to the kitchen area.

The bartender then ambled in my direction with an inquiring look.

"I'll have a wine spritzer," I said.

A skinny guy with a guitar case came into the bar behind me. When the bartender saw him, he grinned. "Hey, how's it goin'? How's Fresno?"

They shook hands and the guy took a stool two down from mine. "Hot. And dull, but Mary Jane's was fine. We really packed 'em in."

"Smirnoff on the rocks?"

"Nah, not today. Gimme a beer instead. Bud'll do."

The bartender pulled one for him and set his drink on the bar at the same time I got mine. I wondered what it must be like to hang out all day in saloons, nursing beers, shooting the shit with idlers and ne'er-do-wells. The waitress came out of the kitchen, tying an apron around her waist. She took a sandwich order from the guys at the far end of the bar. The other fellow and I both declined when she asked if we were interested in lunch. She began to busy herself with napkins and flatware.

The bartender caught my eye. "You want to run a tab?"

I shook my head. "This is fine," I said. "I'm trying to get in touch with a guy who was in here last night."

"Good luck. The place was a zoo."

"Apparently, he's a regular. I thought you might identify him from a description."

"What's he done?"

"Not a thing. From what I was told, he picked up a young lady and ran out on her afterward. She wants to get in touch with him, that's all."

He stood and looked at me. "You're a private detective."

"That's right."

He and the other fellow exchanged a look.

The fellow said, "Help the woman. This is great."

The bartender shrugged. "Sure, why not? What's he look like?"

The waitress paused, listening in on the conversation with interest.

I mentioned the first name and description Mona'd given me. "The only other thing I know about him is he drives an old silver Jaguar."

"Gage Vesca," the other fellow said promptly.

The bartender said, "Yeah, that's him."

"You know how I might get in touch?"

The other fellow shook his head and the bartender shrugged. "All I know is he's a jerk. The guy's got a vanity license plate reads STALYUN if that tells you anything. Besides that, he just got married a couple months back. He's bad news. Better warn your client. He'll screw anything that moves."

"I'll pass the word. Thanks." I put a five-dollar bill on the bar and hopped down off the stool, leaving the spritzer untouched.

"Hey, who's the babe?" the bartender asked.

"Can't tell you that," I said, as I picked up my bag.

The waitress spoke up. "Well, I know which one she's talking about. That girl in the green-sequined dress."

I went back to my office and checked the telephone book. No listing for Vescas of any kind. Information didn't have him either, so I put in a call to a friend of mine at the DMV who plugged the license plate into the computer. The name Gage Vesca came up, with an address in Montebello. I used my crisscross directory for a match and came up with the phone number, which I dialed just to see if it was good. As soon as the maid said "Vesca residence," I hung up.

I put in a call to Mona Starling and gave her what I had, including the warning about his marital status and his character references which were poor. She didn't seem to care. After that, I figured if she pursued him, it was her lookout . . . and his. She thanked me profusely before she rang off, relief audible in her voice.

That was Saturday.

Monday morning, I opened my front door, picked up the paper, and caught the headlines about Gage Vesca's death.

"Shit!"

He'd been shot in the head at close range sometime between two and six A.M. on Sunday, then crammed into the trunk of his Jaguar and left in the long-term parking lot at the airport. Maybe somebody hoped the body wouldn't be discovered for days. Time enough to set up an alibi or pull a disappearing act. As it was, the hood had popped open and a passerby had spotted him. My hands were starting to shake. What kind of chump had I been?

I tried Mona Starling's number and got a busy signal. I threw some clothes on, grabbed my car keys, and headed over to the Frontage Road address she'd given me. As I chirped to a stop out front, a Yellow cab pulled away from the curb with a lone passenger. I checked the house number. A duplex. I figured the odds were even that I'd just watched Mona split. She must have seen the headlines about the same time I did.

I took off again, craning for sight of the taxi somewhere ahead. Beyond the next intersection, there was a freeway on-ramp. I caught a flash of yellow and pursued it. By keeping my foot to the floor and judiciously changing lanes, I managed to slide in right behind the taxi as it took the airport exit. By the time the cab deposited Mona at the curb out in front, I was squealing into the short-term lot with the parking ticket held between my teeth. I shoved it in my handbag and ran.

The airport at Santa Teresa only has five gates, and it didn't take much detecting to figure out which one was correct. United was announcing a final boarding call for a flight to San Francisco. I used the fifty bucks Mona'd paid me to snag a seat and a boarding pass from a startled reservations clerk and then I headed for the gate. I had no luggage and nothing on me to set off the security alarm as I whipped through. I flashed my ticket, opened the double doors, and raced across the tarmac for the plane, taking the portable boarding stairs two at a time. The flight attendant pulled the door shut behind me. I was in.

I spotted Mona eight rows back in a window seat on the left-hand side, her face turned away from me. This time she was wearing jeans and an oversized shirt. The aisle seat was occupied, but the middle was empty. The plane was still sitting on the runway, engines revving, as I bumped across some guy's knees, saying, "'scuse me, pardon me," and popped in beside Ms. Starling. She turned a blanched face toward me and a little cry escaped. "What are you doing here?"

"See if you can guess."

"I didn't do it," she whispered hoarsely.

"Yeah, right. I bet. That's probably why you got on a plane the minute the story broke," I said.

"That's *not* what happened."

"The hell it's not!"

The man on my left leaned forward and looked at us quizzically.

"The fellow she picked up Friday night got killed," I said, conversationally. I pointed my index finger at my head like a gun and fired. He decided to mind his own business, which suited me. Mona got to her feet and tried to squeeze past. All I had to do was extend my knees and she was trapped. Other people were taking an interest by now. She did a quick survey of the situation, rolled her eyes, and sat down again. "Let's get off the plane. I'll explain in a minute. Just don't make a scene," she said, the color high in her cheeks.

"Hey, let's not cause you any embarrassment," I said. "A man was murdered. That's all we're talking about."

"I know he's dead," she hissed, "but I'm innocent. I swear to God."

We got up together and bumped and thumped across the man's knees, heading down the aisle toward the door. The flight attendant was peeved, but she let us deplane.

We went upstairs to the airport bar and found a little table at the rear. When the waitress came, I shook my head, but Mona ordered a Pink Squirrel. The waitress had questions about her age, but I had to question her taste. A Pink Squirrel? Mona had pulled her wallet out and the waitress scrutinized her California driver's license, checking Mona's face against the stamp-sized color photograph, apparently satisfied at the match. As she passed the wallet back to Mona, I snagged it and peeked at the license myself. She was twenty-one by a month. The address was the same one she'd given me. The waitress disappeared and Mona snatched her wallet, shoving it down in her purse again.

"What was that for?" she said sulkily.

"Just checking. You want to tell me what's going on?"

She picked up a packet of airport matches and began to bend the cover back and forth. "I lied to you."

"This comes as no surprise," I said. "What's the truth?"

"Well, I did pick him up, but we didn't screw. I just told you that because I couldn't think of any other reason I'd want his home address."

"Why *did* you want it?"

She broke off eye contact. "He stole something and I had to get it back."

I stared at her. "Let me take a flyer," I said. "It had to be something illegal or you'd have told me about it right up front. Or reported it to the cops. So it must be dope. Was it coke or grass?"

She was wide-eyed. "Grass, but how did you know?"

"Just tell me the rest," I replied with a shake of my head. I love the young. They're always amazed that we know anything.

Mona glanced up to my right.

The waitress was approaching with her tray. She set an airport cocktail napkin on the table and placed the Pink Squirrel on it. "That'll be three-fifty."

Mona took five ones from her billfold and waved her off. She sipped at the drink and shivered. The concoction was the same pink as bubble gum, which made me shiver a bit as well. She licked her lips. "My boyfriend got a lid of this really incredible grass. 'Non Sung Smoke' it's called, from the town of Non Sung in Thailand."

"Never heard of it," I said. "Not that I'm any connoisseur."

"Well, me neither, but he paid like two thousand dollars for it and he'd only smoked one joint. The guy he got it from said half a hit would put you away so we weren't going to smoke it every day. Just special occasions."

"Pretty high-class stuff at those rates."

"The best."

"And you told Gage."

"Well, yeah," she said reluctantly. "We met and we started talking. He said he needed to score some pot so I mentioned it. I wasn't going to sell him ours. I just thought he might try it and then if he was interested, maybe we could get some for him. When we got to my place, I went in the john while he rolled a joint, and when I came out, he was gone and so was the dope. I had to take a cab back to Mooter's to pick up my car. I was in such a panic. I knew if Jerry found out he'd have a fit!"

"He's your boyfriend?"

"Right," she said, looking down at her lap. She began to blink rapidly and she put a trembling hand to her lips.

I gave her a verbal nudge, just to head off the tears. "Then what? After I gave you the phone number, you got in touch with Gage?"

She nodded mutely, then took a deep breath. "I had to wait till Jerry went off to work and then I called. Gage said—"

"Wait a minute. He answered the phone?"

"Uh-uh. She did. His wife, but I made sure she'd hung up the extension and then I talked so he only had to answer yes and no. I told him I knew he fucking stole the dope and I wanted it back like right then. I just screamed. I told him if he didn't get that shit back to me, he'd be sorry. He said he'd meet me in the parking lot at Mooter's after closing time."

"That was Saturday night?"

She nodded.

"All right. Then what?"

"That's all there was," she said. "I met him there at two-fifteen and he handed over the dope. I didn't even tell him what a shitheel he was. I just snatched the baggie, got back in my car, and came home. When I saw the headlines this morning, I thought I'd die!"

"Who else was aware of all this?"

"No one as far as I know."

"Didn't your boyfriend think it was odd you went out at two-fifteen?"

She shook her head. "I was back before he got home."

"Didn't he realize the dope had disappeared?"

"No, because I put it back before he even looked for it. He couldn't have known."

"What about Mooter's? Was there anyone else in the parking lot?"

"Not that I saw."

"No one coming or going from the bar?"

"Just the guy who runs the place."

"What about Mrs. Vesca? Could she have followed him?"

"Well, I asked him if she overheard my call and he said no. But she could have followed, I guess. I don't know what kind of car she drives, but she could have been parked on a side street."

"Aside from that, how could anyone connect you to Vesca's death? I don't understand why you decided to run."

Her voice dropped to a whisper. "My fingerprints have to be on that car. I was just in it two nights ago."

I studied the look in her eyes and I could feel my heart sink. "You have a record," I said.

"I was picked up for shoplifting once. But that's the only trouble I was ever in. Honestly."

"I think you ought to go to the cops with this. It's far better to be up front with them than to come up with lame excuses after they track you down, which I suspect they will."

"Oh, God, I'll die."

"No, you won't. You'll feel better. Now do what I say and I'll check the rest of it from my end."

"You will?"

"Of course!" I snapped. "If I hadn't found the guy for you, he might be okay. How do you think I feel?"

I followed the maid through the Vescas' house to the pool area at the rear, where one of the cabanas had been fitted out as a personal gym. There were seven weight machines bolted to the floor, which was padded with rubber matting. Mirrors lined three walls and sunlight streamed in the fourth. Katherine Vesca, in a hot-pink leotard and silver tights, was working on her abs, an unnecessary expenditure of energy from what I could see. She was thin as a snake. Her ash-blond hair was kept off her face by a band of pink chiffon and her gray eyes were cold. She blotted sweat from her neck as she glanced at my business card. "You're connected with the police?"

"Actually, I'm not, but I'm hoping you'll answer some questions anyway."

"Why should I?"

"I'm trying to get a line on your husband's killer just like they are."

"Why not leave it up to them?"

"I have some information they don't have yet. I thought I'd see what else I could add before I pass on the facts."

"The facts?"

"About his activities the last two days of his life."

She gave me a chilly smile and crossed to the leg-press

machine. She moved the pin down to the hundred-and-eighty-pound mark, then seated herself and started to do reps. "Fire away," she said.

"I understand a phone call came in sometime on Saturday," I said.

"That's right. A woman called. He went out to meet her quite late that night and he didn't come back. I never saw him again."

"Do you know what the call was about?"

"Sorry. He never said."

"Weren't you curious?"

"When I married Gage, I agreed that I wouldn't be 'curious' about anything he did."

"And he wasn't curious about you?"

"We had an open relationship. At his insistence, I might add. He was free to do anything he liked."

"And you didn't object?"

"Sometimes, but those were his terms and I agreed."

"What sort of work did he do?"

"He didn't. Neither of us worked. I have a business here in town and I derive income from that, among other things."

"Do you know if he was caught up in anything? A quarrel? Some kind of personal feud?"

"If so, he never mentioned it," she said. "He was not well liked, but I couldn't say he had enemies."

"Do you have a theory about who killed him?"

She finished ten reps and rested. "I wish I did."

"When's the funeral?" I asked.

"Tomorrow morning at ten. You're welcome to come. Then maybe there'll be two of us."

She gave me the name of the funeral home and I made a note.

"One more thing," I said. "What sort of business are you in? Could that be relevant?"

"I don't see how. I have a bar. Called Mooter's. It's managed by my brother, Jim."

When I walked in, he was washing beer mugs behind the bar, running each in turn across a rotating brush, then through a hot water rinse. To his right was a mounting pyramid of drying mugs, still radiating heat. Today he wore a bulging T-shirt imprinted with a slogan that read: ONE NIGHT OF BAD SEX IS STILL BETTER THAN A GOOD DAY AT WORK. He fixed a look on my face, smiling pleasantly. "How's it going?"

I perched on a bar stool. "Not bad," I said. "You're Jim?"

"That's me. And you're the lady P.I. I don't think you told me your name."

"Kinsey Millhone. I'm assuming you heard about Vesca's death?"

"Yeah, Jesus. Poor guy. Looks like somebody really cleaned his clock. Hope it wasn't the little gal he dumped the other night."

"That's always a possibility."

"You want a spritzer?"

"Sure," I said. "You have a good memory."

"For drinks," he said. "That's my job." He got out the jug wine and poured some in a glass, adding soda from the hose. He added a twist of lime and put the drink in front of me. "On the house."

"Thanks," I said. I took a sip. "How come you never said he was your brother-in-law?"

"How'd you find out about that?" he asked mildly.

"I talked to your sister. She mentioned it."

He shrugged. "Didn't seem pertinent."

I was puzzled by his attitude. He wasn't acting like a man with anything to hide. "Did you see him Saturday?"

"Saw his car at closing time. That was Sunday morning, actually. What's that got to do with it?"

"He must have been killed about then. The paper said some-time between two and six."

"I locked up here shortly after two. My buddy stopped by and picked me up right out front. I was in a poker game by two thirty-five, at a private club."

"You have witnesses?"

"Just the fifty other people in the place. I guess I could have shot the guy before my buddy showed up, but why would I do that? I had no axe to grind with him. I wasn't crazy about him, but I wouldn't plug the guy. My sister adored him. Why break her heart?"

Good question, I thought.

I returned to my office and sat down, tilting back in my swivel chair with my feet on the desk. I kept thinking Gage's death must be connected to the Non Sung Smoke, but I couldn't figure out quite how. I made a call to the Vesca house and was put on hold while the maid went to fetch Miss Katherine. She clicked on. "Yes?"

"Hello, Mrs. Vesca. This is Kinsey Millhone."

"Oh, hello. Sorry if I sounded abrupt. What can I do for you?"

"Just a question I forgot to ask you earlier. Did Gage ever mention something called Non Sung Smoke?"

"I don't think so. What is it?"

"A high-grade marijuana from Thailand. Two thousand bucks a lid. Apparently, he helped himself to somebody's stash on Friday night."

"Well, he did have some grass, but it couldn't be the same. He said it was junk. He was incensed that somebody hyped it to him."

"Really," I said, but it was more to myself than to her.

I headed down to the parking lot and retrieved my car. A dim understanding was beginning to form.

I knocked at the door of the duplex on Frontage Road. Mona answered, looking puzzled when she caught sight of me.

"Did you talk to the cops?" I asked.

"Not yet. I was just on my way. Why? What's up?"

"It occurred to me I might have misunderstood something you said to me. Friday night when you went out, you told me your boyfriend Jerry was at work. How come you had the nerve to stay out all night?"

"He was out of town," she said. "He got back Saturday afternoon about five."

"Couldn't he have arrived in Santa Teresa earlier that day?" She shrugged. "I suppose so."

"What about Saturday when you met Gage in Mooter's parking lot? Was he working again?"

"Well, yes. He had a gig here in town. He got home about three," she said in the same bewildered tone.

"He's a musician, isn't he," I said.

"Wait a minute. What *is* this? What's it got to do with him?"

"A lot," he said from behind me. A choking arm slid around my neck and I was jerked half off my feet. I hung on, trying to ease the pressure on my windpipe. I could manage to breathe if I stood on tiptoe, but I couldn't do much else. Something hard was jammed into my ribs and I didn't think it was Jerry's fountain pen. Mona was astonished.

"Jerry! What the hell are you doing?" she yelped.

"Back up, bitch. Step back and let us in," he said between clenched teeth. I hung on, struggling, as he half-lifted, half-shoved me toward the threshold. He dragged me into the apartment and kicked the door shut. He pushed me down on the couch and stood there with his gun pointed right between my eyes. Hey, I was comfy. I wasn't going anyplace.

When I saw his face, of course, my suspicions were confirmed. Jerry was the fellow with the guitar case who'd sat next to me at Mooter's bar when I first went in. He wasn't a big guy—maybe five-eight, weighing in at a hundred and fifty-five—but he'd caught me by surprise. He was edgy and he had a crazy look in his eyes. I've noticed that in a pinch like this, my mind either goes completely blank or begins to compute at lightning speeds. I found myself staring at his gun, which was staring disconcertingly at me. It looked like a little Colt .32, a semiautomatic, almost a double for mine . . . locked at that moment in a briefcase in the backseat of my car. I bypassed the regrets and got straight to the point. Before being fired the first time, a semiautomatic has to be manually cocked, a maneuver that can be accomplished only with two hands. I couldn't remember hearing the sound of the slide being yanked before the nose of the gun was shoved into the small of my back. I wondered briefly if, in his haste to act, he hadn't had time to cock the gun.

"Hello, Jerry," I said. "Nice seeing you again. Why don't you tell Mona about your run-in with Gage?"

"*You* killed Gage?" she said, staring at him with disbelief.

"That's right, Mona, and I'm going to kill you, too. Just as soon as I figure out what to do with her." He kept his eyes on me, making sure I didn't move.

"But why? What did I do?" she gasped.

"Don't give me that," he said. "You balled the guy! Cattin' around in that green-sequined dress with your tits hangin' out and you pick up a scumbag like him! I told you I'd kill you if you ever did that to me."

"But I didn't. I swear it. All I did was bring him back here to try a hit of pot. Next thing I knew he'd stolen the whole lid."

"Bullshit!"

"No, it's not!"

I said, "She's telling the truth, Jerry. That's why she hired me."

Confused, he shot a look at her. "You never went to bed with him?"

"Jesus Christ, of course not. The guy was a creep! I'm not *that* low class!"

Jerry's hand began to tremble and his gaze darted back and

forth between her face and mine. "Then why'd you meet him again the next night?"

"To get the grass back. What else could I do? I didn't want you to know I'd been stiffed for two thousand dollars' worth of pot."

He stared at her, transfixed, and that's when I charged. I flew at him, head down, butting straight into his midriff, my momentum taking us both down in a heap. The gun skittered off across the floor. Mona leaped on him and punched him in the gut, using her body to hold him down while I scrambled over to the Colt. I snatched it up. Silly me. The sucker had been cocked the whole time. I was lucky I hadn't had my head blown off.

I could hear him yelling, "Jesus Christ, all right! Get off. I'm done." And then he lay there, winded. I kept the gun pointed steadily at body parts he treasured while Mona called the cops.

He rolled over on his side and sat up. I moved back a step. The wild look had left his eyes and he was starting to weep, still gasping and out of breath. "Oh, Jesus. I can't believe it."

Mona turned to him with a withering look. "It's too late for an attack of conscience, Jerry."

He shook his head. "You don't know the half of it, babe. You're not the one who got stiffed for the dope. I was."

She looked at him blankly. "Meaning what?"

"I paid two grand for garbage. That dope was crap. I didn't want to tell you I got taken in so I invented some bullshit about Non Sung Smoke. There's no such thing. I made it up."

It took an instant for the irony to penetrate. She sank down beside him. "Why didn't you trust me? Why didn't you just tell me the truth?"

His expression was bleak. "Why didn't you?"

The question hung between them like a cobweb, wavering in the autumn light.

By the time the cops came, they were huddled on the floor together, clinging to each other in despair.

The sight of them was almost enough to cure me of the lies I tell.

But not quite.

ROB KANTNER

LEFT FOR DEAD

Rob Kantner won the 1986 Shamus Award for Best Paperback Novel with The Back Door Man *(Bantam, 1986), his first novel, and the 1986 Shamus Award for Best Short Story with "Fly Away Home," which appeared in* Mean Streets. *His second "Ben Perkins" novel,* The Harder They Hit, *was published by Bantam in 1987, and the third,* Dirty Work, *will appear in December 1988.*

It's rare to find a writer who is so at home with both the novel and short story forms, but then Rob has already proven himself a rare writer.

For further proof, read "Left for Dead."

It wasn't a landing, it was a barely controlled crash. My ultralight hit on all three wheels of the tricycle gear simultaneously and, hurtling entirely too fast along the rock-hard, burned-out field, bounced from one wheel to another in rapid sequence as I fought the stick for control. A quiet voice in my mind speculated quite impersonally that any second a viciously errant gust of wind would catch one of the wings, flip the aircraft over, and smear me into a long red stain on the ground.

But the voice, for once, was wrong. I rolled to a stop, throttled down the 350cc Zenoah engine, and cut the ignition, leaving only the sound of the driving wind.

I clambered out of the open cockpit, shucked off my wool hood and heavy goggles, unzipped my black snowmobile suit halfway, and paced a small circle under the influence of maximum adrenaline, trying to figure out where I was and what the hell I'd do now.

The first part was relatively easy. I was somewhere in the middle of the twenty-five-hundred-acre Southern Michigan Wilderness Preserve, located roughly halfway between Detroit and Sturgis, in Whitlock County near the Ohio line. What the hell I'd do now was, without doubt, wait. Wait for better weather. Even if I had to spend the night in this godforsaken place. I was lucky I'd gotten the aircraft down in one piece as it was.

I stopped pacing, zipped my suit back up against the October chill, and scanned the area. I was near the center of a large flat valley. Behind me was the westernmost fringe of the Irish Hills. Ahead was a mass of forest, as far as the eye could see. Nowhere were there people or signs of habitation. In a month or so the area would be covered with the first dusting of snow and peopled by red-coated hunters taking potshots at anything that moved, especially each other. A month after that there'd be snow on the ground, and crowds of snowmobilers and skiers. Now was the dead time, nobody around but little old me, an unscheduled visitor but pretty damn glad to be there, just the same.

The afternoon was wearing on, getting colder and windier by the moment. I grabbed the ultralight by the downtube and wheeled her along the hard ground till I reached the fringe of thick trees. I folded down the wings and, for extra measure, propped some rocks against the wheels. Then I ventured twenty feet or so into the woods and found a nice comfortable spot against a rock outcropping, the ground covered with a thick layer of leaves and humus, and tamped myself a place to rest. I lay down, propped my head against an old, rotting stump, and relaxed. Nothing to do but kill time till morning, maybe sleep if I could, later.

I had nothing to eat or drink, but I did have a handful of cigars tucked away, so the essentials were certainly taken care of. I extracted one, stuck it in my mouth, then dug beneath the snowsuit into my jeans pocket in search of a light. Found a wad of bills. A dead Michigan Lotto ticket. Some coins. And a loose .45 caliber bullet. Pretty typical pocket inventory—but no matches. I was starting to panic when I found my kitchen matches in the other pocket, sighed in relief, and flared one. I was just getting the cigar going when I heard the far-off scream.

I jerked upright, listening hard. Nothing. Could have been my imagination, I thought. Or maybe an animal. But I'm not known to imagine things. And, though I knew there were no settlements within twenty miles, I felt certain the scream was human. Female, flat, atonal, not expecting to be heard.

I sighed, hoisted myself to my feet, tucked my cigar away, and hoofed into the vast clearing. Still deserted. I stood still for a moment, hearing the scream again in my mind, then turned left and began to hike. I wasn't even sure the sound had come from that direction. I could very well have been wasting my time. But time was something I had plenty of just then, so I set out hiking.

The woods bent away to my left as the valley turned toward the west. I followed the curve down a gentle incline, and as the trees fell back I saw a cabin at the bottom of the slope, hard against a sudden, wooded rise.

I stopped for a minute and surveyed. The cabin looked small, maybe twenty by twenty, weathered planks topped by a rusted tin roof and a stone chimney, no porch. A gaunt wood-slat snow fence, bowed in spots, surrounded it. The dying grass had grown up tall here and was being whipped to and fro by the wind. Overall, the place looked like it had been built as an afterthought and not occupied much since then. Certainly it looked abandoned now.

I set out for it anyway. Even if there was no screamer to be found, a man-made shelter sure beat the hell out of a makeshift camp deep in the woods. As I drew nearer, I saw a narrow gap in the fence about twenty feet from the cabin, and a path beaten in the tall grass up to the door. To the right of the fence gap was a platform of rotting planks, probably the covering of an old disused well. Beyond that, in the corner of the makeshift yard, was a neatly stacked couple of cords of split, well-seasoned firewood. Back of the cabin I caught just a glimpse of a small, leaning, tin-roofed outhouse. Somebody had obviously put in some time here. How long ago, I had no idea.

I slowed my pace as I passed through the fence gap and ventured up to the door. Not a sound from anywhere, nothing but the wind. The rough-hewn plank door stood open a couple of inches. I looked at it for a minute, then pushed it open slowly on groaning iron hinges.

The inside smelled of old wood and mold. A two-man folding cot stood open on the plank floor, covered with a nondescript pile of gray army blankets. To the right, a wood table hung against the wall with a broad ceramic sink built into it, into which an iron hand pump dripped. On the left-hand wall, between the pair of dirty, cobwebby windows, stood a makeshift cabinet, its twin doors hanging open like a dead man's jaw, its contents indistinct in the darkness.

Dead ahead, to the right of the back door, was a large cobblestoned fireplace. Hanging above it was a dusty, rough-

hewn mantel propped up by wrought-iron supports bolted into
the plank wall.

And handcuffed to one of the iron supports was a woman.

Tall. Short blond hair. Thin, frightened, obviously exhausted.
And completely naked.

Her face changed when she saw me, went into shock. "Who
the hell are *you?*"

Who the hell I am is Ben Perkins, and all I'd been trying to do that
afternoon was get myself home after completing a quickie job for
a client.

The night before, I'd been peaceably enjoying game two of the
World Series when Tony Omaha had called, all in a lather. While
the rest of the nation was engrossed in the I-70 Series, Tony was,
as usual, competing in a top-secret, high-stakes poker tourna-
ment held annually at a lodge at Burns Point, down near the Ohio
line. Normally, Tony does pretty well in those things. This time,
he told me tersely, the cards weren't being too friendly. I knew
very well what he meant—though I'm not in Tony's professional
league—having held in my time plenty of hands composed of
unmatched garbage cards.

But in today's session he'd felt the cards turning, he told me in
all seriousness; all he needed was a fresh infusion of capital, and
he'd be able to turn the thing around in the next day's session.

He wasn't putting the arm on me. All he wanted me to do was
deliver some cash to him, cash which his wife had, waiting and
ready. I told him I'd get it to him the next morning, and went back
to the TV to watch the Royals take it on the chin. I didn't give the
errand a second thought. Private detective work isn't all sleuth-
ing; I've sort of broadened the definition to include anything that
turns a more or less honest buck.

I picked up the cash first thing the next morning from Omaha's
suspicious, yet resigned wife, and headed back to my apartment,
having decided to fly down to Burns Point rather than drive. It
was pushing mid-October, stretching the ultralight season a little;
but the weather outlook was good, and this could very well be my
last chance to fly this year. Besides, Burns Point was an eighty-
mile drive, but only a sixty-mile flight. Furthermore, I'd just the
weekend before completed the 350cc engine's five-hundred-hour
rebuild, and a hop like this one would break in the work, securely
reseating the components, just the thing to do prior to putting the
aircraft away for the winter.

And it worked out great, the flight down, anyway. I coasted down at two thousand feet on a due southwest heading, dipped south when I reached the village of Burns Point, then approached the resort from due east and landed on the golf course. My arrival caused something of a sensation—in my snowmobile suit, black wool hood, and heavy goggles I looked a little like a Michigan Ninja—and Tony Omaha, obviously regarding my mode of arrival as a good omen, gave me half a G and urged me to stay for lunch and sit in on a few hands. I accepted the lunch but passed on the poker, refueled the aircraft, and taxied to the number six fairway, a four-hundred-yard par three bearing due west, for takeoff.

Even as the aircraft left the ground, I knew I was in for trouble. The formerly clear western horizon had scudded up with dirty clouds, obscuring the sun. From the powerful lift I felt upon leaving the ground, I knew the wind had picked up. And, as I made the big banking turn to head northeast, I felt an ominous tugging at the aircraft's thirty-eight-foot, nylon-coated wings. Wind gusts, and strong ones. A storm front was pulling in from the west. Fast.

My first thought was to put about five thousand feet beneath me and try to outrun the sucker. But the wind was from the tail, reducing my lift, and I could tell from the way the engine was laboring that I was sucking up a lot of gas. And as I flew, the wind gusts got progressively worse, making it hard to maintain a heading. I was being knocked around in the sky, and try as I might to stay calm, I began to sweat in my snowmobile suit, my heart pounding, every muscle in my body strung tight and trembling. I knew very well that an ultralight is purely for pleasure flying in absolutely benign skies. Any kind of rough weather up there can crumple you up like a paper cup and send you fluttering down in a lethal embrace of aluminum frame and nylon.

Nothing to do, then, but take her in as best I could. I made a long, sweeping, banking turn till I was headed south, and began to descend in a series of abrupt jerks. The land below flowed away on all sides of me in densely wooded hills and valleys as far as I could see. A couple of miles ahead I could see a reasonably wide valley running east-west, ending at a lake to the east and a large hill to the west. Have to take her down there. As to which direction, there was no contest. Left was downwind; in this wind it was practically impossible to land that way. So I began to swing to the right. Right for safe, I thought. Left for dead.

* * *

I didn't answer, being slightly taken aback at finding a naked woman handcuffed in this shack out in the middle of nowhere. She shrieked, eyes wild. "Who *are* you?"

"Perkins," I managed. I jerked a thumb over my shoulder. "I was forced down—I heard—uh—"

She rattled the handcuff. "Get me loose! Please!"

"Oh sure, right." It wasn't quite that easy. There were no tools to be found inside the cabin. I remembered the woodpile, trotted out there, and found an old, heavy, rusted hatchet. She cringed as I approached her with it. "Take it easy," I said. "Stretch the chain tight against that mantel there." She did so and covered her eyes with her free hand. I severed the chain with one hard chop. The woman took two steps, fell to her knees, bent her head nearly to her thighs, and began to cry. I lay the hatchet on the mantel and examined the iron mantel support. It was scratched bright and deep where the cuff hung. There were corresponding scratches, livid ones, on her thin wrist. She'd been tugging at it for a while.

I looked at her. No point in questioning her till she'd calmed down. "How about I step out, and you get yourself dressed."

She tossed her head back, ran her hand through her blond hair, and got clumsily to her feet. "No"—she sniffed—"you just stay put, it's all right." She walked uncertainly to the cot, rifled the blankets, and found jeans and a heavy white ski sweater. She was utterly unselfconscious as she dressed, and gave me an occasional glance out of the corner of her eye, but said nothing. I leaned against the mantel and watched her. She was a long-limbed one, five-eight, one-ten, her hair a straight blond cap around high cheekbones, deep eyes, a generous mouth, and snub nose. Relatively young, in years anyway. Twenty-five, max. Pretty tough, too, to compose herself so quickly after an experience like this. Whatever *that* was.

"What's your name?" I asked.

"Jill. Jill Evans." She slid her bare feet into a pair of worn hiking shoes and began to lace them up. "You're . . . Perkins, you said?"

"Ben." Finished with her work, she clambered to her feet, went to the pump, worked the handle till the rusty flow had passed, then bent under and drank deeply. Wiping her mouth once, she went back to the cot, wadded up a couple of blankets into a makeshift pillow, and lay back with her head propped on them.

Though her face was slack with weariness, her light eyes were sharp and bright on me. "Oh God, that feels good," she sighed.

"How long you been penned up like that?" I asked.

"Two days, two whole days. I couldn't sit down, I couldn't sleep . . . it gets *cold* at night this time of year, and—"

"How'd you get here in the first place?" I interrupted.

"I was kidnaped," she replied. "They held me here till they got the ransom. Then they cuffed me there and split. Left me here, left for dead." She straightened vertical, forearms propped on her knees. "Hey, you got a car out there or something? I want to get the hell out of here."

For something to do, I ambled to the cupboard and peered inside. Not a hell of a lot there by way of food. Canned tomatoes, a couple of cans of SpaghettiOs, a spilled jar of Folger's instant. Some plastic utensils. And four cans of low-alcohol beer. As a matter of policy, I avoid any beer that sends me to the can cold sober; but, any port in a storm. I popped the top, took a slug, and turned to face her. "No car. I was flying an ultralight, the weather forced me down." I gestured at the darkening window. "Day's about gone, no getting out of here before morning."

She barely contained the shrillness in her voice. "I want to go home. My family's got to be scared sick worrying about me." She tossed her head. "Maybe I'll walk out. There's light left."

"Listen up, Jill, it's twenty-plus miles to the nearest phone, and after two days tied up like that you're in no shape to walk it, trust me."

Her face slackened with resignation. "You got that right. Oh well." Her eyes brightened above a narrow smile. "So it's just you and me here for the night, huh?"

"Sure do look that way." Every man's fantasy, I thought with sour amusement. The big heroic rescuer of a helpless kidnap victim, a natural blonde and thoroughly female (both verified beyond dispute), young, yet exuding experience from every pore. To the victor belong the spoils. Ha. I said, "You must be starving. Menu's kinda thin here, but I can hack open a can of SpaghettiOs for you if you want."

"Oh, not right now. I could use one of those beers, though."

I carried one to her. She popped the top and drank. I said, "Easy, now. Don't wanna lose your head or anything." She winked at me and drank some more. I glanced out the back window—sure enough, another woodpile back there, near the outhouse. I looked back at Jill. "Light's going quick. Think I'll fetch in some firewood and get something going. It'll be a cold one tonight."

Before she could answer, I was out the back door. The dead grass was knee high, and I waded through it toward the woodpile. The wind was strong and the temperature was dropping steadily; I began to feel a chill even inside my snowmobile suit. Got to get the fire going quick, I thought. Hope the wood's okay.

I didn't find out right away. Because, halfway to the woodpile, I stopped and froze, staring down. A man lay prone there, face down, inert. His suit jacket was jagged with an array of small, bloody holes, and he was quite dead.

I used the hatchet to whack some thin strips of well-seasoned maple, built a pyramid of them in the fireplace, fired them up with a kitchen match, then patiently began to feed heavier pieces to the gaining blaze as Jill Evans watched me from the cot.

Finally she said, "Aren't you going to ask me about it?"

I carefully laid a four-by-four hunk of wood on the blaze, then used a twig to relight my cigar, and faced her. "Ask you about what?"

"The body out there."

"Which body."

"The dead body."

"Oh, *that* body." I exhaled smoke and cleared my throat. "I figured you'd get around to it sooner or later."

The skin stretched taut over the good bones of her face, making her eyes look larger in the half-darkness. "He was one of the kidnapers," she whispered.

"How'd he get dead?" I asked.

"Some kind of argument with the other two men. I'm not sure what it was about . . . I was only half-listening. . . . Suddenly they hustled him out there and I heard shooting. . . . He never came back in. The others tied me up and left right after that. I assumed he was dead. I didn't ask. I was—I was scared they'd kill me, too."

"Might have been more merciful if they had, rather than leaving you tied up to freeze to death."

She got to her feet and walked over and sat cross-legged next to me in front of the growing fire. "You're probably right," she murmured. "But you know? All I wanted to do was live. For the next minute, the next hour, the next day." She leaned her head onto my shoulder and took my left hand in both of hers. "I had no way of knowing someone like you would happen along. But you did."

I squeezed her hand, broke from her gently, and stood. "Getting warm in here. Think I'll shuck the suit."

"All right." I didn't have to look to see her smile.

I unzipped my black snowmobile suit down to the crotch and, dancing awkwardly on each foot in sequence, tugged it off. Jill rose, too, and stood very close to me, watching me with her unreadable eyes, lips parted. As I tossed the suit away, Jill reached up and began to unbutton my chambray shirt, the handcuff clinking like a cheap bracelet on her wrist. I made no move to interfere, just reached behind to the waistband of my jeans and pulled out my .45 automatic. She stepped back from me suddenly as I hefted it. "I'd better secure this somewhere."

She laughed nervously. "Packing, huh? How come?"

"Private detective. Standard equipment." I went to the cupboard, laid the weapon down on the shelf, grabbed a large can of SpaghettiOs, and began to wipe the dust off it with my shirttail. "Hungry yet?"

She exhaled impatiently, then grabbed the hem of her sweater, shimmied it off over her head, tossed it toward the cot, and shook her head to loosen her fine blond hair. The firelight ran whitish-gold fingers over her smooth shoulders, her up-aimed, arrogant breasts. She threw her shoulders back and hooked her hands in the empty belt loops of her jeans. "This answer your question?"

It was indeed a transfixing vision: the young half-dressed woman, framed in the blaze of the fire which filled the cabin out in the middle of darkening nowhere with sweet-smelling heat. I grinned. "Look, it's been two days, you gotta eat. Get some of this in you, then we'll sort out the other."

Long pause, then she sighed impatiently. "Oh, all right then." She went to the cot, sat, flung one leg over the other; then, for good measure, she pulled the ski sweater back on even though, by then, it was getting quite warm in there.

I cleaved the top of the SpaghettiOs can with the hatchet, wedged a respectable opening, then took it to her along with a reasonably clean plastic fork and a freshly opened can of designer beer. "Eat hearty," I advised. "Every bite now." She nodded glumly at me and began to eat, taking about four swallows of beer for every bite of cold spaghetti.

I took my time about stoking up the fire with fresh logs. It was roaring now, popping and sizzling, so hot that each fresh log fairly exploded into flames as I tossed it in. I sat down, leaning against the far wall, and smoked my cigar as Jill finished the spaghetti and tossed the empty can into the fire. She took a long draft of beer and licked her lips. Her eyes looked glassy as she said through numb lips, "Okay."

"Okay." I stood. "You get yourself ready, I got an urgent errand." She was unzipping her jeans as I went out the back door and pulled it shut behind me. The cold wind was steady and piercing as I loped through the tall grass to the privy. On my way back, I stopped at the body, fired up a kitchen match and, cupping it with my palm, lowered myself for a long look. Then I flipped the match away and walked slowly and deliberately back to the cabin.

Aside from the crackling roar of the fire, all was still and silent inside the cabin. Jill Evans lay sprawled on the cot, white legs spread, jeans hanging forgotten from one bare ankle. I walked softly to the cot and looked down at her for ten long breaths, then gently lifted her legs onto the cot and covered her with two of the blankets. She muttered vaguely and curled into a fetal position and buried her face in the coarse mattress.

I watched her for ten long heartbeats, then went silently out the front door. I was out there for a vigorous quarter hour, and when I got back I had to wash my hands in the icy pump water. Jill slept silently, almost invisible under the blankets. I tossed a couple more logs on the fire, shunted myself back into the snowsuit, stretched out on the hard plank floor by the fire and, using my hands as a wholly inadequate pillow, free-fell into inky black, totally dreamless sleep.

The explosion didn't just rouse me, it sent me nearly to the ceiling. I came fully awake on knees and fingertips, back arched like a bird dog, heart pounding supercharged adrenaline to every nerve. As the sound replayed in my mind, I relaxed. It had been nothing more than a superheated knot exploding in the dying coals of the fireplace.

I sat back on my rump, breathing hard. Dawn shot hard bright fingers of light through the dirty cabin windows. Birds chirped outside. The drone of the wind, a natural part of the environment the night before, was gone. It was early yet, somewhere between six and seven, but with the full break of day I knew that flying weather would be back.

Jill Evans had not moved, but suddenly I realized her eyes were open, and on me.

She pursed her lips, then licked them quite deliberately and rippled the blanket back off her. The ski sweater had bunched up under her breasts, leaving her bare from there down.

She said, "Come on now, Ben."

I got to my feet. "Better throw on a couple of logs. Getting chilly in here." Ignoring her skeptical look, I tossed on the last chunks of split maple, blew the coals, watched as the flames started their reddish-blue licks, then faced her.

She said in a hard voice, "Don't come near me with that damn snowsuit on."

"Oh. Certainly." I unzipped it, peeled it off, kicked it away, then sauntered to her and sat on the edge of the wobbly cot. With a faraway look in her eyes, she wandered her hands up my shirt and began to unbutton it. I said, "Look, I got a confession to make."

"Mm-hm."

"I believe in honesty in relationships."

"That's your confession?"

"Uh-huh. I don't want to get involved with you under false pretenses."

"Ooh." She finished the unbuttoning and ran her hands over my chest. "I'm not as complicated as you. All I want to do is screw."

I bent and gave her a quick, brushing, teasing kiss, and said very softly, "I just can't stop thinking about my daddy."

Her hands had deliberately wandered to my pants and were busily unsnapping and unzipping. "What about your daddy?"

"What he used to say."

"And what was that?"

"My daddy used to say . . . he told me . . . 'Never lay down with a woman who has more troubles than you.' . . . That's what my daddy always said."

She laughed, and prodded me gently, and I lifted myself just enough to enable her to pull my jeans down over my pelvis. "Sounds like good advice. But hey, Ben," she cooed, "I don't have any troubles. You fixed up the worst of 'em yesterday. And what troubles I have left," she breathed as I kicked my jeans back off one leg, then the other, "I think you're about to take care of for me. Mm. Yes, indeedy."

I lowered myself onto her, slid my left arm under her neck, and we enjoyed a long kiss of tongue tips. I looked into her bright eyes. "But see, that's the point. I don't think your troubles are over, I think they're just beginning."

She traced my eyebrows, cheekbones, mouth and chin with just the lightest touch of fingertips, intertwined her ankles with mine, and laughed softly.

I kissed her again, then raised myself on my palms and said in that same light, casual tone: "'Cause you ain't the victim, babe. You weren't the kidnapee. The kidna*per*, more like. Or one of 'em, anyhow."

She tried that laugh again, and though she was good, very *very* goddamned good, it sent back a hollow echo in that little cabin.

I disentangled my legs, negotiated myself a sitting position on the edge of the cot, and began pulling on my jeans. Out of the corner of my eye I saw her frowning as she propped her head on the heel of her palm. "That's a nasty, ugly thing to suggest, Ben Perkins."

"Oh yeah, I couldn't agree more. 'Specially since it happens to be true, now ain't it, little darlin'.'"

"This is starting to perturb me," she said, giving the blanket a deliberate jerk over her, "*totally*. You read me?"

I zipped and snapped my pants shut, stood, took a step toward the fire, then turned and faced her. "'Member what you said when I first busted in here? You said, 'Who the hell are you?' Like maybe you were expecting somebody else. *Not* like you weren't expecting to see anybody at all. Dig it?"

Her face was a smoldering mask, God knows what churning behind her eyes.

"And then that stiff out back," I added, jerking a thumb. "For a helpless, innocent kidnap victim, you were awful casual about that. And how come he's all dolled up in a business suit? A kidnaper, knowing he was going to spend some time out here, wouldn't dress up in some fancy business suit. Nope, he'd've fixed himself up with jeans. And a sweater. And boots. Sort of like *you*, kid . . . Then there was the way you reacted to my pistol. 'Packing, huh?' Not exactly civilian talk. And this seductress routine, that don't hang right with me either."

Her jaw was square and ugly. "I *liked* you, Ben."

"Oh yeah, sure. I don't think I'm completely disgusting to look at, but for a helpless, traumatized kidnap victim you sure seemed awful anxious to get me between the knees. That old soften-up stunt insults my intelligence, kiddo; it's older than running water."

"I won't repeat the mistake," she said pointedly.

"Suits me just fine," I answered, picking up my shirt.

"Me, too," said the male voice from the window. I whirled as glass crashed in, and saw twin shotgun barrels that were so large I almost didn't take notice of the muscle-bound grinner behind them.

Jill Evans jerked upright on the cot. "'Bout time you got here, Darrell!"

He was young, burr-cut, and a weight freak, judging from the way the veins and muscles stood out on his neck and arms. He wore a sleeveless bright orange hunting jacket and a big grin. "Took me some time, Jill. This ape been molesting you?"

"No way," she said disgustedly, then skooched off the cot and began pulling on her jeans. "What kept you?"

I slid my right hand into my jeans pocket.

"Took me a while to get the drop on Edgar," he said, keeping the twin barrels fixed on my chest. "Got it done late last night and drove like hell to get back here. He the one with the plane?"

She snapped her jeans closed. "Yeah, so what."

"Saw it out there, so I circled around with the Jeep and drove cross-country and snuck in here. Figured you had company."

She ignored him. "You got the money then?"

I sorted through my pocket silently and palmed the loose .45 bullet.

"All hundred G worth, out there in the Jeep." He glanced at me. "What do we do with him, tie him up?"

Her look at me was venomous. "I've got bigger plans than that. Get in here, Darrell."

"He got a gun or something?"

"Yeah. Wait a minute, cover him. I'll get it." She trotted to the cupboard and rescued my .45 automatic from the counter and swung around to hold it on me. "Okay. Come on in."

He gave us one appraising look, then disappeared from the window. We heard a clank, a thump, a "son of a bitch!" and as Jill glanced out I tossed the bullet at the fireplace. It landed soundlessly, hopefully—for me, anyway—in the flames somewhere.

Darrell came in the door, shotgun at port arms, grumbling. "Tripped over a damn bucket out there. Can't wait to get out of this pigpen." He stood at the opposite end of the cot from me, shotgun hung under his arm and aimed half downward. Judging from the way he posed, he was proud of his body; every muscle seemed to stand out whether there were clothes over it or not. His grin was bright and giddy and humorless. "So this fella happened by and turned you loose, huh, Jill?"

"No thanks to you, Darrell. I'd given up on you. I thought I was going to die here."

"Well, hey! You shouldn't have wasted old man Simmons."

I said, "Oh, Simmons the stiff lying out back there? The victim?"

"Shut up, Perkins," Jill said.

Darrell beamed. "Yeah, that's him all right; bigshot insurance man, richer'n God. You shoulda seen what Jill did to him. We'd gotten the ransom, we're all set to split; before Edgar and me know it Jill opens the back door and shoves Simmons out. He starts to run. She's carrying this twenty-two target revolver, single-action job, and she draws down on him, and cocks, and *bang*! Cocks it again, just as cool as could be, and *bang*! All six shots, the last four after he's on the ground."

I glanced at Jill, who held the heavy .45 in both hands aimed at me, and wondered how long it would take the bullet to explode, and where it would go when it did.

Darrell continued, "Well, Edgar got madder'n hell. Wasting Simmons wasn't part of the plan. He grabbed Jill and slapped her around and said to me, 'We're leaving this gun-happy bitch here, teach her a nice lesson.'"

"And you went along with him," Jill said hoarsely. "You helped him strip me and tie me up and you drove away with him."

"Hey sweetie, I had to! He had the gun and he'd of hurt me bad if I hadn't fallen into line." His smile became earnest. "You knew I'd come back for you, just as soon as I could."

"Yeah. I knew I could trust you, Darrell," she said sourly. She hefted the .45 and drew a bead on me, eyes narrow. "We'll argue about that later. First, a little target practice with our private detective friend here."

I took a deep breath, wondering *where the hell is that damn bullet*, and said, "Darrell, you better think about what she might do to you once you have your back turned."

He chuckled. "Sounds like one of them cute little private detective–type tricks. Divide and conquer and all that. No thanks." He looked at Jill. "Careful with that thing, babe. Aim low and leave some give in the wrists. That ain't no twenty-two that gives a snap and drills nice neat holes. That thing kicks like a mule. Built to stop, drop, and splatter."

"Good." I braced myself to jump, and then—finally—the bullet in the fireplace exploded.

I don't know where it went and I didn't take time out to check. I jumped as high as I could and came down with both feet on my end of the cot. The other end flew up like a runaway teeter-totter and caught Darrell under the elbows. The shotgun flew sideways and discharged both barrels, blowing out the front window. I had a quick sight of Jill leveling the .45 toward me, but I was nowhere around; I took a running, full-body leap at Darrell and plowed him back against the cabin wall with a crash.

There could be no Marquis of Queensbury niceties with this clown, and, moreover, I had to keep him from grabbing me or I'd be finished. Fortunately, big muscle-bound guys like him aren't all that fast. I came up with a knee to his groin, jinked back and, as he drove at me I took him by an elbow, pivoted, and threw him across the cot onto the floor. Jill danced back toward the fireplace, aiming, trying to get a clear field of fire, but I was on the move again as she aimed for me, diving across at Darrell as he sprang to his feet.

"Hold him still! Hold him *still!*" she muttered as I piled Darrell against the pump. He gave me a shot upside my head with a bricklike fist, and stars spotted my vision as I fell back. I was aware of Jill frozen in place just behind me, aiming for true now, and as Darrell moved in for me I took a wrist in both hands and jumped on one foot with both of mine and flung him toward me as hard as I could, dropping to the floor as I did so.

Completely off-balance, he fell straight at Jill, who apparently had maximum pressure on the trigger of the .45. The gun went off and Darrell flew back over me, clearing me easily, and landed suddenly inert at the wall. Judging from the looks of his head, he'd only been six inches from the .45 when Jill fired. Like the man said: stop, drop, and splatter.

I heard the .45 hit the floor as Jill screamed. I turned to see her holding her right wrist with her left hand, bending and gasping, face twisted with pain. I started for my feet, but she saw me and charged the door and disappeared outside. I stood, in no particular hurry to chase her. From outside I heard a shriek. Then silence.

I took several deep breaths, then put my snowsuit back on, trying not to look at Darrell as I did so. Then I retrieved and secured my .45 and trotted out the back door. It was a splendid Michigan October morning: pale blue sky, bright sun, just a hint of breeze. I had no trouble finding the Jeep back in the woods, and sauntered back to the cabin, carrying a vinyl airline carry-on bag under my arm. I circled the cabin to the front and walked up to the gap in the fence. The ground disappeared at that point, leaving a circle of black. I stepped toward the lip of the old disused well and looked down.

It was maybe fifteen feet deep, its walls old, rough discolored brick. At the bottom lay remnants of the old rotted boards that had covered the top, and atop these lay Jill Evans, on her side, one leg twisted oddly under her.

Her eyes looked very large in her pale pinched face. "You moved the fence," she said.

"Uh-huh. Last night, after you were asleep."

"You knew even then?"

"Let's just say I had my doubts."

"Oh, God." She squirmed and winced. "That was slick. Real slick, how you tricked me, Ben."

"Wasn't that much to it. All I did was move a section of fence, cover the well top with weeds, and tramp a new path up to it from the cabin door."

"I think my leg is broken," she said in a small voice.

"Doesn't surprise me a bit."

"How are you going to get me out?"

"Hadn't planned to, actually."

She swallowed and blinked and licked her lips. "You can't be serious."

"Am, too. You honest to God scare me, kid. I don't want you anywhere near me. Don't trust you, for some damn reason."

Her efforts to remain calm made her voice sound labored. "Is that—is that bag the money?"

"Uh-huh."

"A hundred thousand, cash."

"If you say so."

"We can—we can take it and go away—together, and—"

"Listen, even if I was the larcenous sort, no way am I going to spend the rest of my life with you in my backfield. Get real, here."

I started away. "Wait!" she shouted. I stepped back. Now, for the first time, her voice was crushed, despairing, completely lost. "How can you just leave me here like this?"

I considered. "Well, all I have to do is picture you standing at the door of the cabin, drawing a bead on that poor old man and putting six shots into him as he ran, four after he hit the ground. That's how."

"I'll *die* here!" she sobbed.

"You, die? No way. The cops'll be here by afternoon. You're a pretty tough chick, you'll keep till then."

"Heartless bastard!"

"Takes one to know one."

As I began the long hike toward the ultralight, I heard her screaming obscenities. Gradually the voice faded and then stopped entirely.

As I powered the ultralight into the air and swung northwest, it idly occurred to me that I could, in fact, just keep the money and sort of forget to call the cops. No one would ever know that I'd ever been at the cabin.

Of course I did notify the police once I got home, but not because I felt sorry for Jill Evans.

Quite the opposite.

JOHN LUTZ AND JOSH PACHTER

DDS 10752 LIBRA

John Lutz is presently serving his second term as president of PWA. He is also continuing to produce first-rate novels in two P.I. series—those featuring "Nudger" (Ride the Lightning, St. Martin's Press, 1987), and "Carver" (Scorcher, Henry Holt, 1987). He is a past winner of the Shamus and Edgar awards for short fiction, another example of that uncommon writer adept at both the short and long forms. Here he joins forces with Josh Pachter to give us a truly memorable Nudger story.

Josh Pachter has been writing and publishing short stories since he was eighteen years of age. He is the editor of one of the best anthologies of recent years, Top Crime, and the editor and publisher of The Short Sheet, a publication dedicated to the short story.

Dwight Stone sat hunched over the telephone in the yellow glow from the antique lamp atop his desk. His voice was pitched low but excited. The huge oak rolltop was the dominant feature of Stone's cluttered living room, which also served as his office. Most of the furniture scattered around was ancient, because he couldn't afford anything newer; the desk and lamp, legacies from a long-dead aunt, were the only valuable pieces in the apartment.

A mischievous smile flickered briefly across his lips as he cradled the receiver, but his clear brown eyes were still troubled. He crossed to the tiny cubicle his landlord called a kitchenette, made coffee on a hot plate, and carried a steaming mug back to his desk. He pulled a blank expense account form from one of the drawers and laboriously began to fill it in, now and then darting out a hand for coffee or to work the cantankerous old adding machine at his side. He was a large man, with too much upholstery straining the material of his clothes; he and his overstuffed furniture were perfectly compatible.

In a silence between ratchety growls of the adding machine, Stone suddenly sat up straight. A slight noise from behind had alerted him. He turned, and saw the tarnished brass knob of the front door slowly rotating, heard a floorboard creak outside in the hall. Fear lanced through his bowels like a shaft of ice as he realized that he *had* been followed home, after all.

Fright momentarily numbed him. Like most small-town private investigators, he never carried a gun, didn't even own one. He regretted that now, because he had no illusions about who it was that stood outside his door. Or about what it was the man had come for.

True, the door was locked, but the lock was a joke and would offer little resistance. It would slow down the man outside for a moment, but it wouldn't stop him.

There wasn't much time. Within the next few minutes, Stone knew, he would be out of time forever.

Swallowing his terror, he scribbled hastily at the bottom of the paper he was working on. There was an ominous click from the doorway, and he dropped his pen and reached for one of the desk's many cubbyholes.

Seconds later, the apartment door swung open behind him.

Nudger watched the two detectives nosing around the ransacked apartment. The place was a mess. Stone hadn't been much of a housekeeper to begin with, and whoever had killed him had taken the time to toss the four small rooms with frantic thoroughness.

The policemen were both in their fifties; they moved with the studied nonchalance of the typical small-town cop. They were a team: one was named Byrnes (the plodder, Nudger soon decided), the other was Allen (the brains of the operation). Nudger resisted making the obvious crack about George and Gracie. He didn't figure this pair for a comedy act.

"Go through it again," said Byrnes, standing in the light from the front window. The lamp on the big old rolltop where Stone had died was still on. Nudger had found it on when he'd arrived, an hour earlier, and had left it that way. He hadn't touched the body, either; it lay slumped across the surface of the desk, as he had discovered it. The expression on the half of Stone's face he could see was twisted, terrorized. There was no blood on the desk or the floor, because the small-caliber bullet that had left a neat little hole in the back of Stone's head on entry hadn't come out the other side. Nudger was glad about that; he hated the sight of blood. Murder scared him plenty all by itself, without the accompanying gore.

"Stone had been hired to recover a set of drawings which had been stolen from the office of a fashion designer here in town," he said tiredly, starting in on the story for the third time. "He phoned me in the city last night and told me about the case. He'd only been brought in a couple of days ago, but he'd already managed to get his hands on the drawings. He was worried that the thief would try to get them back again, though, so he'd hidden them someplace where he was sure they'd be safe. He wouldn't tell me where they were, but he seemed pretty clear that the thief would never be able to find them. He was going to work up an expense account, he said, then catch some sleep. He wanted me to meet him here this morning and go with him to pick up the drawings and deliver them to his client. Just in case the thief tried to get him back, he said."

Byrnes and Allen listened impassively.

"When I showed up here," Nudger went on, "he didn't answer my knock. I slipped the lock with a credit card and came in to wait for him."

Byrnes stirred. "That's breaking and entering," he remarked.

Actually it was trespassing, but Nudger decided not to quibble. Somehow the time seemed wrong for a discussion of legal niceties. "Bull," he said. "Dwight Stone and I have been friends for years. I let myself in whenever I came calling and found him out. He didn't mind; he did the same thing at my place." He motioned toward the body at the desk. "Anyway, I found him like that and phoned the police immediately."

Allen's pale blue eyes were unreadable. If he held any particular opinion about Nudger's story, he wasn't letting it show. Byrnes, on the other hand, had a more provincial personality; he was making no effort to conceal his disdain for the hotshot city-slicker P.I.

"You didn't touch anything?" Allen asked.

"Of course not."

"Just like on TV," said Byrnes. Nudger couldn't tell if he was kidding.

"Tell us more about this case Stone was working on," Allen suggested.

"There's not much to tell. Geoffrey Devane's got a small but very successful fashion house here in your town. He does all the designing himself, and employs about two-dozen people to manufacture and market the clothing. When he opened up his safe on Monday morning, the drawings for his spring line were missing. Four of the people who work for him knew the combination of the safe, and Devane figured one of the four must have swiped the designs, planning on selling them to one of the firm's competitors."

"Industrial espionage," Allen murmured.

"Exactly. Devane reported the theft, but the police didn't seem very encouraging, so he decided to bring in a private investigator. He got Stone's number out of the Yellow Pages, and it took Dwight three days to pin down the thief's identity and recover the drawings."

"Only the thief wanted them back"—Allen picked up the narrative—"so he followed Stone home and killed him and turned the place upside down looking for them."

"That's the way I figure it," Nudger agreed.

Allen trudged to the window, gazed outside, then turned to face Nudger. He was framed by sunlight, and Nudger had to squint to look at him. That was the sort of technique cops used on suspects, not fellow professionals. Nudger's stomach twitched out a warning. He thumbed back the foil on a roll of antacid tablets and popped two of the chalky disks into his mouth.

"Nervous?" Allen asked.

"My stomach is. Almost always."

"Ulcer?"

"Don't know. Afraid to find out."

"Dumb."

"I guess."

"You say you used a credit card to slip the lock this morning?"

Nudger nodded. "The killer must have locked the door behind him when he left last night."

"Why last night? Why not this morning, sometime before you arrived?"

"The lamp on the desk," said Nudger. "It must have been dark outside when Stone was shot, that's why he had it switched on."

"You look good for this, you know." Byrnes scowled. "In spite of your pretty story." He seemed to relish the opportunity to speak in Hollywood clichés.

"You mean I'm a suspect?" Nudger asked, as if the thought had just now occurred to him. It was uncomfortable, standing there in a room with two homicide detectives as they plied their trade. It was uncomfortable standing there in a room with a dead body in it. The combination of cops and corpse was lousy. "Don't forget," he said to Allen, who seemed much the more open-minded of the two, "I'm the one who called this in in the first place."

"Subterfuge," Allen suggested. "You and Stone were pals. You figured we'd get around to you sooner or later, so you called in the murder to convince us you had nothing to do with it."

Now they were ganging up on him. It didn't seem fair. "I'm not that devious," Nudger said. "And what about the murder weapon? I'm not carrying a gun, and you haven't found one in the apartment. And the door was locked when I got here."

"That's *your* story," said Byrnes doggedly. He shot a glance at the corpse. "What's *his* story?"

"What about my motive?" Nudger tried.

"We might just find one."

Or invent one, Nudger thought. He popped another antacid tablet into his mouth. Small-town murder, small-town cops, small-town judge and jury. Put it all together and it might spell big-time trouble.

"Mind if I look at the desk for a minute?" he asked.

"Be our guest," Allen told him.

Nudger crossed the room, riffled through the papers on the rolltop's surface, explored its cubbyholes carefully.

"The expense account," he said at last, straightening and looking over at Allen. "Stone told me he was going to work it up for Devane after he got through talking with me, but there's no sign of the form on his desk."

"*You* say he told you," Byrnes reminded Nudger. "What *I* say is that you and Stone were together last night. You had an argument, or you've got some other motive we haven't tumbled to yet. You shot him, then realized we'd tie you to him eventually. So you went away and ditched the gun, then came back this morning so you could 'find' the body and call us in and feed us your carefully rehearsed version of the facts."

Nudger thought back over the last fifteen hours and realized he'd been completely alone between the time he'd hung up the phone after talking with Stone and his discovery of the body this morning. Alone on the phone with Stone; the words ran through his mind and kept him from thinking clearly. The law couldn't prove he was here when Stone was murdered, that was certain—but Nudger couldn't prove he wasn't here, either. His stomach dived and did a few tight loops.

"The fingerprint man and photographer ought to be here soon," Byrnes announced. "When they show up, we'll be leaving."

"I know," Nudger said. "You're going to take me downtown for another little chat."

"This *is* downtown," Allen told him. "You can call your lawyer from headquarters."

"I'll wait until I'm charged before I do that," Nudger muttered. He wasn't at all sure Byrnes and Allen had enough evidence to hold him on a murder rap.

Allen shrugged. Byrnes smiled. Nudger figured they probably thought they had enough.

Staring at the big rolltop desk and the position of the body, he had an idea. Or maybe it was just a final straw to clutch at before drowning in a sea of lawyers, judges, and jurors. And then jailers.

"Maybe he hid it," he said.

"Hid what?" That was Allen, of course. Byrnes had better things to do than pay attention to anything Nudger might offer.

"The expense account form. Stone was sitting at his desk when he was shot. What if he heard someone at the door behind him? He might have had just enough time to scrawl a message on that form and hide it from his killer."

"That's right," said Byrnes, deadpan, "he was working on his expenses when he bought it."

"Which would explain how come there's no expense account form in plain view on the desk now," Nudger continued. "He wrote a message on it and hid it before the killer entered the apartment."

That line of reasoning seemed to sway Allen slightly. He gave Nudger an encouraging smile. Byrnes looked like he was wishing they could wind this whole thing up, so he could file his report and head for home. Police work, this minor matter of the rest of Nudger's life, was apparently annoying him.

Nudger walked back to the desk, and neither officer moved to stop him.

"We looked and you looked," Byrnes said.

"Can I look again?"

"Why not?" Allen shrugged. "With a minimum of touching, please."

Nudger stood back from the desk and scanned it carefully.

Nothing he could see even remotely resembled an expense account form.

"We already checked under the body," said Byrnes, hoping to hurry things along. "We did everything but take the damn desk apart."

"You didn't look where you couldn't see, though, did you?"

"What do you mean?" Allen's forehead wrinkled with puzzlement.

Ignoring him, Nudger stepped to the desk and eased the rolltop down as far as possible, almost to the point where it would have touched Stone's body.

A printed form was attached to the accordion S-roll of the retractable top with a bit of cellophane tape. Stone must have had just enough time to use the tape, then push the rolltop up and out of sight before his murderer came into the room.

Nudger tore the form away from the wooden rolltop triumphantly. Byrnes and Allen had already moved to flank him, and the three of them read the combination of letters and numbers scribbled across the bottom of the sheet:

DDS 10752 LIBRA

"Libra," said Byrnes, with a disgusted look at his partner. "Don't tell me this turns out to be another one of your damn zodiac cases."

"'Zodiac cases'?" Nudger repeated, turning the words into a question.

Allen frowned. "A couple years back," he explained, "I solved a case where a dying man's last word was *Gemini,* and Byrnes here thinks that makes me some kind of astrology expert."

"Libra," Byrnes grumbled. "And DDS. And 10752. What the hell's it all supposed to mean?"

Nudger fumbled with his roll of antacid tablets, then changed his mind and slipped the roll back into his pocket. "The DDS part I understand," he said. "Stone once told me he was born during Eisenhower's first presidential campaign. His parents were staunch Republicans, so they named him Dwight David. Which made his initials DDS."

"And," Allen mused, "he was born during Ike's campaign." He bent over the body and slid a thin billfold from the dead man's hip pocket. Unfolding it, he leafed through its half-dozen plastic windows until he located Stone's driver's license. "Uh-huh. He was born on October seventh, 1952: that's 10/7/52."

"Which makes him a Libra, all right," Byrnes contributed. "Same as my wife." Suddenly he faced Nudger and snapped, "What's *your* sign?"

"No smoking," Nudger told him.

"Get serious, tough guy."

"I'm not tough and I am serious. I don't have any idea what my sign is. My birthday's September thirteenth, does that help any?"

"Virgo," said Byrnes, as if a lot of things had just been explained.

"So the letters are his initials, the numbers are his birthdate, and Libra is his astrological sign," Allen nodded. "But—I mean, so *what*?"

"Maybe the killer was a Libra, too," Byrnes suggested feebly.

"Or a dentist," said Nudger, glad to see that the focus of the investigation had shifted away from him for a change. "DDS might stand for Doctor of Dental Surgery, you know, instead of Dwight David Stone."

Before Byrnes could formulate an appropriately snide comeback, the fingerprint man and photographer arrived. They turned out to be the same man, a wiry scarecrow with bristling gray hair and a genuine Speed Graphic camera, like the press used to rely on in the thirties and forties. Then a second man turned up, the county's medical examiner and town's mortician. There was a lot of versatility in this backwater. Stone hadn't had any family, and the M.E. was sizing up the furniture to see how big a funeral the estate could be expected to cover.

While the experts went about their tasks, Nudger, Byrnes, and Allen turned back to Dwight Stone's last desperate message.

"We oughta check his horoscope for today," Byrnes proposed.

Nudger thought that was as logical an idea as he'd heard so far.

"Never mind that," Allen said, snapping his fingers. There was a hunter's gleam in his eye. "Let's go."

"Go?" Byrnes asked gruffly. "Go where?"

"You'll see," said Allen. "And you're not going to like it when I tell you Nudger here gave me the idea."

"Me?" Nudger looked around blankly, making sure there was nobody else with that name in the apartment. "What'd I say?"

"You said maybe the killer was a dentist." Allen smiled mysteriously, and they couldn't get another word out of him. They left Stone's apartment and crossed the street to a dusty unmarked car parked illegally next to a fire hydrant. Halfway to their destination, Nudger finally realized where they were headed, and why. He was impressed. Maybe there was something to be said for small-town detective work, after all.

If Allen turned out to be right, that is.

The building was suitably quiet. There were people there—old ladies in padded armchairs devouring Barbara Cartland romances, college types copying term papers from assorted encyclopedias, a prim woman with her hair in a bun pulling outdated periodicals out of plastic covers and replacing them with more recent issues—but all of them went about their business in silence.

It took only a few moments for Allen to find the shelf he was looking for, and he ran his index finger along the spines of the books lined up there until he reached one whose white gummed label read 107.52 and, beneath that, Mol. He eased the book from the shelf and pronounced its title aloud: "*Teaching Philosophy*, by Vincent Molloy. Should make fascinating reading, if that's the sort of reading that fascinates you. Me, I like the 87th Precinct."

There were several sheets of paper sandwiched between the book's removable dust jacket and permanent hard cover. Allen slid them free and unfolded them. Each page displayed a sketch of a woman dressed in delicate pastel clothing, and each drawing had been signed by Geoffrey Devane at the lower-right corner.

On the top sheet, in Dwight Stone's handwriting, the name of Devane's comptroller had been penciled in.

"I'm still not sure I understand it all," Byrnes said, as Nudger and the two detectives sat over coffee in a closet-sized office at headquarters. Luther Higham, Devane's comptroller, had confessed to the theft of the drawings and the murder of Dwight Stone, and was in a holding cell awaiting arraignment on charges of industrial espionage and murder.

Nudger was glad to explain. "Higham opened up the safe and stole his boss's drawings, planning to sell them to a competitor. But unfortunately—for the thief, that is—Stone was able to recover the sketches. He was afraid to keep them in his apartment, though, figuring—correctly, as it turned out—that the thief might know who he was and come after them. So he stashed them at the local library, figuring he and I would pick them up the next morning and deliver them to Devane."

Byrnes finished his coffee and set down his Styrofoam cup, still looking perplexed. "That much I get," he said. "And to make sure he wouldn't forget which book he'd hidden the drawings in, he used the volume whose call number matched his birthdate. But why did he put his initials on that note he left you? And why the hell did he bother writing down his sign?"

"They weren't his initials," said Allen. "And it wasn't his sign, either. It was Nudger who tipped me off to that, when he pointed out that DDS didn't *have* to stand for Dwight David Stone. Well, it didn't stand for a dentist, either: it stood for Dewey decimal system, the cataloging system used for classifying nonfiction books by subject. Stone was telling Nudger that he'd hidden the drawings in the book shelved under Number 107.52 according to the Dewey decimal system."

"But why Libra?" Byrnes demanded.

Nudger grinned. "Stone didn't have time to finish his message *and* hide it away before Devane's comptroller broke into his apartment. It was more important to hide it than to finish it, so he stopped writing, two letters before what he'd intended to be the end of the message, and counted on Nudger to realize what he meant."

"Library," Byrnes sighed. "Dewey decimal system number 107.52, in the public library."

"Only I managed to miss it," said Nudger. "I guess I'm not as bright as Stone thought. Good thing for me your partner worked it out."

Byrnes washed a hand across his face. "Yeah, sure is. Listen, Nudger, looks like I owe you an apology. I jump to conclusions, sometimes. It's a lousy habit, I know, but I do it anyway. Like with that astrology business—"

Nudger stood up from his straight-backed chair, feeling his stomach beginning to react to the acidic coffee he'd only half finished. He smiled and waved a hand negligently and said, "Forget the apology. Let's just say you owe me a decent cup of coffee. That stuff you guys drink is awful."

"Actually, we usually drink tea." Byrnes grinned. "So the Zodiac Detective here can read the leaves."

ARTHUR LYONS

DEAD COPY

Arthur Lyons is a busy man, producing novels featuring his P.I., Jacob Asch (most recently Fast Fade, *The Mysterious Press, 1987), compiling works of nonfiction (*Satan Wants You: The Cult of Devil Worship in America, *The Mysterious Press, 1988), and writing screenplays for his own books.*

He has not written many short stories, however (a notable exception being "Missing in Miami," which appeared in Mean Streets). *We are proud to feature one of those rare and delicious efforts in this volume.*

All in all, it was a perfect day for a funeral. A weepy drizzle fell steadily from the somber sky and there were rumblings of thunder from the north, carrying with them the threat of more gloom.

I didn't need thunder and rain to feel gloomy. As I watched the casket disappear into the ground I felt sad, and at the same time angry. Angry at myself and the capriciousness of the universe. You add up a man's life and what do you get? A hole in a hillside. Ten plus ten plus ten equals zero. The addition was screwy.

Steve Guttenberg and I had been close at one time, but our lives had gone off in different directions over the past six years—his in search of the Big Story, mine in search of whatever anyone paid me to search for, preferably in advance. We had talked on the phone several times during the past few months, always making the proverbial promises to get together for lunch. We never had; something I regretted now but could do nothing about because Steve had stepped off the wrong curb, canceling all future lunches.

The shovelful of dirt rattled off the top of the casket, the rabbi went into his ashes-to-ashes bit, and it was over. I waited for the crowd of well-wishers around Becky to dissipate, then went over.

She had always reminded me of a little doll, tiny and fragile and cute, and she looked even more that way now, even dressed in black. She had cut her dark hair pixie-short and she was very pale, so that her skin and dark red lipstick looked almost like paint. She saw me and her big dark eyes filled with tears. "Oh, Jake. He was only thirty-three."

She fell into my arms and began to cry and I held her, feeling as if she would break if I squeezed too hard. I knew she wouldn't, though. She was a trench fighter. I remembered her eight years ago when Steve had been starting out as a cub reporter for the *Chronicle* and she had been holding down two jobs to keep them in Hamburger Helper.

She backed up and dabbed her eyes with a tissue. "I have to talk to you," she said, sniffling. "It's really important. Will you come over to the house?"

I was depressed enough and didn't feel like dragging out the mood, but there was an urgency in her request I couldn't turn down, and I told her I'd be there.

The house was a small, ranch-style place in the hills above Studio City. I parked the car at the first available curb space I could find and made a fifty-yard dash through the rain, which was heavy now. Becky greeted me at the front door and took my dripping overcoat, then whisked me into the den, past the two dozen or so people in the living room filling paper plates from the buffet table set up in the corner.

The den was a small, bookshelf-lined room with a desk, a small love seat, and a reclining leather chair. A portable electric typewriter sat on the desk—Steve's typewriter—and I felt slightly uneasy listening to its silence. She told me to sit down, which I did, and she shut the door. When she turned around her face looked feverish. "It wasn't an accident," she said quietly, locking stares with me. "They killed him, Jake. That car ran him down on purpose."

"Wait a minute," I said, trying to catch up. "Who is 'they'?"

"That's what I want you to find out." Her face was deadly serious. She sat down next to me on the love seat. "Steve was working on something, Jake. Something big. He said it was going to shake a lot of people up, and one of them was going to be Irving Sappherstein."

The name jarred me. Irving Sappherstein's legal clients included some of the West Coast kingpins of organized crime, and it was even rumored that the lawyer-businessman was in charge of all Syndicate financial investments from L.A. to Denver. But in spite of the fact that his name cropped up regularly in every major federal and local investigation of organized crime activity in southern California, no law enforcement agency had ever come close to making any allegations against Sappherstein stick. "What did Steve have on Sappherstein?"

"I don't know. All I know is that he was working day and night on it. He didn't come home until nearly two all last week. Whatever it was, something was supposed to be happening with it the day he died."

"Do you know what?"

She shook her head and looked down at the handkerchief she was twisting in her lap. "No, but it was something major, I think. Two days before he was killed he started acting real strange, as if something were really bothering him. I asked him what it was, but all he would say was that he couldn't tell me then, that I'd hear about it one way or another on Friday."

"The day he died," I said, mulling that one over. "What about his notes? Didn't he keep any about what he was doing?"

"Yes, but trying to decipher them is another thing. Joe Fitzpatrick is trying to do that now."

Another name that surprised me. "Joe Fitzpatrick the Pulitzer prize winner?"

She nodded. "Harry, Steve's editor, turned the notes over to him. He says Fitz was closer to what Steve was working on than anyone. Steve consulted him several times about it, I guess."

"Do the cops know about this?"

"I told Lefferts, the detective in charge of the case," she said in a slightly resentful tone, "but he didn't seem very impressed."

"Have they determined what Steve was doing at Plummer Park at ten-thirty at night?"

"Nobody has any idea. And the only people who saw him there were a young couple too distracted with each other to pay attention. They said they thought the car that hit him pulled out from the curb, but they weren't sure. They were pretty far away and it happened so fast."

I really didn't see what I could do about it that the entire staff of the *Chronicle* couldn't. "Fitzpatrick is one of the best around, Becky. If there's something wrong, he'll find it."

"*You're* the best," she said firmly. "Steve always said so. He said you were his mentor."

"Steve liked to exaggerate. I showed him a few tricks of the trade when he was starting out, that was all. Within a few months, he was making up his own."

"I'll pay you." Her eyes had that helpless, wounded look in them I hated to see.

"That isn't the point—"

"The point is he was your friend," she said, her voice suddenly brittle.

She was right, of course. I owed him that much. At the end of my career at the *Chronicle*, when I had been a rather unfashionable cause, Steve had never balked at backing me up even when it put him into direct conflict with management. Perhaps there was nothing to it. Perhaps he had just been the victim of some strung-out drunk driver who was on a bender because his wife had left him for a lineman for the phone company. But he had been a friend and I owed him a look-see. He would have done it for me.

I pointed at the closed door. "Is Fitzpatrick in there?"

"No. He was at the funeral, but he had to get back to the paper."

"Tell you what," I said. "I'll drop by and talk to him and see what he's gotten from Steve's notes."

"You don't have to," she said, getting up and walking around the desk. From the middle drawer, she pulled out a manila envelope and put it on top of the typewriter. "Steve always made an extra copy of his notes, in case something happened to the original."

She had me now. I told her to tend to her guests and shoved her out the door.

She was right about the notes—they were a mess—but after two hours, I'd managed to come up with a couple of intriguing items. Steve seemed to have been taking a close look at three companies—Thompson Paint and Varnish, Wil-Stick Glue Company, and Apex Steel Drum—in which Sappherstein was a major stockholder. Although Sappherstein was not an officer in any of the corporations, he did appear as an original incorporator of one, Apex. Indeed, Apex seemed to have been the focus of Steve's investigation; a log among the notes indicated that he had staked out the company on five different nights during the week prior to his death, which would be why he hadn't been getting home until two. Apparently nothing much had happened on those nights and the reason for the stakeouts was not among the notes. One thing that *was* among the notes that seemed totally unconnected to the rest of the file was one of the articles from Fitzpatrick's

Pulitzer prize–winning series on cocaine smuggling. It had appeared last year in the *Chronicle*. Passages in the text had been underlined, and in the margin Steve had scribbled, "S.B. 109." After unsuccessfully dwelling on the significance of S.B. 109 and the underlined passages for ten minutes or so, I put everything away in the desk drawer and went out to the living room.

The crowd had boiled down to half-a-dozen diehard friends and Becky managed to detach herself from their sympathetic cooing long enough to come over. "Well?"

"I'll do some nosing around and see what I can come up with."

She put a hand on my arm and smiled gratefully. "Thank you."

Her eyes were starting to get watery again. I told her I'd keep her informed and got out of there before the floodgates opened.

They had already opened outside, and all the way downtown my wipers fought a losing battle with the rain. From a pay phone in the lobby of the *Chronicle* I called Detective Lefferts at the LAPD, and found his interest in Becky's murder theory at least as tepid as she'd described. He seemed to get irritated when I brought it up, saying that he intended to look into it as soon as he checked out every body-and-fender shop in town for a late-model, green GM car, which was what they'd determined had hit Steve. He became even more irritated when I suggested they'd find the car about the time his seven-year-old needed a new pair of Nikes, and hung up on me.

The city room upstairs had the usual aura of frenzy when I popped in. There were a lot of new faces manning the desks, but some I knew, and others I could have happily gone another eight years without seeing. I recognized Fitzpatrick from the funeral. He had a long, narrow face with too much chin, and a long bony nose on which sat a pair of rimless glasses. His brown hair was parted on the side and slicked down, its neatness contrasting with the rumpled white shirt rolled up to the elbows and spotted with various stains.

He stood up and offered a thin, pale hand. "Sit down, Mr. Asch. It's a pleasure to finally meet you."

"Finally?" I asked, pulling up a chair.

He smiled and waved a hand at the reigning chaos. "You've achieved a permanent measure of fame around here. The man who went to jail before revealing his news sources, and all that. What can I do for you?"

"I understand Steve Guttenberg's notes have been turned over to you."

Behind the glasses, his small eyes were shiny and hard, like the backs of two brown beetles. "That's right."

"Have you determined yet what connection Steve was trying to make between Irving Sappherstein and Apex Steel Drum?"

The beetles jumped. "How did you know about that?"

"Becky has asked me to look into Steve's death. She has a copy of his notes."

He didn't seem too pleased about that, but I hadn't expected him to be. Investigative reporters as a rule don't like other people digging around in their stories. He shrugged and began toying with a pencil on the desk. "On paper, at least, Apex seems to be legit. It's a company that buys, repairs, and resells chemical storage drums. Aside from being a major stockholder, Sappherstein doesn't seem to have any interest in it."

"You say it's legit on paper. What about off paper?"

"I don't know."

"Why was Steve surveilling the place?"

"I don't know that, either."

"What did Steve talk about when he consulted you about the piece?"

He put down the pencil and began rubbing the back of his neck. "I've done a few organized crime pieces. Steve threw out some names and wanted to know what I knew about them."

"What names?"

"Sappherstein and a few of his business associates. Manny Rothstein, Jimmy Carnera."

"Did he ask any questions about drug connections?"

His tone grew wary. "Drug connections? No, why?"

"Your cocaine piece was in with his notes."

The beetles sought refuge in the cracks as the eyelids narrowed. "I don't know why. Steve never mentioned anything about drugs, if that's what he thought was going on."

"He'd written on the clipping," I said. "'S.B. 109.' Does that mean anything to you?"

"No."

I had a feeling he knew more than he was telling, but there was no way he was going to give it to me, so I thanked him and stood up. To ease his reporter's paranoia, I said, "I reread your Pulitzer piece this afternoon. You're a hell of a writer. I just want you to know that if I find out anything, you'll get the exclusive."

His expression seemed to relax a bit. "I appreciate that," he said, offering his hand.

* * *

The rain had stopped late in the afternoon but the cloud cover was still thick at ten that night, which was good for me. The street I was parked on was wide and unlighted, lined with grimy industrial warehouses and storage yards, and Apex fit right in. A high wooden fence ran around the perimeter of the property, but I could see the hangarlike building through the chain-link gates pulled across the driveway. Two hours ago, two men had driven a four-ton, open-bed truck through the gates and had disappeared into the building. That had been the only activity of the night.

I unwrapped the ham sandwich I'd brought from home and had started to take a bite when headlights in my rearview mirror sent me sliding down in my seat. When the car drove by, I sat up and watched it pull over to the curb a hundred feet ahead, and its lights and engine go off. The car was easily in range of the 300mm lens attached to my Starlight Scope, and after getting the license number, I focused through the back window and waited for the driver to turn around. After a minute or two he did, and I unscrewed the bulb from the overhead light and slipped quietly out of the car.

Fitzpatrick jumped about a foot off the seat when I opened the passenger door of the Granada and got in. He let out the breath he was holding and said in an annoyed tone, "You scared the hell out of me. Where did you come from?"

"You know how sneaky we detectives are," I said, grinning. "I just thought since we both had the same idea, we might pool our efforts. Stakeouts can get pretty boring alone."

The wary look was back. He said hesitantly, "Okay, but I expect you to keep your word about me getting the exclusive."

"You got it."

He glanced down at the equipment in my hand. "What kind of camera is that?"

"Canon 35mm with a 300mm lens attached to a Starlight Scope with a focal plane iris for reading license plates."

"You like to come equipped."

"Boy Scout training."

We shared several Thermos cups of coffee laced with 100-proof bourbon and a lot of conversation over the next hour and a half, while we waited for something to happen. I found out he was thirty-nine and from Nebraska, a Columbia graduate, and had come West to work for the *Chronicle* three years ago after making a rep for himself as A Big Story man at the *Washington Post*. He had

tried marriage for a short time but had given it up when he found
it interfered with his work, which was his life. His goal had
always been the Pulitzer and he had his break last year when he
fell in with a group of coke smugglers and they had allowed him
to accompany a shipment from South America.

At twelve-forty, conversation was put to an end by the sound of
a motor starting up. I trained my scope on the building. A
heavyset, dark-haired man opened the gates and the big open-
bed truck rumbled through and stopped, heading away from us. I
read off the license number to Fitzpatrick as the heavyset man
repadlocked the gate and trotted to the truck. After they had gone
down the street, we flipped a U and followed without lights until
they turned right onto Santa Fe. The area was still heavily
commercial and we hung back and tried to blend in with the few
other headlights on the street. We crossed under the freeway and
after half a mile, the truck's running lights disappeared. Fitzpatrick speeded up, then took his foot off the gas as we passed a big
brick building sitting back from the street. The sign on the
building said THOMPSON PAINT AND VARNISH. The truck was
nowhere to be seen.

"I have one of those feelings," Fitzpatrick said.

"Yeah," I agreed.

We parked on a dark side street across from the building and
waited. Twenty minutes later, the truck pulled out of the
driveway of Thompson Paint and Varnish and headed back in the
direction from which it had come. At the freeway, it got onto the
westbound ramp.

The truck's running lights made it easy to follow and we were
able to drop way back. Five miles later it swung onto the junction
for the San Diego Freeway heading north, and we had to close
some distance to make sure we didn't lose it. At the top of the
Sepulveda pass the truck's blinker flashed, and it got off at the
Mulholland exit.

A few turns later, and the city was only a memory. The fresh
smells of the rain-soaked chaparral filled the car as we followed
the narrow, two-lane road twisting into the hills. On our left the
canyon dropped away sheerly, and occasionally, far down, I could
see the rectangular light from a window. The truck was lost in the
curves and we were traveling blind. Then suddenly, as we came
around a hairpin, there it was right in front of us.

The truck was parked on a dirt turnout, its back end hanging over the edge of the canyon. The heavyset man and the driver were outside the cab and they watched us suspiciously as we passed. Around the next curve Fitzpatrick let me out and took off. I slid down the wet embankment and made my way as quietly as I could through the weeds, back toward the truck. The camera made it clumsy going, but that couldn't be helped; I had a feeling I was going to need it.

The two men were standing stiffly by the truck, listening to Fitzpatrick's engine die in the distance. When they were satisfied he wasn't coming back, they hopped up onto the truck bed and began shoving the half-dozen twenty-gallon steel drums they were carrying over the side of the canyon. They spent five minutes dumping the load and I spent an entire roll of film.

Ten minutes after they had gone Fitzpatrick pulled up, and I got in the car and asked for a flashlight. He said there was one in the glove compartment. I found it under a car rental receipt, snatched up the Thermos and, while Fitzpatrick rummaged around in his trunk for tools, started the long slide down the side of the canyon. Luckily, I didn't have to go to the bottom; one of the drums had lodged against a boulder halfway down the slope. Fitzpatrick joined me and together we pried off the lid.

"What do you think it is?" he asked as we were knocked back by the strong chemical smell. The liquid had an oily, green look to it.

"I don't know," I said, as I carefully ladled some of the stuff into the Thermos with the plastic cup. "I just hope it doesn't eat through the Thermos."

He shook his head. "I must admit I had my doubts, but I guess this clinches it. They must have spotted Steve tailing them one night and decided to have him hit."

"Maybe."

"What do you mean, 'maybe'?" he asked, almost angrily. "Do you know how much money is at stake here? The bastards have to be saving thousands a load dumping it this way instead of at a licensed toxic waste dump."

"If he tailed them, why wasn't it in his notes?"

"Maybe he didn't have time to write it down. Maybe they got to him before he could."

"If these guys hit Steve, they're either incredibly stupid or incredibly cocky. They know somebody is onto them and they conduct business as usual without taking the most minor security precautions? They let us follow them all over town without even checking to see if somebody is behind them? I don't buy it."

"Why should they check? They think they've eliminated the problem."

"Come on, Joe. Sappherstein is not dumb. He has to know that the *Chronicle* is not going to let one of its people get wiped out without looking into what he was working on."

He shook his head. "It's Sappherstein. I can feel it."

"Maybe you want to feel it."

His tone turned belligerent. "What do you mean by that?"

"Think what a story it would make. ORGANIZED CRIME'S POISONOUS ROOTS EXTEND ALL THE WAY DOWN TO THE WATER TABLE. Quite a byline."

"Sappherstein had Steve killed," he said positively. "And I'm going to prove it. With or without your help."

The Thermos was still intact when we got back to the car, but my lungs felt as if they were going through a major meltdown. Fitzpatrick must have said a total of six words all the way back to Apex, which was all right with me. I had some thinking to do.

The next morning, I stopped at the camera store and put a rush on the film, then took the Thermos over to a lab and waited for the analysis. When it came in, I called Fitzpatrick. "Toluene, carbon tet, and cadmium," I read from the report. "Nice poisons all."

"I *knew* it," he said gleefully.

"You find out anything?"

"Some good, some bad. Alex Tartunian, the president of Apex, and Sappherstein were both officers in a plastics manufacturing business that went bankrupt a few years ago. That gives him a connection to management. But proving either of them are behind the illegal dumping is going to be tough. Apex leases its building and equipment and another company pays its payroll. If we're going to tie Sappherstein into it, we're going to have to establish a stronger connection than we have." His tone was friendly and he was talking in "we's." He must have forgotten our little difference of opinion last night. "You up for another stakeout tonight?"

"Eight o'clock?"

"Fine," he said. "Oh, and Asch, you know the paper will pay you a nice chunk of change for those pictures."

I couldn't keep the grin off my face. "I already thought of that."

The grin didn't last long. I was still bothered by the carelessness of those men last night. I called Becky and drove out to the valley.

I wanted to go through Steve's notes again, just to make sure I hadn't missed something.

When I related what we had found out, she wanted to immediately get on the phone to the cops. I told her that after discussing it, Fitzpatrick and I had decided to wait until we found out what other companies Apex was illegally dumping for and hand it to them in a nice, neat package they couldn't screw up. She reluctantly went along with the program and left me alone in the den.

Two hours later, I'd gone through Steve's notes three times without finding any indication Steve had witnessed a midnight dumping or had been spotted while surveilling Apex. He could have been spotted without knowing, of course, but if that had been the case, why didn't they take care of business there and then? Why wait until a day or two later, when he could have blown the whistle on the operation? Had it taken that long for the decision to be made and the order passed down? And if that had been the way it had happened, why hadn't Sappherstein or whoever tried to plug the leaks before ordering Steve hit? Sappherstein was a careful man; he would have wanted to find out what kind of incriminating evidence Steve had left behind before ordering something as drastic as an execution.

I picked up Fitzpatrick's cocaine article and stared at it. I could not shake the feeling that it was a missing piece of the puzzle. Why had Steve put it with his notes? The incongruity of it irritated me. I shifted my gaze to the bookcase next to the desk and let my eyes wander aimlessly, with my thoughts. They stopped wandering when they landed on a paperback book lying horizontally on top of the upright volumes. *Snow Bound* by Hugh Harris. I pulled it off the shelf.

It had been published four years ago, by a publishing house I had never heard of. There was a bookmark sticking out of the text. I knew what page it would be on and I knew what would be on the page, but I turned to it anyway.

Fitzpatrick was parked across from Apex when I pulled up and parked. It was eight-ten and the half moon put a silvery backing on the dissipating clouds. It was a fine night. Fitzpatrick greeted me cheerfully as I opened the door of the Granada. He offered me a cup of coffee from a new Thermos.

"No, thanks," I said, glancing across the street. "Any action?"

"Not yet." He looked at my empty hands. "You didn't bring your equipment?"

"I'm not going to be staying that long." I opened the glove compartment and pulled out the rental receipt I'd run across last night. "You rented this car on Saturday. What happened to your car? The 1963 green Firebird?"

His eyes became small and hard again. "It's being repaired. I blew a piston."

I put the receipt back and slammed the box shut. "Really? Where is it being worked on? Mexico? It couldn't be being done around here, unless, of course, you're chummy with some hot-car boys who don't advertise their skills."

He stiffened and looked at me as if I was wearing a bunch of bananas on my head. "What are you talking about?"

"The front end of your car is being repaired, not a piston. You hit Steve with it."

He kept the look on his face. I didn't mind. I went on: "I couldn't figure why Steve had your cocaine article among his notes. My mistake was thinking it had something to do with Apex. He consulted with you on the Wednesday he died, all right, but not to talk about Sappherstein. He wanted to talk about the fact that your Pulitzer story had been lifted from a little-known book called *Snow Bound*. It was all a lie. You never traveled with any coke dealers. Steve must have had his notes with him when you two met, and stuck the article among them."

His expression went blank and he turned away, rigidly. I said to his back: "Steve told his wife she would know all about what was bothering him on Friday. What did he do, give you a deadline to expose yourself?"

He turned back. The surface of his face rippled, then broke in a wave of anguish. "He gave me forty-eight hours to break the story any way I wanted, then he was going to break it himself. It would have made me a laughingstock. My career—my life—would have been over."

"So you killed him . . . then talked your editor into turning Steve's notes over to you. You had to find out if there was anything incriminating in them."

He grabbed the sleeve of my jacket and held on desperately. He looked dazed, like a punch-drunk fighter. "I didn't mean to. It just happened. We arranged to meet at Plummer Park that night to discuss things. I was already there when he got there. He got out of his car and started toward mine. I don't remember anything after that until I was miles away. I swear to God, I don't remember running him over."

He choked down a sob. I didn't know if he was telling the truth or getting his plea ready, although it didn't matter much. He went on: "That was the only time in my career I ever did anything like that, Asch. I was just all written out and I had a deadline. I'm sorry now the damned article attracted so much attention. The Pulitzer was something I'd wanted my whole life, and once I got it, it turned out to be a curse."

He was sorrier about the article than he was about the fact that he had killed a man. It made me feel good that I was out of the business. "Steve gave you forty-eight hours," I said, getting out of the car. "I'm giving you zip."

He called out to me as I walked back to my car, but I didn't turn around. I kept a keen ear for the sound of his engine starting, just in case he decided to go for two out of two, but nothing happened. He was still parked there when I drove away.

I called Becky from home and told her the story, then made myself a stiff drink and went to bed.

The next morning, I opened the paper to a black-and-white photograph of a smashed-down sardine can that had once been a car. The story beneath it said that Pulitzer prize–winning reporter Joe Fitzpatrick had been killed shortly before ten last night when his automobile had gone out of control and struck a freeway abutment. He should have been proud, wherever he was; he had made Page One.

BILL PRONZINI

INCIDENT IN A NEIGHBORHOOD TAVERN

Bill Pronzini's "Nameless" detective is one of the more enduring P.I.s of the genre; he has been appearing in short stories and novels since the late 1960s.

Bill received a Shamus Award for Best Novel with Hood-wink *(St. Martin's Press, 1981); for Best Short Story with "Cat's Paw" (1983); and in 1984 became the youngest recipient of PWA's Life Achievement Award, the "Eye." He also served as PWA's very first president.*

Many of us presently toiling in the genre learned a lot about writing the P.I. story from reading Bill Pronzini. Now it's your turn to read—and enjoy.

When the holdup went down I was sitting at the near end of the Foghorn Tavern's scarred mahogany bar talking to the owner, Matt Candiotti.

It was a little before seven of a midweek evening, lull-time in working-class neighborhood saloons like this one. Blue-collar locals would jam the place from four until about six-thirty, when the last of them headed home for dinner; the hard-core drinkers wouldn't begin filtering back in until about seven-thirty or eight. Right now there were only two customers, and the jukebox and computer hockey games were quiet. The TV over the back bar was on but with the sound turned down to a tolerable level. One of the customers, a porky guy in his fifties, drinking Anchor Steam out of the bottle, was watching the last of the NBC national news. The other customer, an equally porky and middle-aged female barfly, half in the bag on red wine, was trying to convince him to pay attention to her instead of Tom Brokaw.

I had a draft beer in front of me, but that wasn't the reason I was there. I'd come to ask Candiotti, as I had asked two dozen other merchants here in the Outer Mission, if he could offer any leads on the rash of burglaries that were plaguing small businesses in the neighborhood. The police hadn't come up with anything positive after six weeks, so a couple of the victims had gotten up a fund and hired me to see what I could find out. They'd picked me because I had been born and raised in the Outer Mission, I still had friends and shirttail relatives living here, and I understood the neighborhood a good deal better than any other private detective in San Francisco.

But so far I wasn't having any more luck than the SFPD. None of the merchants I'd spoken with today had given me any new ideas, and Candiotti was proving to be no exception. He stood slicing limes into wedges as we talked. They might have been onions the way his long, mournful face was screwed up, like a man trying to hold back tears. His gray-stubbled jowls wobbled every time he shook his head. He reminded me of a tired old hound, friendly and sad, as if life had dealt him a few kicks but not quite enough to rob him of his good nature.

"Wish I could help," he said. "But hell, I don't hear nothing. Must be pros from Hunters Point or the Fillmore, hah?"

Hunters Point and the Fillmore were black sections of the city, which was a pretty good indicator of where his head was at. I said, "Some of the others figure it for local talent."

"Out of this neighborhood, you mean?"

I nodded, drank some of my draft.

"Nah, I doubt it," he said. "Guys that organized, they don't shit where they eat. Too smart, you know?"

"Maybe. Any break-ins or attempted break-ins here?"

"Not so far. I got bars on all the windows, double dead-bolt locks on the storeroom door off the alley. Besides, what's for them to steal besides a few cases of whiskey?"

"You don't keep cash on the premises overnight?"

"Fifty bucks in the till," Candiotti said, "that's all; that's my limit. Everything else goes out of here when I close up, down to the night deposit at the B of A on Mission. My mama didn't raise no airheads." He scraped the lime wedges off his board, into a plastic container, and racked the serrated knife he'd been using.

"One thing I did hear," he said. "I heard some of the loot turned up down in San Jose. You know about that?"

"Not much of a lead there. Secondhand dealer named Pitman had a few pieces of stereo equipment stolen from the factory outlet store on Geneva. Said he bought it from a guy at the San Jose flea market, somebody he didn't know, never saw before."

"Yeah, sure," Candiotti said wryly. "What do the cops think?"

"That Pitman bought it off a fence."

"Makes sense. So maybe the boosters are from San Jose, hah?"

"Could be," I said, and that was when the kid walked in.

He brought bad air in with him; I sensed it right away and so did Candiotti. We both glanced at the door when it opened, the way you do, but we didn't look away again once we saw him. He was in his early twenties, dark-skinned, dressed in chinos, a cotton windbreaker, sharp-toed shoes polished to a high gloss. But it was his eyes that put the chill on my neck, the sudden clutch of tension down low in my belly. They were bright, jumpy, on the wild side, and in the dim light of the Foghorn's interior, the pupils were so small they seemed nonexistent. He had one hand in his jacket pocket and I knew it was clamped around a gun even before he took it out and showed it to us.

He came up to the bar a few feet on my left, the gun jabbing the air in front of him. He couldn't hold it steady; it kept jerking up and down, from side to side, as if it had a kind of spasmodic life of its own. Behind me, at the other end of the bar, I heard Anchor Steam suck in his breath, the barfly make a sound like a stifled moan. I eased back a little on the stool, watching the gun and the kid's eyes flick from Candiotti to me to the two customers and back around again. Candiotti didn't move at all, just stood there staring with his hound's face screwed up in that holding-back-tears way.

"All right all right," the kid said. His voice was high pitched, excited, and there was drool at one corner of his mouth. You couldn't get much more stoned than he was and still function. Coke, crack, speed—maybe a combination. The gun that kept flicking this way and that was a goddamn Saturday Night Special. "Listen good, man, everybody listen good I don't want to kill none of you, man, but I will if I got to, you believe it?"

None of us said anything. None of us moved.

The kid had a folded-up paper sack in one pocket; he dragged it out with his free hand, dropped it, broke quickly at the middle to pick it up without lowering his gaze. When he straightened again there was sweat on his forehead, more drool coming out of his mouth. He threw the sack on the bar.

"Put the money in there Mr. Cyclone Man," he said to Candiotti. "All the money in the register but not the coins; I don't want the fuckin' coins, you hear me?"

Candiotti nodded; reached out slowly, caught up the sack, turned toward the back bar with his shoulders hunched up against his neck. When he punched No Sale on the register, the ringing thump of the cash drawer sliding open seemed overloud in the electric hush. For a few seconds the kid watched him scoop bills into the paper sack; then his eyes and the gun skittered my way again. I had looked into the muzzle of a handgun before and it was the same feeling each time: dull fear, helplessness, a kind of naked vulnerability.

"Your wallet on the bar, man, all your cash." The gun barrel and the wild eyes flicked away again, down the length of the plank, before I could move to comply. "You down there, dude, you and fat mama put your money on the bar. All of it, hurry up."

Each of us did as we were told. While I was getting my wallet out I managed to slide my right foot off the stool, onto the brass rail, and to get my right hand pressed tight against the beveled edge of the bar. If I had to make any sudden moves, I would need the leverage.

Candiotti finished loading the sack, turned from the register. There was a grayish cast to his face now—the wet gray color of fear. The kid said to him, "Pick up their money, put it in the sack with the rest. Come on come on come on!"

Candiotti went to the far end of the plank, scooped up the wallets belonging to Anchor Steam and the woman; then he came back my way, added my wallet to the contents of the paper sack, put the sack down carefully in front of the kid.

"Okay," the kid said, "okay all right." He glanced over his shoulder at the street door, as if he'd heard something there; but it stayed closed. He jerked his head around again. In his sweaty agitation the Saturday Night Special almost slipped free of his fingers; he fumbled a tighter grip on it, and when it didn't go off I let the breath I had been holding come out thin and slow between my teeth. The muscles in my shoulders and back were drawn so tight I was afraid they might cramp.

The kid reached out for the sack, dragged it in against his body. But he made no move to leave with it. Instead he said, "Now we go get the big pile, man."

Candiotti opened his mouth, closed it again. His eyes were almost as big and starey as the kid's.

"Come on Mr. Cyclone Man, the safe, the safe in your office. We goin' back there *now*."

"No money in that safe," Candiotti said in a thin, scratchy voice. "Nothing valuable."

"Oh man I'll kill you man I'll blow your fuckin' head off! I ain't playin' no games I want that money!"

He took two steps forward, jabbing with the gun up close to Candiotti's gray face. Candiotti backed off a step, brought his hands up, took a tremulous breath.

"All right," he said, "but I got to get the key to the office. It's in the register."

"Hurry up hurry up!"

Candiotti turned back to the register, rang it open, rummaged inside with his left hand. But with his right hand, shielded from the kid by his body, he eased up the top on a large wooden cigar box adjacent. The hand disappeared inside; came out again with metal in it, glinting in the back bar lights. I saw it and I wanted to yell at him, but it wouldn't have done any good, would only have warned the kid . . . and he was already turning with it, bringing it up with both hands now—the damn gun of his own he'd had hidden inside the cigar box. There was no time for me to do anything but shove away from the bar and sideways off the stool just as Candiotti opened fire.

The state he was in, the kid didn't realize what was happening until it was too late for him to react; he never even got a shot off. Candiotti's first slug knocked him halfway around, and one of the three others that followed it opened up his face like a piece of ripe fruit smacked by a hammer. He was dead before his body, driven backward, slammed into the cigarette machine near the door, slid down it to the floor.

The half-drunk woman was yelling in broken shrieks, as if she couldn't get enough air for a sustained scream. When I came up out of my crouch I saw that Anchor Steam had hold of her, clinging to her as much for support as in an effort to calm her down. Candiotti stood flat-footed, his arms down at his sides, the gun out of sight below the bar, staring at the bloody remains of the kid as if he couldn't believe what he was seeing, couldn't believe what he'd done.

Some of the tension in me eased as I went to the door, found the lock on its security gate, fastened it before anybody could come in off the street. The Saturday Night Special was still clutched in the kid's hand; I bent, pulled it free with my thumb and forefinger, broke the cylinder. It was loaded, all right—five cartridges. I dropped it into my jacket pocket, thought about checking the kid's clothing for identification, didn't do it. It wasn't any of my business, now, who he'd been. And I did not want to touch him or any part of him. There was a queasiness in my stomach, a fluttery weakness behind my knees—the same delayed reaction I always had to violence and death—and touching him would only make it worse.

To keep from looking at the red ruin of the kid's face, I pivoted back to the bar. Candiotti hadn't moved. Anchor Steam had gotten the woman to stop screeching and had coaxed her over to one of the handful of tables near the jukebox; now she was sobbing, "I've got to go home, I'm gonna be sick if I don't go home." But she didn't make any move to get up and neither did Anchor Steam.

I walked over near Candiotti, pushed hard words at him in an undertone. "That was a damn fool thing to do. You could have got us all killed."

"I know," he said. "I know."

"Why'd you do it?"

"I thought . . . hell, you saw the way he was waving that piece of his . . ."

"Yeah," I said. "Call the police. Nine-eleven."

"Nine-eleven. Okay."

"Put that gun of yours down first. On the bar."

He did that. There was a phone on the back bar; he went away to it in shaky strides. While he was talking to the Emergency operator I picked up his weapon, saw that it was a .32 Charter Arms revolver. I held it in my hand until Candiotti finished with the call, set it down again as he came back to where I stood.

"They'll have somebody here in five minutes," he said.

I said, "You know that kid?"

"Christ, no."

"Ever see him before? Here or anywhere else?"

"No."

"So how did he know about your safe?"

Candiotti blinked at me. "What?"

"The safe in your office. Street kid like that . . . how'd he know about it?"

"How should I know? What difference does it make?"

"He seemed to think you keep big money in that safe."

"Well, I don't. There's nothing in it."

"That's right, you told me you don't keep more than fifty bucks on the premises overnight. In the till."

"Yeah."

"Then why have you got a safe, if it's empty?"

Candiotti's eyes narrowed. "I used to keep my receipts in it, all right? Before all these burglaries started. Then I figured I'd be smarter to take the money to the bank every night."

"Sure, that explains it," I said. "Still, a kid like that, looking for a big score to feed his habit, he wasn't just after what was in the till and our wallets. No, it was as if he'd gotten wind of a heavy stash—a grand or more."

Nothing from Candiotti.

I watched him for a time. Then I said, "Big risk you took, using that .32 of yours. How come you didn't make your play the first time you went to the register? How come you waited until the kid mentioned your office safe?"

"I didn't like the way he was acting, like he might start shooting any second. I figured it was our only chance. Listen, what're you getting at, hah?"

"Another funny thing," I said, "is the way he called you 'Mr. Cyclone Man.' Now why would a hopped-up kid use a term like that to a bar owner he didn't know?"

"How the hell should I know?"

"Cyclone," I said. "What's a cyclone but a big destructive wind? Only one other thing I can think of."

"Yeah? What's that?"

"A fence. A cyclone fence."

Candiotti made a fidgety movement. Some of the wet gray pallor was beginning to spread across his cheeks again, like a fungus.

I said, "And a fence is somebody who receives and distributes stolen goods. A Mr. Fence Man. But then you know that, don't you, Candiotti? We were talking about that kind of fence before the kid came in . . . how Pitman, down in San Jose, bought some hot stereo equipment off of one. That fence could just as easily be operating here in San Francisco, though. Right here in this neighborhood, in fact. Hell, suppose the stuff taken in all those burglaries never left the neighborhood. Suppose it was brought to a place nearby and stored until it could be trucked out to other cities—a tavern storeroom, for instance. Might even be some of it is *still* in that storeroom. And the money he got for the rest he'd keep locked up in his safe, right? Who'd figure it? Except maybe a poor junkie who picked up a whisper on the street somewhere—"

Candiotti made a sudden grab for the .32, caught it up, backed up a step with it leveled at my chest. "You smart son of a bitch," he said. "I ought to kill you too."

"In front of witnesses? With the police due any minute?"

He glanced over at the two customers. The woman was still sobbing, lost in a bleak outpouring of self-pity; but Anchor Steam was staring our way, and from the expression on his face he'd heard every word of my exchange with Candiotti.

"There's still enough time for me to get clear," Candiotti said grimly. He was talking to himself, not to me. Sweat had plastered his lank hair to his forehead; the revolver was not quite steady in his hand. "Lock you up in my office, you and those two back there . . ."

"I don't think so," I said.

"Goddamn you, you think I won't use this gun again?"

"I *know* you won't use it. I emptied out the last two cartridges while you were on the phone."

I took the two shells out of my left-hand jacket pocket and held them up where he could see them. At the same time I got the kid's Saturday Night Special out of the other pocket, held it loosely pointed in his direction. "You want to put your piece down now, Candiotti? You've not going anywhere, not for a long time."

He put it down—dropped it clattering onto the bartop. And as he did his sad hound's face screwed up again, only this time he didn't even try to keep the wetness from leaking out of his eyes. He was leaning against the bar, crying like the woman, submerged in his own outpouring of self-pity, when the cops showed up a little while later.

ROBERT J. RANDISI

THE VANISHING VIRGIN

Nick Delvecchio's first appearance in a novel was No Exit
From Brooklyn, *published by St. Martin's Press in 1987.
His very first appearance was in a short story called "The
Snaphaunce," which appeared in Wayne Dundee's* Hard-
boiled, *and was nominated for a Shamus Award as Best P.I.
Short Story of 1985.*

*Join Delvecchio in Brooklyn as he looks for "The Vanishing
Virgin."*

1

"One of my virgins has vanished," the man sitting across the
table said.

I frowned at him. I'd heard of men collecting women before—
harems, and all that—but virgins? What would one do with
them?

"Perhaps I'd better explain," George Vanguard said.

"It would be appreciated."

I didn't usually talk like that, but there was something about
Vanguard that brought it out in me.

He had called me earlier and asked for an appointment; I lied
and told him that he was in luck, I'd had a cancellation. His name
was George Vanguard and he was a playwright with a problem.

"You see," he began, "in my new play—which is now in
rehearsals, by the way—the three central characters are virgins."

In this day and age? "Is it a fantasy?"

"How did you know?" he replied, looking at me with surprise
and something akin to respect. It never hurts to impress a
potential client early.

"I guessed. Go on, please."

"Yes, well, the girl who plays one of the virgins hasn't shown up for rehearsal in two days. It's wreaking havoc with my schedule, as I'm sure you can imagine."

The guy came off like a daisy, but I wanted to give him the benefit of the doubt—which was kind of hard to do with a fellow who wears a pink shirt and lavender jacket with matching kerchief.

"Indeed," I said.

"Well, that's it," he said, shrugging. "We simply *cannot* find her," he added, for dramatic effect.

"Have you tried her home?"

"Well, we've *called*, of course."

"You haven't gone to her place to check?"

"I simply don't have the *time*," he explained. "We're running rehearsals around her, but we can't do that *forever*. I'd like to hire you to find her within the next two days."

"Why the time limit?"

"Well, I don't *want* to replace her, she's *perfect* for the part, but in a few days that will be a moot point. I will simply be *forced* to replace her and continue rehearsals. We open next month, you know."

"On Broadway?"

"Off Broadway," he said, as if he were implying *who wants to be on Broadway?*

"I see. Do you have her address with you?"

"Well, of *course*," he scolded. His nose wrinkled when he scolded. I decided he was definitely gay—that's why I'm a *detective*.

He rattled off her address and I wrote it down on the doodle pad I carry in my pocket. It was in Manhattan, and *I* wrinkled *my* nose at the prospect of going across the bridge.

"My fee," I told him, "is twenty dollars an hour, plus expenses."

"My backers will pay it."

"I'll need a retainer," I said, firmly.

He wrinkled his nose and took out a checkbook. He signed with a flourish of loops and circles. It was a lavender check for three hundred and twenty dollars. Sixteen hours' work. I wondered if he expected those hours to be spread over two days. I've been known to work on a case like this for four hours a day, or even two, in which case it stretched out. It depended on whether or not I had other cases.

Which, at the moment, I did not.

Accepting the check I asked, "What about her friends?"

"What about them?"

"Who are they?"

"How should I know that? I don't socialize with the girl, for heaven's sake," he said, as if the very thought of socializing with a *woman* was appalling. "As for the other girls in the show, you can come to the theater and I'll introduce you."

"Where are you rehearsing?"

He wrinkled his nose again.

"We simply could not get a theater in Manhattan, so we're using an old movie theater in Bay Ridge. Do you know where Bay Ridge is?"

"I can find it," I said, with my tongue in my cheek.

He gave me the address, a small theater on Third Avenue.

"When will you come down?"

"Are you rehearsing today?"

"Well, of *course*. That's where I should be *now*."

I checked my watch. Twelve-forty.

"After I check out the girl's apartment I'll come right over. What's her name, by the way?"

"Oh, of course," he said, almost simpering, "how silly of us. Her name is Amy Butterworth."

"What does she look like?"

"Oh, I'm terrible at describing *women*. I can do men much more easily."

I believed him.

I smiled and said, "Give it your best shot."

"Let me see," he said, looking at the ceiling. "She's about twenty-two, built rather petitely except for her breasts, which are rather large for a girl her size. She's just right for the part, you know, virginal, but with a touch of wanton, do you know what I mean?"

"I believe so."

"She has blond hair, long," he said, touching his shoulders, "blue eyes, and she laughs a lot. Does that help?"

"It'll do. I'll probably drop by the theater somewhere around three, after I've been to her place and talked to the police."

"The police?" he said, alarmed. "Oh dear, we shouldn't have any bad publicity."

"I'm just going to check with them and see if she's . . . turned up, anywhere, like in a hospital."

"Oh, I see. That makes sense."

"Thank you."

He rose and extended his hand for me to shake. I had already done that when he arrived, and I dreaded doing it again. He was tall, about six-one, but very thin, like a blade of pink-and-lavender grass. His eyes were a pale gray and slightly watery and he seemed as if he'd be the nervous type even under normal circumstances. His handshake hadn't gotten any firmer since his arrival, when it had felt like a warm, moist dishrag.

"Thank you ever so much, Mr. Delvecchio," he gushed, pumping my hand. I hate men who gush. "I'm sure my cast is just going to love you, but remember—my business before your pleasure, eh?" he said, trying in his own way to be slightly bawdy—I think.

"I'll keep that in mind."

2

The girl who opened Amy Butterworth's door had long dark hair, elegantly thin red lips, and two of the biggest breasts I'd ever seen. I got a real good look at them, too, because she was wearing a thin T-shirt on which someone had stenciled the words "Fly Me." Below that she was wearing tight designer jeans, no shoes, and red nail polish on her toes.

The apartment was on West Fifty-sixth Street in Manhattan, and I'd had to walk up four flights of stairs to knock on the door. I was acutely aware of the fact that I was soaking wet from perspiration, not all of it from exertion. I was experiencing the usual heebie-jeebies from crossing the bridge from Brooklyn to "the City."

"Hello," she said, cheerfully. "Can I help you?"

"Soon as I get my breath back you can," I said.

"You'll have to do better than that before I invite a strange man into my apartment," she said, thinking it was a compliment.

"The climb," I said, panting.

"Oh."

"And this heat doesn't help, either. Why don't they air-condition these halls?"

"Are you kidding? I had to buy my own window air conditioner."

I could feel the cool air coming out of her apartment, feeling cooler yet on my wet face.

"My name is Delvecchio, Nick Delvecchio. I'm a private investigator looking for Amy Butterworth."

"Do you have some I.D.?" she asked, like a true New Yorker.

I showed it to her and she stepped back and said, "All right, come on in and cool off."

"Thank you."

I entered and she shut the door behind us. She was tall, about five-nine in her bare feet. With heels she would be taller than me.

"I'm Amy's roommate. What's this about?"

"Have you seen her lately? Over the past few days?"

"No, I haven't seen her for three or four days, but that's not unusual."

"Oh? Why not? Does she stay away for days at a time?"

"No, I'm a stew."

"Pardon?"

"A stewardess—or flight attendant, as they now call us. I haven't been in town for days. I just got back today from London. Has something happened to her?"

"I hope not. May I sit down?"

"Oh, sure, sorry, please," she said, nervously. "My name's Lucy, Lucy Mills."

"Nick Delvecchio," I said.

"Can I ask who hired you to look for Amy, and why?"

"Sure. Do you know George Vanguard?"

"The playwright?"

"Yes. He's the man who hired me. Seems Amy hasn't shown up for rehearsals for two days, and he's worried."

"About his play, I'll bet."

"That may be, but he did hire me."

"He's a fag," she said with distaste. "He probably hassled Amy and she took off for a couple of days."

"You're not worried, then?"

"No," she said, shrugging. "She's an actress, isn't she? And she's everything an actresss should be: temperamental, sensitive, and a little nutty. She'll be back."

"Well, if you don't mind," I said, handing her one of the business cards I'd just had printed up. All they had on them was my name, my occupation, and home phone. "If she shows up within the next couple of days, would you give me a call?"

"I'm flying out again tomorrow night, but if she shows by then I'll call you."

"I appreciate it."

She walked me to the door and said, "When I get back why don't I check in with you again and see if you've found her. If not, you might want to talk to me again."

I wondered if it would be presumptuous of me to read something else into her offer. I figured I'd just have to wait and see.

"That'd be fine," I said, and left.

3

Before going to the theater I called a detective in Missing Persons I used to work with when I first became a cop. I asked if they had anything on an Amy Butterworth, or anyone who fit her description. Their listing was citywide, and if she'd been in a hospital or morgue in any of the boroughs, they would have known about it.

They didn't, which meant she wasn't in one of those places—or maybe just not yet.

I got to the theater a little after three and rehearsals were in full swing. I took a seat about halfway down and watched for a while, waiting for an opening. It was hot as hell in there, and obvious the air-conditioning was out of order. Still, I felt a lot better just being back in Brooklyn.

"I won't tell them why you're here," Vanguard said, sitting next to me. "You can do that individually."

"Fine."

"Until you speak to them privately, they'll probably just assume that you're another backer."

"Good enough."

"Lord, I wish they'd fix the air-conditioning in here," he bitched.

"It could be worse," I said. "We could be in Florida in July instead of New York."

"True."

A woman started up the aisle toward us and Vanguard started

to get up, saying in a low tone, "Maybe I'd better introduce you to my director."

"Nick Delvecchio," he said aloud, "this is my assistant director, Sherry Logan."

"Mr. Delvecchio," she said, extending her hand as a man would.

Her grip was surprisingly firm. She was auburn-haired, with green eyes and a wide, full-lipped mouth. She reminded me very much of an actress I had seen in a private-eye movie my friend Billy Palmer had showed me, once. The film was called *P.J.*, and the actress's name was Gayle Hunnicut.

Unlike the actress, however, she was not tall—maybe five-four—and she was slim and small-breasted. Her mouth was very sensuous; the upper and lower lip were of equal fullness. A tendril of hair was plastered to her forehead by perspiration.

I placed her age at about twenty-eight, but she could have gone a couple of years in either direction with no problem. What with her job I figured her for closer to thirty than not.

"I'm pleased to meet you, Mr. Delvecchio. Are you interested in the theater?"

"Not particularly. Theater people, yes, but not the theater itself. I have to meet a few of the people here, but perhaps we could talk later, say over dinner?"

She frowned at my abrupt offer and asked, "About what?" She was polite, because she still wasn't sure that I wasn't a backer.

"Oh, about theater people."

Her puzzled frown turned shrewd.

"Anyone in particular?"

I handed her one of my cards and said, "Amy Butterworth."

She read the card and turned to Vanguard. "Oh, George, you didn't."

"I certainly did," he replied haughtily. "Cooperate with him, Sherry. Let me introduce him around and then you can talk to him."

"If you don't mind," I added. I didn't want her to be hostile.

She looked at me, parting her full lips and tapping her front teeth with my card.

"No, I guess I don't mind. I'll wait for you, Mr. Delvecchio, but this dinner is going to cost you."

"That's okay," I said, "I'm on an expense account."

Vanguard frowned, and then led me toward the stage. He introduced me around without saying who and what I was, and I could tell by the polite reception that he'd been right about everyone assuming I was a backer.

The male lead in the play was a fairly young, tall, slim, somewhat effeminate-looking man named Harry Wilkens. His handshake was firmer than Vanguard's, but not as firm as Sherry Logan's.

The second lead was a huskier man who seemed a bit old to be second lead actor in an off-Broadway play. His name was Jack Dwyer and he studied me long enough to make me uncomfortable. I had the feeling he wasn't accepting me for what I appeared to be.

Next I met the other two virgins.

Linda Pollard was a petite blonde with light blue eyes and a small mouth, kind of like Lana Turner when she was real young. She was extremely slim and delicate looking and—if her breasts hadn't been so small—she could have fit Amy Butterworth's description.

The other virgin was quite different; probably, I figured, by design. Her name was Onaly O'Toole, and I had to have that repeated to me before I understood that it was her stage name.

"I was an on-aly child," she said, as if she'd been explaining it for years.

She had the blackest hair I've ever seen, worn long and parted in the center. She was tall, about five-eight, and had an arresting face. Her eyes were brown and set just a bit too far apart. Her nose was too big, but not so much so that it would hamper her career any. She was as full-breasted as Linda Pollard was petite. *Virgin* was the last word that would come to mind to describe Onaly O'Toole.

It was obvious that this was not a dress rehearsal, as virtually all of these people were wearing T-shirts and jeans.

"Those are our lead players," Vanguard said after the intros had been made. "Now that they've met you they won't question your presence in the theater. You can talk to them now or at your convenience, just please keep in mind that there is a time limit. This is Wednesday. If you can't find Amy in time for Saturday rehearsal, I'm going to have to replace her."

"I understand."

He stepped away into the center of the stage and clapped his hands, reminding me very much of a teacher I'd had in the third grade. Thinking back, I could swear that he'd been gay, too.

I became aware of a presence behind me at that point and turned to find Sherry Logan.

"I don't mind an early dinner," she said.

"Doesn't he . . ."

"George can handle this himself. Besides, I want to talk about Amy."

"Why?"

"I want this show to go on without a hitch," she said. "It's important to me. Helping you find Amy can accomplish that."

"All right," I said, "an early dinner, it is."

4

She took me to a restaurant in the area—an air-conditioned restaurant—and after we ordered a couple of iced teas she said, "So tell me how I can help you?"

"Do you know Amy well?"

"Not very well. We've worked together once or twice before, but we're not what you'd call friends."

"Had she ever done a disappearing act any of those other times you worked with her?"

"Let me think." The waitress brought our drinks. "I'm sure she missed a rehearsal or two on occasion, but I wouldn't say it was a habit with her."

"Do you know any of her hangouts?"

"Only the usual theater places," she said, mentioning a few. "Some of the others might know something more specific."

"Who are her friends in the show? Who is she close to?"

"Linda," she said, without hesitation. "Linda and Amy are *very* close."

"I think you're trying to tell me something without telling me something," I said.

She smiled and said, "You really are a detective."

"Are you telling me that Linda and Amy were an item?"

"Well, it's pretty common knowledge that Linda and Amy were—are—lovers."

"You're sure of that?"

"They don't flaunt it, but yes, I'm sure."

"Is Vanguard aware of this?"

"Georgie is only aware of his performers as performers, not as people."

"Well then, I guess my next step is to talk to Linda."

"Take it easy on her, Nick," she said, using my first name very easily. "She's very young, and she's as fragile as she appears to be."

"Isn't that a hazard in your business?"

"Yes," she said, as our dinner arrived.

We talked about other things: my former profession as a boxer, and hers as an actress, before she decided to "switch sides," as she put it. This was actually her first chance to direct on her own—although it hardly seemed that way to me. She said that Vanguard was taking a big chance with her.

"It'll keep his budget down," she explained, being realistic. She seemed to have both feet firmly planted on the ground, and I liked that about her.

"As producer and author, Georgie will always be around with his two cents anyway, but I really am grateful for the opportunity he's given me."

"I wish you luck."

"Thank you."

"Can you tell me anything about the other people in the show?"

"Personal things, you mean?"

"That's what I mean, all right. What about Harry Wilkens? Is he involved with anyone? Or Onaly O'Toole?"

"Isn't that a great name?" she asked. "Her real name's Ann, but Onaly is a wonderful stage name." She shook her head and got back to my question. "Onaly keeps to herself, so I can't help you there—but Harry?" she said, smiling. "Georgie and Harry are *very, very* close."

"I see."

"Jack is this guy from the Midwest who was recommended to Georgie. I don't know much about him."

"I'll just have to ask him, then."

"There's only one thing I do know about him for sure."

"What's that?"

"He's not gay. He's been after me since we first met."

"Has he caught you?"

"Can I tell you anything else?"

"Yes," I said, "tell me about this play."

5

I got Linda's address from Sherry and decided to go and see her after our early dinner. The fact that Sherry insisted she go straight home—where her work awaited—certainly had a bearing on my decision.

"I'll see you tomorrow at the theater," she said, and we went our separate ways.

It was after six, but the heat was persisting.

Linda Pollard lived in an apartment on the Upper East Side of Manhattan, one that she should have had trouble paying for if she did not have a roommate, a rich daddy, or a sugar daddy. From what Sherry had told me about Amy and Linda, though, the latter seemed remote.

When she answered the door I had to explain who I was before she recognized me.

"I'm sorry," she said, frowning, "but what are you doing here?"

"I'd like to come in and talk to you, if I may."

Her eyes widened and she said, "I'm sorry, mister . . . ?"

"Delvecchio."

"I'm sorry, but maybe one of the other girls would—I mean, I don't—"

"You don't understand. I want to talk to you about Amy."

"Do you know Amy?" she asked. "Do you know where she is?" Her tone was desperate.

"No, but I'm looking for her." I took out my I.D. and showed it to her. "Vanguard hired me to try and find her."

"A private detective," she said, frowning at the card.

"May I come in?" I asked again, and this time she nodded and backed away from the door.

"Miss Pollard—"

"Linda, please."

"Linda . . . when was the last time you saw Amy?"

"We went shopping together three days ago."

"Where?"

"Oh, Fifth Avenue, Thirty-fourth Street, like that. Amy doesn't have any money, but I get some from . . . from home, so we shopped and I bought her something."

"And after that?"

"We had dinner, and then we went home. We had an early call the next morning."

"When you say you went home, does that mean . . ."

"She went to her apartment, and I came here."

"I see."

"She didn't show up the next day, or yesterday. I'm real worried. She really wanted this part. She wouldn't walk away from it, Mr. Delvecchio, not willingly."

I started to say "I see" again, but stopped myself and just nodded.

"Was anyone bothering her lately?"

"Georgie was yelling at her, but he does that sometimes."

"No, I mean were there any men following her, or calling her?"

"No, not that she mentioned."

"Would she have mentioned it to you?"

"Oh, definitely, either to me or Lucy. That's her roommate."

"I've met her." I hadn't asked her that question, though. It was as good a reason to go back as any.

"Amy didn't talk about leaving town?"

"She'd never leave, Mr. Delvecchio—"

"Nick."

"She wants to be an actress so much. This part meant *everything* to her."

This time I did say "I see," and immediately grimaced.

"Is there somewhere she would go if something was bothering her?"

"If something was bothering her, she'd come to me . . . Nick."

I stood and said, "Well, thank you for your help, Miss—Linda."

"If you find her, you'll let me know?"

"Yes, and if you hear from her, call me at this number," I said, giving her one of my cards. "Oh, by the way. Does she have any family in town?"

"She has no family anywhere, Nick. Neither of us do. That's why we became such good friends."

I nodded and said, "Thanks, Linda."

"Please," she said, grabbing my arm, "find her."

"I'm going to do my best."

I went home from Linda Pollard's apartment and ran into Sam in front of the building. Sam is Samantha Karson, my neighbor across the hall. She's a romance writer who uses the name "Kit" Karson on her books. A pale blonde who reminds me of a prettier Sissy Spacek, she invited me to have a drink with her, and I accepted. We went to a place that had opened up nearby called the Can-U-Drop-Inn and sat at the bar.

"What do you know about the theater?" I asked her.

"Nothing."

"Big help."

"I try," she said.

I told her about the case and she listened quietly. She was real good at listening. She wanted to break into the mystery field, and she saw me as the source of her plots.

I finished my beer and climbed down off my stool.

"Going?"

I nodded. "I'm wiped. This heat wrings me out."

"Working tonight?" she asked.

I shook my head. "I'll go back to the theater in the morning and talk to everyone. There's no point in pussyfooting around this thing. If any of them know where she is, they'll tell me. If they don't, it'll hold up the show."

"Good luck. I'm going to have another drink and get to know the bartender."

"Why?" I asked. "This place will be closed in a month."

She shrugged and said, "I need a couple of drinks before I get to work tonight."

Sam did most of her writing at night. Sometimes, if I listen real hard, I can hear her typewriter going at three in the morning.

"Okay," I said. "I'll see you sometime tomorrow."

"I'll be in after three."

I nodded, shook hands, and went out into the waning heat. By eight or nine o'clock, maybe it would even be down to eighty.

6

The next morning I had breakfast and headed for the theater. When I got there, all the doors were open and the people inside were complaining.

"Not only is it the heat," someone up on the stage was yelling, "but now we've got this smell."

Vanguard called back petulantly, "I've opened the windows and doors. What more do you want?"

"Get somebody in here to find out what that smell is." I saw now that it was Onaly O'Toole who was complaining.

"Onaly—"

"God," she said, "it smells like something curled up in a corner and died."

I was halfway down the aisle now and the smell hit me. I stopped short, took a wary breath, and my stomach sank.

"George," I said.

He turned and saw me, waved a hand for me to wait.

"Vanguard!" I said, moving to him and grabbing his arm.

"What is it?"

"Get everyone out of here."

"What?"

"Out!" I said. "Get everyone out . . . now!"

"Why?"

"Take a deep breath, George."

He did and said, "I smell it, for heaven's sake; what can I do—"

"Get everyone out and I'll find out what the smell is. If it's what I think it is . . ." Actually, I knew what it was because I'd smelled it plenty of times when I was a cop.

"Oh my Lord," he said, his eyes widening.

"Exactly. Now come on, get everyone outside."

"All right, people," he shouted, "take five. Everyone outside."

The complaints started, but he was doing a good job of herding them out. As he passed me on his own way out I stopped him again.

"George, who's not here?"

"Uh, Dwyer, Jack Dwyer. He's not here yet, but I assumed he was just late."

"Where's the smell coming from?"

"There's a stairway backstage—stage right—that goes downstairs. It seems to be coming from there."

"What's down there?"

"It's used for storage."

"Okay. Go outside and wait for me."

. He nodded and turned away, and I heard him say, "Linda, come on, love; let's go outside. You don't want to stay in here . . ."

". . . looking for my purse . . ."

The rest of what they were saying got lost as I made my way to the stage. I hopped up and went backstage. I made like Snagglepuss—"Exit, staaage right!"—and found the stairway.

He was right. The smell was stronger here, and was rising. I went downstairs, breathing as shallowly as possible. I knew that a civilian would be choking by now. I found myself in a small hallway with two doors on the right and one on the left, directly under the stage.

I checked the two on the right and found small storage rooms. The smell was no stronger in either of them. That left the door under the stage.

When I opened it I was hit first by a wave of air that might have been coming from a furnace, and then by the smell. I took out my handkerchief, held it over my mouth, and went inside.

I found her fairly easily. Someone had piled debris on top of her, but the smell and insect activity led me right to her.

Whoever had killed her and put her down there had probably figured to come back eventually and move her. What they hadn't counted on was the air-conditioning going on the fritz. Amy—if it was Amy, and I felt sure it was—had swelled up like a balloon and done what a balloon does when it's filled too much. She was as ripe as they come.

When I was on the job and we were called to the scene of a D.O.A. what we usually did was drop a handful of coffee into a frying pan. In moments the strong smell of burning coffee would help dilute the odor of the corpse. I knew some cops who could eat their lunch in the same room while waiting for the M.E. and never miss a swallow. I wasn't one of them.

I turned to leave and saw her in the doorway.

"Linda," I said.

"My God," she said, "it smells terrible."

"Didn't expect that, did you?" I asked.

She had one hand over her mouth. In her other was a .22 caliber revolver.

"Where did you get the gun, Linda?"

"My father gave it to me when I told him I was moving to New York. I carry it with me everywhere."

"And how did you come to use it on Amy?"

"We had a fight."

"Over . . . someone else?"

"I see you've heard the stories," she said, bitterly. "Amy and I weren't lovers. In fact, we were hardly even friends. We just had a lot in common."

"What changed that?"

"When she got the role as the first virgin, and I got the role as the third."

"And the second?"

"Onaly."

"What happened between you and Amy?"

"She got uppity when she landed the role of first virgin. That night we stayed to go over some lines, and we got into a fight. She said I was third virgin because I had third-virgin talent."

"That wasn't fair."

"No, it wasn't. I told her I could very easily be second virgin. She sneered and said the only way I could do that was if Onaly died."

"And you showed her different, didn't you?"

"That's right, I did," Linda Pollard said. "I showed her that I could move up by her dying."

"And how would you have moved up to first virgin, Linda? By killing Onaly?"

"I wouldn't kill Onaly," she said, staring at me strangely. "She's a nice girl."

"And Amy wasn't."

"No," Linda Pollard said. "She was a snot."

"Did you drag her down here by yourself?"

"I dragged her to the stairs and pushed her down, then pulled her in here and covered her. I didn't know where else to put her!"

Her eyes were tearing now from the smell, as mine were. I was so wet from perspiration that I felt as if I were standing in a pool.

"Come on, Linda. Let's go upstairs."

"No," she said, choking a bit, "you'll tell them."

"I'll have to."

"No!"

"Are you going to kill me, too?" I asked. My stomach was one big knot, waiting for her to pull the damned trigger.

"I . . . don't know."

She coughed then and I said, "Let's get out of here so we can talk, Linda."

"No, no!"

"Linda—"

I'd never seen anyone with such vacant eyes before. I knew she was going to fire and that there was nothing I could do about it. I leaped for her anyway, just as an arm came through the doorway behind her and a hand took hold of her arm as she squeezed the trigger. Jack Dwyer pushed her arm up and her shot went into the ceiling. He reached around with his other hand and twisted the gun away from her.

"Jesus Christ," he said, "let's get out of here!"

7

Dwyer had indeed arrived late and, when he saw everyone outside and smelled the scent of a ripe one, he knew what was going on. He asked Vanguard about it, and George had told him that I'd gone downstairs to find the source of the smell. As it turned out, he was an ex-cop, too, as well as sometime actor and sometime P.I. It was just coincidence that he happened to land this role, so that he could be around to save my life. He'd told George to call the police, and come downstairs after me.

He told me all this at the Can-U-Drop-Inn over a beer, after the police had come and taken Linda Pollard away. Vanguard gave everyone the day off so that the theater could be cleared of the smell, and maybe even get the AC fixed.

"Why did she go down there?" Dwyer wondered aloud.

"I guess she was afraid I'd find the body."

"And it never occurred to her that that's what smelled?"

I shrugged and said, "I guess she'd never smelled a ripe one before, Jack. A lot of people haven't had that pleasure. Speaking of ripe ones, what'll happen to the show now?"

"I guess Vanguard will find himself two more virgins," Dwyer answered.

"And what about you?"

"I've about had it with this show. Vanguard's a prima donna, the leading man's gay, Onaly's number one virgin now, and she can't act worth a damn. I think I'll head back home."

"That means he'll have to replace you, too."

"That shouldn't be too hard. Mine wasn't much of a part, anyway." He swirled the beer at the bottom of his bottle and said, "They never are."

"Well," I said, "you've got my vote for performer of the year, the way you performed in that basement. I can't give you a Tony Award, but I can buy you another drink."

"Well," he said fatalistically, "I guess that's a start."

JAMES M. REASONER

THE SAFEST PLACE
IN THE WORLD

James Reasoner and his wife, L.J. Washburn, represent the first husband-and-wife team to appear in a PWA anthology. They also represent two very special writing talents.

James's 1980 first novel Texas Wind *(which introduced his Texas P.I. "Cody") has become something of a cult classic, and is to be reprinted by Black Lizard Books. Cody appears here in a PWA anthology for the first time.*

The eye squinting at me over the sights of the automatic weapon was pale gray and insane. One burst would just about cut me in half.

The things a private eye gets into for his clients . . .

It began simply enough. All I would have to do, Connie Lamb had said, was make friends with her ex-husband Roy. Roy had legal custody of their son Jeremy, and Connie wanted to get the boy back before Roy turned him into a killer.

She was pretty upset when she came into my office on Camp Bowie Boulevard, on the west side of Fort Worth on the edge of the museum district. Sensing that just being in a private investigator's office was adding to her nervousness, I took her a couple of doors down the street to an ice cream place and calmed her down over a couple of bowls of Fudge Ripple. It was summer, after all, and what could be more soothing than a bowl of good ice cream?

"Roy didn't have any trouble getting custody," Connie said. "He did find me in bed with another man, after all. And I don't have the greatest background in the world." Her spoon rattled against the bowl as she put it down. "Before I was married I did a

183

lot of drugs and got busted for it a few times. I just thank God I didn't mess up my chromosomes and stuff. Jeremy was always a healthy little kid."

His mother was pretty healthy, too, I thought. She was a tall brunette, her hair cut fairly short, and though she had to be in her early thirties she looked ten years younger than that. Her figure was striking, to say the least, especially in tight blue jeans and a sleeveless jersey top. I told myself sternly that I should not be thinking semilecherous thoughts about a potential client in distress.

"Roy's lawyer brought all of that up, of course," she was saying. "I never had a chance. And naturally he made Roy sound like Ward Cleaver or somebody. It was disgusting." She looked out the window toward the traffic passing by on Camp Bowie, but I don't think she was seeing the cars. "I never had a chance. He's a goddamned *accountant*, after all."

I waited a moment, then asked, "How old is Jeremy now?"

"He's twelve. Roy's had him since he was nine. I guess Roy thought he wasn't old enough to brainwash until now."

"Brainwash is a strong word," I pointed out. "I suppose all parents try to mold their children in one way or another."

"He's taking Jeremy with him to that camp on weekends! He's taking him out there and teaching him how to kill!"

The ice cream parlor was doing brisk business on a hot afternoon like that one, and several people turned to look at our table. Connie's voice wasn't loud, but it carried a lot of intensity. I said, "Take it easy. I can understand you wanting to get your son back. Maybe I can help you."

"You can. If you can just get proof that Roy's getting Jeremy involved with all that paramilitary crap, I'm sure any judge would give him back to me."

I had an image in my mind of a twelve-year-old in fatigues and helmet, carrying an M-16. Maybe she had a point. A lot of judges I knew wouldn't look kindly on that sort of parental influence. If she could prove that she had cleaned up her act and wasn't sleeping around or doing drugs, she could stand a good chance of regaining custody.

"Tell me more about Roy," I said.

It was a common enough picture: Roy Lamb was an accountant, as she had told me, and worked at the livestock exchange for one of the cattle companies headquartered there. During the week he fit the stereotypical mild-mannered image of his profession. It was only on the weekends that he became a raving gun-nut, to hear her tell it. He and some friends of his gathered out in the boonies in Wise County, northwest of Fort Worth, and shot off their rifles and machine guns, practiced military maneuvers, and generally prepared themselves to survive once the godless Communists came in and took over the United States.

"He thinks he's going to be a damned guerrilla fighter," Connie said bitterly. "Either that, or the Russians will drop the bomb and he'll be a survivalist. He's got his basement stocked with all kinds of survival gear and food, and he's talking about buying a place out in the country and building an underground bunker. Then he'll move all the stuff out there. I tell you, Mr. Cody, it's kind of scary."

"Was your husband like that before you married him?"

Connie shook her head. "It started about five years ago. I put up with it for a couple of years, thinking that maybe Roy would grow out of it. It was almost like he was a little kid playing soldier. But he never changed. I was going to divorce him, but well, he kind of got the goods on me first, if you know what I mean."

I knew what she meant, all right. And I wasn't sure that Jeremy Lamb wouldn't be just as well off with his father as with her. That wasn't my decision to make, though. My job was just to gather evidence and turn it over to her. After that it was all up to her and her ex-husband and the judicial system.

"Will you take the case?" she asked, staring pitifully across the empty ice cream bowl at me.

"I'll look into it for you," I told her. I quoted her my daily rate and she nodded and reached for her purse.

"I'll give you a check," she said.

"Let's walk back down to the office. We'll fill out a contract, and you can give me a retainer then."

Back in the office, the business taken care of, she stood up and extended a hand to me. I shook it, still vaguely uncomfortable after all these years about shaking hands with women, and told her I'd call her when I had something to report. She had already given me Roy Lamb's address and phone number and told me where he worked. All that information was written down in my notebook. We were through for now, and I should have been ready to go to work.

Her hand was cool and soft, though, and as she smiled at me across the desk and said, "I know this will all work out," I knew distinctly that I didn't want her to go yet. I wanted to come up with some reason for her to stay a little longer, so that I could talk to her and look into her dark brown eyes.

I kept my mouth shut and let out a sigh of relief when the door shut behind her. The appeal she had been oozing had probably been totally unconscious on her part, but I knew one thing.

I was too damned old for that sort of stuff.

Cowtown, the city where the West begins. That's what they used to call Fort Worth. Still do, in the chamber of commerce brochures. And the name is authentic enough. The Old West is still alive in the spirit of the town, even after the influx of Yankees during the seventies and eighties. The livestock industry has been a vital part of the economy for over a hundred years.

But in some parts of town, Fort Worth is the city where the Hype begins.

I sat in a restaurant in the Stockyards area and watched the tourists in newly bought Stetsons as they gawked at longhorns mounted on the walls and sat on bar stools shaped like saddles. I was in a booth next to the wall, drinking dark beer and waiting for Roy Lamb.

The livestock exchange building was only a few blocks away, and Connie had told me that Roy often had lunch here. The day before I had followed the same routine, but he hadn't shown up.

Today he did. He came in about ten minutes after noon, wearing a suit and carrying a small briefcase. He was alone, so maybe he planned on getting a little work done while he ate. He was a little over six feet, with the beginnings of a paunch. His light brown hair was carefully styled and brushed, and the horned-rim glasses he wore were just the right touch with the conservative gray suit. Just like Connie had described him. He looked honest. I might have even trusted him with my money.

Of course, his honesty wasn't what was in question.

He cooperated by sitting at one of the tables between the bar and the wall, where he would have a good view of the booth where I was waiting. He set his briefcase down on the red-and-white-checked tablecloth and sprung it open, taking out a sheaf of papers. A waitress came over, and he ordered quickly, without consulting a menu.

I picked up one of the magazines I had brought with me and opened it up, holding it so that the cover was visible. I sipped my beer and began reading an article about combat shotguns and how they were perfect weapons for defending your family when it came time to ensure their survival.

I didn't look at Roy Lamb as I read.

I made it through that article and a couple of others on how to build a radiation detector from items you could find in an ordinary kitchen or some such, while Roy Lamb ate a chef's salad and drank a glass of iced tea. It looked like he wasn't going to pay any attention to me, and I was starting to wonder how many days I might have to do this.

But then he put his papers back in the briefcase, closed it, stood up. His eyes lit on the cover of the magazine, and he smiled.

A couple of steps brought him over beside my booth, and he said, "Say, I hate to bother you, but isn't that the new issue?"

I looked over the top of the magazine, keeping my face neutral, and said, "What? Oh, the magazine. Yeah, I just picked it up."

"I subscribe. My copy must be late this month. Hell of a magazine, isn't it?"

I laid the magazine down on the table, keeping my place with a finger. "Sure is," I agreed. "Lots of good information. We'd be better off if more people knew what was going on in the world."

"That's the truth," he said emphatically. He stuck out his hand. "Roy Lamb."

I shook hands and told him my name, then gestured at the other magazines on the seat beside me. "You read these, too?"

He leaned over slightly so that he could see their titles. "You bet. They're good magazines."

I nodded to the seat on the other side of the table. "You're welcome to look at these if you want. They're all new issues, and I'm just killing time waiting for a guy."

"Well . . ." Roy looked at his watch, and for a second I thought he was going to say that he had to get back to work. But then he said, "I don't have to get back right away. I got some work done while I was eating, so I think I can justify taking a few minutes off."

The few minutes turned out to be almost half an hour. He sat across from me and let me buy him another glass of iced tea, though he turned down my offer of a beer. We hit it off right away, flipping through the magazines and making comments on the articles. I'm no weapons expert, but you can't be in my line of work and not know something about guns, so I was able to keep up with what he was saying and add some remarks of my own. Anyway, Roy did most of the talking.

He was everything that Connie had told me he was. On the surface, a normal, likable guy, but his interest in guns bordered on passion. And his politics followed right along with the philosophies of the magazines. It all came down to us versus the Russians and us versus the subversive elements in our own country who wanted to bring us down. Of course, it was always possible that a great natural disaster, like the shifting of the earth's magnetic poles, would come along first and plunge the world into chaos, beating World War III to the punch.

Whatever catastrophe happened, it was going to be up to the average man to be prepared to defend himself and his family. To *survive* . . .

And I couldn't say, even to myself, that he was necessarily wrong. Something about his attitude made me a little uncomfortable, though. It was like he was anxious for something to happen, so that he could demonstrate just how well prepared he was.

You can make friends in a hurry if you get a man to talking about his hobby. By the time Roy had to get back to the livestock exchange building we were buddies, at least in his eyes. I told him I had lunch there frequently, and he said that he did, too. Even as I said, "Maybe we'll run into each other again," I knew damn well that we would.

That was a Tuesday. By Thursday night, when Connie Lamb called me wanting to know how things were progressing, I had had lunch with Roy twice more. He had told me about his son and the breakup of his marriage, and I had heard all about how Connie cheated on him, neglecting him and Jeremy to run around with men she met in bars. As I talked to Connie on the phone, I could hear talking and laughter and hard-driving music in the background, and I thought it was safe to assume she wasn't home studying her Sunday-school lesson.

None of my business.

I assured her that the job was going well. I had dropped a few hints already about wishing I could find a group in the area who thought the way I did, and Roy had said noncommittally that he had heard of such a group. I was sure that he was just checking with the leaders to make sure it was all right before he told me about it.

"Be sure you let me know what happens. They'll be going out to their camp this weekend. I'm certain of that. They always do."

"I'll keep you advised," I told her.

She partially covered the phone and yelled at somebody to hold on, that she was almost through, then said, "Thanks again, Mr. Cody. You don't know how much this means to me."

I told her she was welcome and hung up. I was earning my money on this one.

At lunch the next day, Roy was excited. Maybe it was the prospect of the weekend, maybe it was the fact that he was going to recruit a new member for his group.

"I spoke to some friends of mine," he told me, "some guys I go out in the field to train with. They said I could bring you with me this weekend."

"You're talking about organized survival training?" I asked.

"That's right. We rent a place out in the country, an old farm with about two hundred acres of land. It makes a great staging area."

"Military maneuvers?" I kept my voice down.

Roy nodded. "We've got a target range and an obstacle course and plenty of room for war games. It's quite a setup."

"Who runs it?"

"The commander is a man named Brian Hayes. He was a Green Beret colonel in 'Nam. Great guy. He's an expert in everything from demolitions to unarmed combat."

"Sounds great," I said enthusiastically. "What do I have to do to join?"

"Well, one of the troop has to sponsor you, but that's no problem. I'll be your sponsor. You come out this weekend and take part, and we see if you fit into the group. If you do, that's all there is to it. If for some reason you don't like it, well, there's no hard feelings. There are just a couple of things."

"Like what?"

"It'll cost you a couple hundred dollars."

"For a weekend?" I tried to sound suitably put out.

"It's worth it, Cody. The group furnishes all the uniforms and equipment."

"Including weapons?"

He nodded. "If you don't have your own. A lot of the guys already have their own armaments."

"Well, that sounds a little more reasonable, if the fee covers all that. What's the other thing?"

"Just a little background info on you, mainly your place of employment."

I was ready for that question, even though it hadn't come up so far in our conversations. A friend of mine who worked at one of the downtown banks was prepared to tell anybody who asked that I was part of their security force. I told Roy the same thing, and he nodded happily. He would pass it along to someone higher up in the group, probably this Brian Hayes who ran the thing. If the checking up didn't go too deep—and I had a feeling it wouldn't—my story would be accepted, and so would I.

"How do I get to the place?" I asked.

"I can come by and pick you up," Roy said. "That is, if you don't mind riding up with me."

"Not at all. That sounds fine."

"That'll give you a chance to meet my son Jeremy. He'll be going with us."

I smiled. "After all you've told me, I'm looking forward to meeting him."

"Yeah, he's a great kid. Twelve years old. Just the right age to start teaching him how to be a real man."

"Damn right," I said.

He left first, heading back to his office. I stayed where I was for a long time, drinking beer and watching the tourists soak up the phony Western culture.

Jeremy was fairly tall for his age, with a touch of the gangliness that went with being twelve. His hair was blond and short, and his face had a scattering of freckles. He shook hands with me and said he was glad to meet me, and I did the same.

"Didn't I tell you he was a great kid?" Roy asked, parental pride strong in his voice.

Jeremy rode in the backseat of Roy's Volvo. Roy drove northwest out of Fort Worth toward Decatur. It was a typical summer Saturday, already hot enough to make you sweat if you were outside more than a minute. The sky was high and clear, the air almost bone-dry.

Just the kind of day to go out in the country and play war.

Roy talked quite a bit, obviously excited at the prospect of training over the weekend. He already had his camouflage fatigues on, as did Jeremy, and I could see that the mental image I had had of the boy as I talked to his mother a few days before hadn't been far wrong. There was something ridiculous about the whole situation.

"How many members do you have?" I asked Roy as we drove through a little town called Alvord. There was a nudist colony nearby, I remembered, where one of my more embarrassing cases had taken me.

"We have forty in the group right now," Roy replied, "but it's growing all the time. Small but vital, that's us."

Forty members at two hundred dollars a head. That was eight thousand dollars every weekend. Not a bad business. It sounded like ex-colonel Brian Hayes might be cleaning up.

Jeremy hadn't said much. I half-turned in the seat and asked him, "You enjoy the training, Jeremy?"

"You bet," he said. "Dad's teaching me how to shoot, and Colonel Hayes has already taught us how to kill an enemy with our bare hands, three different ways!"

There was a disturbing amount of enthusiasm in his voice, and suddenly Connie Lamb's barhopping didn't sound so much like a bad influence.

Roy said, "It's important to be prepared for the dangerous times that are coming, of course, but you'll see that one of the best things about the camp is that you can put all the mundane little details of your everyday life in perspective. For instance, I've been working on a deal for my bosses all week that's been a real killer. They're buying a big herd up in Jack County, and I've been putting the figures together for them. You wouldn't believe how many details there are to consider in a hundred-thousand-dollar deal, especially when it's a cash sale. But I can put all that behind me while I'm training this weekend."

He rattled on some more, but I didn't pay much attention. As far as I could tell, Jeremy was healthy and well cared for, at least physically. Roy and I had never talked about how much money he made, but he had to be doing all right to afford four hundred dollars every weekend for the two of them to go out to the camp. I knew he loved the boy, and Jeremy seemed to like him. I could see why a judge had given custody to Roy in the divorce action.

If it wasn't for all the paramilitary survivalism, I would have said that Jeremy would be a lot better off staying right where he was.

But I just couldn't reconcile that thinking with teaching a twelve-year-old three different ways to kill with his bare hands.

Roy turned off the highway onto an asphalt-topped county road and followed that for several miles, then turned again onto a dirt road. After a mile or so, I noticed that the land to the left of the road was now fenced. A high chain-link fence, in fact, that looked like it should have been topped with barbed wire but wasn't.

"That must be the place," I said, nodding toward the fenced-off property.

Roy glanced at me. "How did you know?"

"Lucky guess." I shrugged. "Figured you'd want your privacy. That's why the fence is there, isn't it?"

"Survival training is serious business," he said solemnly. "We don't want any of the locals blundering in and getting hurt. We get enough bad publicity."

"Boy, that's the truth." I made my voice sound bitter. "Damned newspaper and TV reporters never get things right. They always make things sound worse than they are."

"You are absolutely right, Cody. I've got a feeling you and the colonel are going to get along just fine. You'll be a regular in the group before you know it."

There was an open gate in the fence a little farther on. Roy turned in there. I was a little surprised there was no guard on the gate, but I thought I saw movement in a clump of oaks nearby. A hidden guard? That was a possibility.

The narrow driveway led through more trees, across a little dry wash, and up a hill. The old farmhouse sat among trees at the top of the hill. There were a couple dozen cars parked around on the grass.

The farmhouse looked like it had been there a long time, but it had been restored. Either that, or it had been cared for with great diligence. The wooden siding on its walls appeared newly whitewashed. The trim was painted dark brown. There were two floors, and a big porch ran the entire width of the house. A small group of men sat there in rocking chairs, waiting for something.

The something must have been us, because the men stood up and came to the edge of the porch to greet us. In the lead was a man in his forties, tall and athletic, with sandy hair and a heavy moustache. He wore dark, aviator-style sunglasses. The other men were a little younger, but they were cut from the same mold. A couple had short, neat beards. All of them wore fatigues and looked like they had probably been born in them.

The leader snapped a casual salute, which Roy and Jeremy returned crisply. He said, "Mornin', Mr. Lamb, Jeremy. This the new man you told me about?"

"That's right, Colonel," Roy said. He quickly introduced us, and the leader turned out to be Brian Hayes, as I had suspected.

His handshake was hard, almost painful, and I let myself wince a little bit.

"Glad to meet you, Mr. Cody," Hayes said. "It's always a pleasure to meet another man who believes in good old-fashioned American values."

"Nothing wrong with being a good old-fashioned American," I said.

"Of course there's nothing wrong with that. You have the fee for the weekend, I believe?"

I pulled out my wallet, gave him nine twenties and two tens. He took the bills and passed them on to one of the other men. A slight smile tugged at his lips. "We'll get you all set up," he told me. "Roy, why don't you and Jeremy go on down to the staging area after you draw your weapons from the armory. The rest of us will be down shortly, and we can get underway."

Hayes and one of the other men took me into the house while the rest of them marched off somewhere. The place was well appointed, especially the huge dining room which had been made by knocking out some walls and combining rooms. It was paneled in dark wood, with animal heads mounted on the walls, along with a collection of antique weapons. The long table was massive, made of thick slabs of wood. There was something about it that reminded me of an ancient mead hall, where the Viking warriors could gather and carouse after a hard day of pillaging.

In the back part of the house was another large room lined with metal lockers that would have looked right at home in any junior high. I was told that I could leave my clothes and personal possessions there.

They outfitted me with a set of fatigues. I felt silly, but I tried not to let that show. Get into the spirit of things, that's what I had to do. Get in there and play soldier with the rest of them.

I got the feeling that Hayes and his cadre weren't playing, though.

The armory was behind the house and had been a barn at one time. One of the men who had been on the porch was waiting there for us. He issued me an M-16. I checked the magazine. Empty.

"You'll be issued ammo for target practice later," Hayes told me. He picked up a bulky weapon that looked more like a kid's toy. "For maneuvers, we use these. They fire paint balls. I'm sure you've heard of them."

I had. They were a standard part of all these civilian war games. I had to admit, though, I was a little surprised they didn't use regular weapons and blanks. The atmosphere around the place was serious, almost grim.

Almost like it was the real thing, and not just play.

I was starting to get a bad feeling about this setup. I told myself I'd seen too many hokey TV shows that used paramilitary groups as villains, read too many action novels in that same vein. But something sure as hell wasn't right.

We went down the hill to the staging area.

Nearly all the group must have been in attendance that weekend, because there were at least thirty-five men waiting for the training to get underway. I saw a few teenagers, but no one else as young as Jeremy. And there were no women there, either. That made sense, though. To their way of thinking, it was part of a man's duty to protect defenseless females.

The men were all shapes and sizes, but they had one thing in common. With the exception of Hayes and his lieutenants, all of them looked out of place in the camouflage fatigues. They were trying hard to look like hardened survivalists, but something about them just didn't cut it. They looked like accountants and merchants and computer salesmen wearing funny outfits. I watched them as one of Hayes's subordinates put us through several drills, and though the members of the troop tried hard and made the right moves, there was more than a touch of clumsiness about them.

Maybe in a year or so, these guys might shape up and become good civilian soldiers. Maybe. Until then, they were no threat to godless Communists or anybody but themselves.

And Hayes and his men never stopped praising them and telling them what good fighting men they were turning into.

It was a scam, all right, I decided as I went through the drills and workouts with the rest of them. I was willing to bet that Hayes owned this place and that most of the eight thousand bucks a week went right into his pocket. He and his buddies, probably all of them combat vets from the same unit, had set up this deal to bilk a bunch of average guys who wanted to play at being commandos and guerrilla fighters. Not a bad idea, and obviously successful.

The most interesting part was that I couldn't see one damn thing illegal about it.

Nobody had hired me to get the goods on ex-colonel Brian

Hayes, though. I could testify in court that Roy Lamb was taking his son to a survival training camp where he was being taught how to kill some hypothetical "enemy." That was the extent of my job.

In the meantime, though, I was stuck out here for the rest of the weekend.

Late Saturday morning, unarmed combat training came up on the schedule. So far, I had managed to blend in with the other guys, but now Hayes surprised me by calling my name. "You're a newcomer here, Mr. Cody," he said with a tight little smile, "so I'm sure you won't mind if we see just what you can do."

I shrugged my shoulders. "You're in charge, Colonel."

He nodded. "That's right, mister." He gestured at one of his men. "You and Lieutenant Starnes here can put on a demonstration for us."

Starnes was a whipcord-thin man of medium height, quite likely fast and mean. He grinned at me and stepped forward.

I wiped sweat off my forehead. Starnes was eight or ten years younger than me and quite a bit lighter. But I didn't want to back down. Stupid male pride, maybe.

I grinned right back at him and handed my empty M-16 to Roy Lamb, who was standing nearby. "Sure, be glad to," I said.

"Be careful, Cody," Roy whispered to me. "Starnes is good."

I just nodded and turned back to face the lieutenant.

"You can start it off, mister," he rasped at me.

I didn't wait any longer. I swung a roundhouse punch, telegraphing it badly.

He twisted and let my fist go by, then lashed out and chopped me in the side. Pain shot through me. I tried to turn around and block the next blow, but it slipped past my guard and drove into my belly. Air puffed out of my lungs, leaving me gasping.

I saw the arrogant grin on Starnes's face as he moved in for the kill. So far, I hadn't put up much of a fight.

That was the way I had intended for it to go. I wanted to look just as clumsy and ineffectual as the rest of the troop. But Starnes had hurt me, and he had enjoyed it. I forgot what I had planned and let my instincts take over.

The punch he aimed at my jaw found only air.

Instead of letting him polish me off, I drove inside, putting my shoulder into his belly and bulling him backward. His balance went and he fell, and I landed right on top of him. I brought my right elbow up under his chin, knocking his head back so that it bounced off the hard ground. His throat was wide open, and I could have crushed his larynx and left him there to suffocate slowly.

My brain started functioning again just in time, and I slipped awkwardly off his body, making it look like I lost my balance. He hit me savagely in the kidney, and the groan I let out was genuine. I rolled away as he tried to stomp me in the head.

Then two of the other lieutenants had hold of his arms, dragging him back, and Hayes was stepping forward with a grin on his face. "You see what happens when you lose your temper, men," he called out. "Cody had an advantage for a moment, but he lost it because he wasn't in control of his anger. You have to channel your emotion, make it work for you, rather than letting it take control of you."

I knew it was bullshit, and maybe he did, too. The only one who had lost control was Starnes.

I got up and brushed myself off, retrieving my rifle from Roy Lamb. Hayes went on with the training schedule, and the little incident between me and Starnes was quickly forgotten.

Almost forgotten. There was an ache in my side that kept reminding me when I moved wrong.

Lunch in the big dining room was simple fare, light because of the heat. We got a short rest period after we ate, and then it was back to work. In the middle of the afternoon, I got a chance to talk to Jeremy alone, as both of us took a five-minute break under the shade of an oak tree.

"You enjoy this kind of stuff, Jeremy?" I asked him.

"Sure." He shrugged. "It's fun, shooting and fighting and things like that. It's important, too. Besides, it gives me a chance to spend more time with my dad."

"What do you do during the week? Don't you go to ball games or anything like that?" My old-fashioned attitudes were cropping up again, but I couldn't help it.

Jeremy shook his head. "I have to spend a lot of my time studying, you know. And Dad's always busy with his work, or with things like checking our food supply and replenishing it."

I looked away from him and grimaced. He sure as hell didn't sound much like a kid. I glanced back at him and asked, "Studying? You going to summer school or something?"

"No, sir. My dad gives me books and articles to read on survival preparedness and then quizzes me on them."

"We've got to be ready for whatever comes," Roy Lamb said from behind us.

I glanced up, wondering how much of the conversation he had overheard and whether he thought I was meddling. "You're sure right," I agreed with him. "Can't be too prepared."

He gave me a funny look anyway.

I was starting to wonder if it would be possible to get out of here tonight. My job was done, and I didn't see any point in prolonging it.

Hayes called us back into formation, and that ended my speculation for the moment.

I was sore by the time the day was over. As the sun finally set, Hayes gathered the whole group together and made a little speech to get our minds off our aching muscles.

"You'll read articles and hear people talk about where the safest place to be is in case of war, nuclear or otherwise. Well, I don't care if they say Australia or Idaho or Timbuktu." His voice rose in stirring tones. "The safest place in the world is the place a man is willing to defend with his life! Remember that the next time you look around your home."

It was effective rhetoric, and as we went in to supper, I could see the smiles on the faces of the men. They believed in what they were doing and in what they were hearing. Maybe, in the long run, it didn't really matter that Hayes was taking them for a ride.

Maybe they were getting their money's worth in heroic dreams alone.

Our time was our own after supper, so I decided to take a walk around the farm. There was no particular reason for it, just something to do to kill time. I didn't feel like sitting in the makeshift barracks on the second floor of the farmhouse and joining in one of the ongoing poker games.

I had showered and put my own clothes back on, and I suppose in the back of my mind was the thought that I could hike back to the highway and catch a ride back to Fort Worth, leaving this phony training camp behind me.

That was before I spotted the helicopter, though.

It was parked about a hundred yards away from the house in a little clearing in the trees. I hadn't spotted it earlier because it was covered with camo netting. I wouldn't have seen it now if I hadn't nearly run into one of the landing skids.

"What the hell?" I muttered.

There was nothing unusual in a helicopter, of course. It was a good-sized chopper, a four-man job, and that was about all I could tell about it under its camouflage. I couldn't help but wonder why it was hidden. Nobody had said anything about using a helicopter in our training, but maybe we just hadn't gotten to that yet.

The man behind me was good. I barely heard him in time to dodge the knife he tried to put in my back.

I went down, scissoring with my feet and catching his left leg at the knee. He stumbled and fell, but he held on to the knife and came back up onto his feet at the same time I did.

"This time I'll kill you, you son of a bitch!" Starnes hissed at me.

I held up my hands, palm out. "Wait a minute, Starnes!" I said quickly. "I was just taking a walk. No need to get upset."

"Don't give me that crap! What are you, a cop? You're sure as hell not one of those lard-ass toy soldiers!"

I shook my head. "I don't know what you're talking about."

"You could have had me this morning. You could have killed me, and you know it! The colonel told me to keep an eye on you."

So my bad feelings had been from more than the mild swindle Hayes was working on his "recruits." Starnes wanted me dead, and there had to be a reason for that.

"You'd better drop that knife, mister," I said coldly. "I'm from Military Intelligence, and we know all about your operation here."

He laughed.

It had been worth a try. Not much of one, maybe, but a try.

Starnes came at me, fast and vicious.

There was enough moonlight so that we weren't fighting in darkness, but it was still a desperate struggle among shadows. I blocked his first thrust and tried to get a hand on his wrist, but he was too slippery. He squirmed away and lashed at me back-handed. The point of the knife ripped my shirt and laid a shallow scratch across my stomach.

He was out of position for a split second, though. I kicked, burying the toe of my boot in his groin. He gave a strangled scream and hacked at me with the knife as I drove in on him. I knocked the blade aside and caught him flush on the jaw with a punch, putting all of my weight behind the blow. He went down hard and stayed down. I clutched my throbbing hand and hoped I hadn't broken a knuckle.

I hadn't, I decided after a few moments. Starnes was unconscious but alive. He'd probably be out a good while. The longer the better, as far as I was concerned. My shirt was wet with the blood leaking from the wound he had given me, and I didn't feel one damn bit guilty about kicking him in the balls.

There was a possibility that Starnes was just crazy and had decided to kill me because he thought I had shown him up that morning. I didn't think so, though. My gut told me that Hayes had given him the orders to kill if I got too close to something I shouldn't.

I suddenly wanted to get back to that armory and get my hands on a gun.

The armory was locked, so I had to give up that idea. Given time, I might have been able to pick the heavy padlock on the door, but I didn't think I had that much time. I circled around the house instead, finding a lighted window on the first floor. I was glad that the simulated hardships of survival training meant that there were no air conditioners in the place. The glass was up, and I could hear everything that Hayes and a couple of his men were saying inside.

"They're all accounted for except that Cody," one of the lieutenants said. "Everybody else is upstairs."

"I sent Starnes to keep an eye on Cody," Hayes told him. "He should be back soon."

"You think Cody's a cop?"

"It's possible," Hayes admitted. "More than likely, though, he's just a nosy bastard. He never should have taken Ed down like that in the unarmed combat drill. Ed'll kill him if he's got the least excuse."

"We don't need that," another voice said.

"We can handle it," Hayes assured him. "There are plenty of places on this farm where an unmarked grave will never be found. I grew up here, remember."

That confirmed one of my guesses. This was Hayes's place.

I heard the rattle of papers. "All right," Hayes went on, his voice stern now like he was conducting an operations briefing. In a way, I guess he was. "Here are the details of the deal. The meeting is at the main ranch house at eleven o'clock next Wednesday. Lamb's bosses will arrive right at eleven, and they'll have the cash with them. We land right behind their car, blocking them in. We waste them, take the briefcase with the money, and we're gone. Less than a minute on the ground if everything goes according to plan, and we'll practice enough Monday and Tuesday so that it *will* go according to plan. Once we're airborne again, we put napalm into the house so that there won't be any witnesses left. Any questions?"

"Sounds good, Colonel," one of the other men said. "Lamb doesn't suspect anything?"

"Hell, no," Hayes snorted. "I'm his trusted commanding officer. He thought I was sympathizing with him when he was bitching about setting up this cattle sale."

"Just like all the others," a man said, chuckling.

"Right. Just like all the others."

And they had thought that I was a security officer at a bank, with access to all sorts of information about money transfers and things like that. I wondered suddenly what kinds of jobs the other "troops" had. I was willing to bet that a lot of them involved money.

Targets for armed robberies from the sky, carried out with military precision.

I remembered hearing about a couple of heists like that over the last year or so, and as far as I knew, the men who had been responsible for them had never been caught. It wasn't the kind of deal you could pull all the time, but two or three jobs a year, if they were big enough, would make all this phony survival training worthwhile. Plus they were taking in the fees from the suckers who were unwittingly helping them.

This had gotten a lot more grim than just a custody hassle.

"Don't move, you son of a bitch!" a voice grated behind me.

Slowly, I turned my head, not wanting to alarm him. Starnes had come to sooner than I had hoped, and he had gotten a gun from somewhere. This wasn't an army-surplus M-16, though, but a full-sized Ingram MAC-10. And as I said, the eye squinting at me over the sights was pale gray and insane.

I stood as still as possible, trying not to even breathe.

"I oughta blow you away," Starnes rasped. "Now get inside, and keep your damn mouth shut!"

I walked slowly away from the window, Starnes right behind me, prodding me every few steps with the hard barrel of the Ingram.

I was getting mad again. I forced it down. There was no way in hell I could spin around and disarm him before he could squeeze off a burst.

We went up onto the porch and inside the house; the screen door slammed behind us. Starnes marched me down the hall toward the room where Hayes and the others had been having their meeting. They all jerked their heads around and stared when Starnes shoved me through the door.

"He was listening outside the window," Starnes said, "and he found the helicopter."

Hayes's face was tightly drawn as he looked at me. He had finally taken off the sunglasses, and I could see that his eyes were blue.

"All right," he said after a moment. "Take care of him, Starnes." There was no mercy on his face or in his voice, and the other men looked the same.

Starnes caught my collar and hustled me back outside.

I wasn't going to just stand still and let him kill me. Even if it was futile, I had to do *something*. I waited, trying to control my fear and anger, waited for the best moment.

It never came.

"I'm going to enjoy this," Starnes growled, pushing me into the woods behind the house, toward the chopper. "You been askin' for it, you goddamn smart ass."

"Cody!" a voice yelled behind us. "Hit the dirt!"

I reacted instinctively, doing like the voice said, diving to the ground as Starnes spun around and looked for a target. We both spotted him at the same time, standing about twenty yards away, a rifle in his hands. Starnes fired as I launched myself toward him.

I hit his knees as the Ingram ripped off a burst. He went down and I was all over him, clubbing my hands together and driving them into the back of his head. His face smashed into the ground, and I grabbed his hair and lifted him back up and slammed him down again several times. It wasn't until I rolled his limp body over and saw the blood and the distorted features that I saw the rough chunk of rock on the ground. The stains on the rock were dark in the moonlight.

I picked up the Ingram and ran over to where Roy Lamb writhed on the ground, his legs blown out from under him by the heavy slugs. The empty M-16 lay on the grass beside him.

Roy was crying almost silently. I knelt beside him, and he opened his eyes, focusing on me after a few seconds.

"Cody . . . ," he gasped. "Saw you and . . . Starnes . . . from the window . . . thought something was wrong . . ."

"You were right," I told him. "He was going to kill me."

"Wh-why . . . ?"

"Too long a story," I told him. "Hayes and the others, they're the bad guys, Roy. They're the real enemy. I've got to stop them, so I'll have to leave you here for a little while." I didn't like the way he was bleeding, but there was nothing I could do about extensive wounds like he had suffered.

"Jeremy . . . he's back there . . ."

"I'll get him out," I promised. "And then I'll come back for you."

His hand caught my arm, dug in painfully. "I . . . I'm sorry . . ."

"You saved my life, Roy. It's not your fault—"

I broke off. He was unconscious, his hand slipping off my arm.

I went back toward the house at a run, the Ingram cradled in my arms. I had fired one once, with a cop friend of mine at the police firing range, but I wasn't real confident about handling it. Maybe I wouldn't have to do any more shooting.

As I neared the porch, a shape came out of the shadows, and Hayes called to me, "Is that you, Starnes?"

I brought the Ingram up. "Hold it, Hayes!"

He went for the pistol holstered on his hip, and I knew it wasn't loaded with blanks. I hesitated, and he had the .45 all the way out of the holster before I pressed the trigger of the machine gun.

The recoil threatened to push the muzzle up. I held it down, squeezing off short bursts that chewed up the porch of the old house. Hayes grunted and folded up, the pistol falling from his hands and bouncing down the steps to the ground.

His men came boiling out of the house, but so did the trainees. I covered all of them with the Ingram and yelled for nobody to move. I spotted Jeremy in the crowd on the porch and called out to him. "Your dad's in the woods, Jeremy," I told him. "He's been hurt."

He came off the porch and ran past me while I kept the rest of them under the gun. I backed off, then turned and hurried into the darkness after Jeremy.

There was plenty of confusion behind me, and I expected Hayes's men to be after me in a matter of minutes. Moving Roy Lamb might not be a good idea, but I didn't see that I had any choice.

I found Jeremy beside him. I pulled the kid to his feet and shoved the Ingram into his hand. "You've fired a gun before," I told him. "Just be careful." Then I bent to pick up Roy, who was still out cold. I had in mind that we'd head for the helicopter. I didn't think they'd risk shooting it up.

I heard car doors slamming, the roar of engines. Headlights lanced through the woods, then turned and went away, and all I could see was the red glow of taillights as the cars raced toward the highway.

They were pulling out.

All of them.

I figured it was a trap, but with Hayes dead, the others must have thought it made more sense to cut and run. With everything that had happened, there would be no chance of continuing with the survival camp scheme.

I would have liked to wait until morning before catfooting back up to the house, but with Roy badly injured, there wasn't that much time. I found that I was worried for nothing. The place was deserted, and the phone still worked. I got hold of the operator and started yelling for help as loud as I could.

Then I went back into the woods to wait with Jeremy and his father.

"What do you mean you won't testify?" Connie Lamb asked me, her voice rising stridently. "It's not bad enough that the damn reporters are making out that Roy's a hero, and now you say you won't tell the truth!"

"The truth is your husband saved my life," I told her flatly. "He's going to be in a wheelchair the rest of his life as it is. I'm not going to help take his son away from him."

She leaned over the desk in my office, glaring at me. "He wouldn't have gotten shot if he hadn't been out there at that camp with those other lunatics!"

"You may have a point there," I admitted. "But he went up against one of those lunatics armed only with an empty rifle he was using to practice field-stripping methods. And he saved my life."

"You keep coming back to that!"

"It is pretty important to me," I said.

"I'll have you subpoenaed."

I shrugged. "Go to it. But it won't look good, having to haul me into court. And once I'm on the stand, I'll have to offer my testimony that Roy saved my life and helped capture a band of ruthless criminals. That won't help your case, either."

She stared at me for a long moment, then turned and stalked out of the office. Even after all that had happened, I couldn't help but admire the rear view.

The rest of Hayes's men had been rounded up, and a few of the recruits had even come forward to tell the cops about the operation of the camp. It was going to be a nice mess before it was all cleaned up, but I had a feeling when the investigation was over, there would be several military-flavored robberies cleared up.

As for me, I was back in Fort Worth, definitely not a safe place. Less than ten miles from my office was Carswell Air Force Base, with its long-range bombers that made it a prime target for a Russian attack. Not to mention the damage that would be done to the agriculture and oil industries if the city was suddenly vaporized by the godless Communists. The safest place in the world? Not here.

Besides, my office rent was due in a few days and Connie Lamb had decided not to pay me the rest of the money she owed me. Unless another case came along in a hurry, I was going to be in trouble.

I locked the door and went across the street to commune with the spirits of Remington and Russell. Then, maybe, a bowl of ice cream . . . ?

L.J. WASHBURN

HOLLYWOOD GUNS

We are proud to be able to claim that we introduced L.J. Washburn's P.I. Hallam, in The Eyes Have It, *with her story entitled simply "Hallam."*

Since then this cowboy who has outlived the days of the old West to become a gun-toting P.I. and stuntman in 1920s Hollywood has appeared in Hardboiled, A Matter Of Crime, *and in his first novel,* Wild Night *(Tor, 1987). A second Hallam novel has also been scheduled to be published by Tor.*

Now Hallam is back—still the freshest, most original P.I. to appear in some years.

Hallam's Colt jammed just as he was about to shoot William S. Hart.

Hallam said, "Dammit!" and glared down at the revolver. Bill Hart, who was directing as well as starring in the picture, merely shrugged his shoulders and called, "Cut!" in that deep, resonant voice of his.

"Sorry, Bill," Hallam said as he drew back the hammer of the Colt and studied it. "Looks like the sear's busted."

"Don't worry about it, Lucas. The script called for you to miss me anyway," Hart pointed out. He held out his hand. "Mind if I take a look?"

Hallam handed over the Colt, knowing that Hart was a westerner like himself and not some play-acting dude from back East. Hart handed the weapon back after a moment's study of it and agreed with Hallam's conclusion.

"I imagine that old hog-leg's seen a lot of use," he said.

Hallam grinned, hefting the Colt. "Had it, man and boy, nigh onto forty years."

"I have a pair of six-shooters that belonged to Billy the Kid. Did you and young Bonney ever cross paths, by any chance?"

Hallam shook his head. "He was a few years before my time. Not much, mind you."

Nearby, an assistant director sweated and watched the two older men talking. He was wearing an open-throated sport shirt and jodhpurs, which was quite a contrast to the dusty range clothes worn by Hallam and Bill Hart. In the wilds of Bronson Canyon, where the company was shooting today, the A.D. looked more like he was in costume than Hallam and Hart did.

They looked right at home.

"Excuse me, Mr. Hart," the A.D. finally said. "Are we going to try to set up for another shot?"

Hart glanced around at the crowd of people, momentarily forgotten as he and Hallam had looked at the broken gun. He looked back at Hallam. "Feel like doing the scene with another gun, Lucas? We could start from the top so there wouldn't be any problem with continuity."

Hallam removed the battered, broad-brimmed hat from his head and ran his fingers around the inside of the band, wiping away the sweat. His craggy face with its drooping gray moustache was thoughtful. "Wouldn't really seem right," he said after a moment.

Hart nodded. "That's what I thought. Man gets used to his own gun." He turned to the A.D. "Might as well get the chase out of the way, Marty."

The young man nodded, hurrying off to confer with the cameraman and round up the riding extras that would be needed to film the scene. Hallam slid the Colt back in its holster and said, "Reckon it won't matter while I'm just ridin'. I can get it fixed tomorrow."

"Are you going to take it to Old Bob?" Hart asked.

"Where else? Old Bob's the best damn gunsmith in Hollywood."

The sign painted on the window of the little shop read HOLLYWOOD GUNS. The place was far out on Sunset, on the edge of town in an area where the rents were low. Inside, it was musty and a little gloomy, but as Hallam opened the door the next day, he thought that it was one of his favorite places in California.

There were guns everywhere you looked in the front part of the store, rifles and shotguns in racks along the walls, handguns of all kinds in glass-topped display cases. A wooden counter ran through the middle of the room. The back section was cluttered with metal racks and workbenches and guns in various states of disrepair. That was where Old Bob did his gunsmithing. There was also a small back room where ammunition was stored.

Hallam had never heard Old Bob called anything else. He didn't know the man's last name. But he was a familiar figure as he sat on a tall stool behind the counter, fiddling with a little nickel-plated .25. He was a small, wizened man in his sixties, with a few strands of hair plastered across a bald head and a wispy growth of whiskers on his chin. His dark eyes lit up as he saw Hallam come into the shop.

"Well, if it ain't the actor!" he said mockingly. "How's the picture business, Fairbanks?"

Hallam grinned, used to the old codger riding him. Of course, Bob wasn't that much older than Hallam himself. But hell, Hallam didn't mind being a codger.

He hauled out the broken Colt and laid it on the counter. "Got a busted sear," he said. "Reckon you can fix it?"

Old Bob snorted derisively. "Can I fix it? Of course I can fix it!" He picked up the Colt and sniffed it, wrinkling his nose. "Don't you ever clean this damn thing?"

Hallam ignored the question and said, "Time's money. How soon can you have it ready?"

"You picture people," Old Bob growled. "Hurry up, hurry up. That's all you do. Then you stand around."

Hallam put his hands on the counter. "How long?"

Old Bob shrugged and said, "Give me a couple of hours."

Hallam nodded. He turned to leave the shop, but he paused in front of a small stretch of wall where there were no gun racks. Instead, the wall was covered with yellowed newspaper clippings, some of them dating back to the 1870s. Hallam always got a kick out of reading them. Old Bob had one interest besides guns, and that was outlaws.

The stories had been cut out of papers all over the country. Evidently Old Bob had traveled a lot in his younger days. The clippings told of bank robberies and stagecoach holdups, train robbers and shootists and road agents. All the famous desperadoes were there—the James boys, the Daltons and the Youngers, Bill Doolin, Bitter Creek Newcomb, Jake Fentress and his backshooting brother Leroy, the Wild Bunch, Ben Thompson, King Fisher, John Wesley Harding . . . Nearly every outlaw Hallam had ever heard of was up on that wall, represented by the colorful writing of the journalists of those wild days.

Hallam had crossed paths with a few of those lawbreakers, had traded lead with some of them. In fact, one of the clippings contained a group photograph of the posse that had rounded up a gang of train robbers in Arizona, and Hallam was right there, a lot of years younger and serving as a deputy. Old Bob had been excited to meet one of the men pictured in his collection, and it had been an even bigger thrill when Hallam had brought Al Jennings around to meet him. Hallam didn't know the Oklahoma badman well, but he had made a few pictures with him.

"Relivin' past glories, Lucas?" Old Bob asked from his seat behind the counter, and the irascible tone was gone from his voice now.

Hallam shook his head. "Them days weren't so glorious, most of the time. Lots of hard work and gettin' shot at."

"You still a detective?"

"When somebody wants to hire me," Hallam said, nodding. He divided his time between movie work and being a private detective. Between the two jobs, he made a decent living.

Old Bob shook his head. "Must not be much of a challenge, chasin' crooks these days. The country's grown up a mighty sorry crop of desperadoes."

"Oh, there's still a few wild and woolly ones out there," Hallam said.

"Not like the old days," Old Bob insisted.

"Hell," Hallam said with a grin, "what is?"

With a wave of his hand, he went out the door and wandered down the street.

There was a diner a couple of blocks away, and he settled in there to drink several cups of coffee and read a paper that a previous customer had left behind. There was a lot of tension in the world, as usual. That seemed to be something that just went with modern times. Back East in New York and Chicago the gangsters were shooting each other up, also as usual. Hallam was glad he was in sunny Southern California.

There was crime out here too, though. As he scanned the paper, he saw stories about a man going insane and shooting his wife and in-laws, a payroll robbery in Glendale, a gun battle between two rival groups of rumrunners, and a swindle that had left several people penniless. Only the lunatic had been caught. The cops were still looking for the folks who had pulled all the other jobs.

Hallam turned the pages to the trade news. A new studio had

opened for business down on Poverty Row, and he was sure they'd be grinding out Westerns, just like all the other Gower Gulch outfits. Good news for him and all the others like him, the riding extras and the wranglers and the stuntmen who had found a home in the moving pictures.

It was hot in the diner, the one fan not stirring up much air. Hallam was used to heat, though, having lived in the Southwest most of his life. Hollywood was nothing compared to the deserts of Texas and New Mexico and Arizona. The time passed fairly quickly and when he checked his turnip, he saw that he ought to be heading back to Old Bob's to check and see if the Colt was ready.

Before, the old man had been alone in the shop. This time there was another customer, a tall man in a suit who was studying some of the pistols in the display cases. He glanced up at Hallam and then went back to looking at the guns.

Old Bob was sitting stiffly on his stool, and he didn't return Hallam's nod of greeting. He was probably feeling touchy again, Hallam thought. "Got the Colt ready yet?" he asked.

Old Bob squinted at him. "What's that name again?" He held up a hand as Hallam frowned. Before Hallam could say anything, Bob went on, "Oh, yeah, I remember now. Fentress, ain't it? Had a Colt with a busted sear."

Hallam nodded slowly. "That's right."

"Got 'er ready for you, Mr. Fentress." Old Bob reached under the counter and pulled out Hallam's Colt. "Be five dollars," he said as he handed it over.

Hallam took the gun and pulled out his wallet, gave a five-dollar bill to Old Bob. "Thanks," he said.

"Welcome," the gunsmith grunted. Hallam turned to go out, but Old Bob stopped him by saying, "You wouldn't be any relation to Leroy Fentress, would you?"

Hallam shook his head. "Never heard of him."

"Thought you might've been. I seen ol' Leroy not long ago."

Hallam smiled politely. "'Fraid I don't know the man, friend."
He left the shop after nodding politely to the other customer.

Hallam walked to his flivver parked at the curb nearby, got in, drove away. He turned at the next corner and went around the block. There was a vacant lot behind the shop called Hollywood Guns. Hallam parked next to it, then reached into the glove box and took out a box of shells. He thumbed the cartridges into the cylinder of the Colt.

He wished there was more cover leading up to the back door of Old Bob's place. There was only one window on the rear wall, though, and it was fairly grimy. He'd just have to chance it.

Hallam got out of the car, went toward the building at a run.

He lifted a booted foot and drove it against the back door, his heel slamming into the panel beside the knob. The wood splintered and the door smashed back against the wall.

Hallam went through low, the boom of a gun filling his ears. He saw the muzzle flash off to his left and dove to the floor, rolling and tracking the Colt in that direction. He just had time to hope that Old Bob had done a good job repairing it before he triggered off two fast shots.

Both of them hit their target, smashing into the chest of the man crouched in the shadows of the back room and driving him back against the wall. The pistol he held slipped from his fingers and thudded to the floor. The man slid down the wall into a sitting position. His eyes were staring at Hallam, but they weren't seeing him. All the life was gone from them.

Hallam was back on his feet before the echoes of his shots had died away. A thick curtain covered the opening in the partition between the back room and the rest of the shop. Hallam bulled through it, his eyes scanning the room and finding the man who had pretended to be a customer. The man had a pistol out now and was trying to find something at which to fire it.

Old Bob was still on the stool. Hallam kicked out, upsetting the stool and sending the old man flying. He crashed behind the relative safety of the counter as Hallam leveled the Colt at the other man and yelled, "Hold it!"

The man jerked his gun toward Hallam and got off a shot. The slug whined past Hallam's head and punched through the partition behind him. Hallam fired once. The heavy bullet from the Colt caught the man in the shoulder, shattering bone and shredding muscle. The man flopped to the floor, his gun spinning away. He gobbled in pain for a few seconds before shock knocked him out.

From the floor behind the counter, Old Bob looked up at Hallam and asked, "T'other one?"

"Dead in the back," Hallam said shortly. His face was grim as he looked at the sprawled figure of the second gunman. "What the hell was that all about?"

Old Bob got to his feet, brushing himself off. He reached under the counter and brought out a bulky machine gun. "Feller got too

attached to his gun," he said. "Thing kept jammin' up on him, so
he brought it in to be fixed before him and the other one took off.
They was on the run, somethin' about a payroll robbery they
pulled in Glendale. Been layin' low for a few days, but the cops
were closin' in on them. They were goin' to try to head back East,
where they come from. Right talkative pair. 'Course, they
figgered to kill me when they left, so's I couldn't send the cops
after 'em."

Hallam shook his head. "Damned foolish."

"That they were," Old Bob agreed.

Hallam glared at him. "I'm talkin' about *you*. Startin' a shoot-
out in here like that."

"Hell, boy, I knew you'd pick up on it when I called you by Jake
Fentress's name. I just threw in that bit about Leroy so's you'd
know there was one hidin' in the back. Knew you'd remember
the Fentress boys and understand what I was gettin' at."

"I'd've looked a mite embarrassed if that gent had turned out to
be a real customer." Hallam grimaced. "I'm gettin' too old to be
goin' around bustin' in doors and wavin' guns around. Besides,"
he added, "what if them two had dropped me, instead of the
other way around? Then there'd be two of us dead."

Old Bob shook his head slowly. "I knew you could take 'em.
Ain't I been tellin' you? These owlhoots today ain't real des-
peradoes! Now if it had been Frank and Jesse James, or the
Daltons . . ."

Hallam just shook his head and went to see if he could keep the
wounded man from bleeding to death before the cops and
ambulances got there.

The Mysterious Library offers enduring works of reference, biography, and fiction covering the entire spectrum of crime and supense literature.

Eric Ambler: HERE LIES: AN AUTOBIOGRAPHY

The Edgar Award-winning autobiography of the man Graham Greene called "our greatest thriller writer." ILLUSTRATED.
$8.95

Robert Barnard: A TALENT TO DECEIVE: AN APPRECIATION OF AGATHA CHRISTIE

The definitive critical study and celebration of the lady whose name is synonymous with mystery, by the distinguished mystery author.
$8.95

Raymond Chandler: RAYMOND CHANDLER'S UNKNOWN THRILLER: THE SCREENPLAY OF "PLAYBACK"

An entirely new story—in the form of a never-produced screenplay—by one of the 20th century's most influential authors.
$9.95

Carroll John Daly: THE ADVENTURES OF SATAN HALL (A *Dime Detective Book*)

A series of 1930s novellas featuring "The Man Police and Gangdom Alike Feared," by the most popular writer of pulp detective stories.
$8.95

Norbert Davis: THE ADVENTURES OF MAX LATIN (A *Dime Detective Book*)

Novellas from the 1930s and '40s featuring a most unusual private eye, by one of the most talented of the pulp writers. With an introduction by John D. MacDonald.
$8.95

Patricia Highsmith: THE ANIMAL-LOVER'S BOOK OF BEASTLY MURDER

A series of extraordinary murder tales, each featuring a protagonist who is not man but beast.
$8.95

Patricia Highsmith: LITTLE TALES OF MISOGYNY

Seventeen bizarre, sophisticated, ironic, and humorous stories about women who destroy their men and women who destroy themselves.
$8.95

Patricia Highsmith: SLOWLY, SLOWLY IN THE WIND
A dozen short stories which explore the guilt—or lack of it—in their characters, and justice—or the lack of it—in their world.
$8.95

Peter Lovesey: BUTCHERS AND OTHER STORIES OF CRIME
The award-winning author's first collection of short stories. "One of the most amusing, original, and surprising writers in the crime field."—*Police*
$9.95

Gregory Mcdonald, ed. LAST LAUGHS:
THE 1986 MYSTERY WRITERS OF AMERICA ANTHOLOGY
Fourteen unusual mystery stories which prove that even crime may be humorous.
$8.95

Frederick Nebel: THE ADVENTURES OF CARDIGAN
(A *Dime Detective Book*)
A series of 1930s private eye novellas by one of the finest practitioners of the Dashiell Hammett school of pulp writing.
$9.95

William F. Nolan: THE BLACK MASK BOYS: MASTERS IN THE HARD-BOILED SCHOOL OF DETECTIVE FICTION
The story of the men who invented and refined the hard-boiled form and created the fabled *Black Mask* magazine.
$8.95

Bill Pronzini: GUN IN CHEEK
A delightful exploration of "alternative" crime fiction—the most inept writing in the genre.
$9.95

Bill Pronzini: SON OF GUN IN CHEEK
Taken with its companion volume, this study provides a hilarious crash course in the worst crime fiction of the 20th century.
$8.95

Robert J. Randisi, ed.: THE EYES HAVE IT
The first anthology from the Private Eye Writers of America, bringing together the most distinguished practitioners of the genre.
$8.95

Robert J. Randisi, ed.: MEAN STREETS
The second anthology from the Private Eye Writers of America
continues to showcase the work of today's best hard-boiled writers.
$8.95

Hank Searls: THE ADVENTURES OF MIKE BLAIR
(A *Dime Detective* Book)
A collection of hard-boiled novellas which provide a fascinating
look at the pulp apprenticeship of one of today's most
accomplished suspense authors.
$8.95

Ralph B. Sipper: ROSS MACDONALD'S INWARD JOURNEY
A collection of essays by and about one of the greatest of
modern-day mystery writers. ILLUSTRATED.
$8.95

Vincent Starrett: THE PRIVATE LIFE OF SHERLOCK HOLMES
Written by the most distinguished of all Sherlockian scholars, this
is the first comprehensive biography of the world's most famous
detective. ILLUSTRATED.
$8.95

Julian Symons: CONAN DOYLE: PORTRAIT OF AN ARTIST
A brilliantly concise and readable introduction to the man and his
work, by the well-known author/critic. ILLUSTRATED.
$9.95

Colin Watson: SNOBBERY WITH VIOLENCE: CRIME STORIES
AND THEIR AUDIENCES
The noted mystery author examines the detective story and thriller
in sociological context. A classic of literary and social history.
ILLUSTRATED.
$8.95

To order by mail, simply send title and retail price, plus $3.00 for the first
book on any order and 50¢ for each additional book on that order, to
cover mailing and handling costs. New York State residents add applica-
ble sales tax. Enclose check or money order to: *Mysterious Press Mail
Order, 129 West 56th Street, New York, New York 10019.*